LITTLE BLACK DOTS

LITTLE BLACK DOTS
A Short Story Collection

By: Peter Barlow

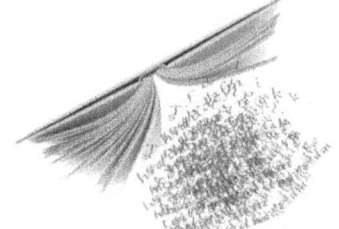

Chatter House Press
Indianapolis, Indiana

Little Black Dots
A Short Story Collection

Copyright© 2017 by Peter Barlow

For information:

Chatter House Press
7915 S Emerson Ave, Ste B303
Indianapolis, IN 46237

chatterhousepress.com

ISBN: 978-1-937793-40-1
Library of Congress Control Number: 2017943407

DEDICATION

This book, and every story contained within it,
is dedicated to my mother, my father, and my brother.

ACKNOWLEDGEMENTS

"What You're Looking For" first appeared in Rosebud.

"Perhaps, Perhaps, Perhaps" first appeared in The Other Herald.

"Liberty Bell" was previously anthologized in Coming Unglued:
  Six Stories About Things Falling Apart.

"Ghost" first appeared in Bryant Literary Review.

"Sweet" first appeared in Prole.

"Little Black Dots" first appeared in Inwood Indiana.

"Lament" first appeared in Per Contra.

"At Chichén Itzá" first appeared on Black Market Review

"Layover" first appeared in The Puckerbrush Review.

"Great Horny Toads" first appeared in Underground Voices.

"The Guy who Makes the Coffee" first appeared on Zouch Magazine
  and Miscellany.

"Poster" first appeared in The Oklahoma Review.

"The Match" first appeared in The Louisiana Review.

"Lake Effect" first appeared in Spindrift.

"Albert ❤ Julia" first appeared on Orion headless.

"After the War Ended" first appeared on Istanbul Literary Review, and
  later appeared in Ginosko Literary Journal.

"Reservations" first appeared in Ranfurly Review.

"Meeting Monica Seles" first appeared in Chiron Review.

"Tornado in a Box," was previously anthologized in Oh Sandy!: An
  Anthology of Humor for a Serious Purpose.

"Another Sunrise" first appeared in a slightly edited form in Quarterly
  Literary Review Singapore.

"Sea of Tranquility" first appeared in Confluence.

"Besame Mucho" by Consuelo Velazquez. Copyright © 1941 by Promotora
Hispano Americana de Musica S.A. Administered by Peer International Corporation. Copyright Renewed.

"Perhaps, Perhaps, Perhaps" English lyrics by Joe Davis of "Quizas, Quizas,
Quizas" by Osvaldo Farres. Copyright © 1947 by Peer International Corporation
and Southern Music Publishing Co., Inc. Copyright Renewed.

Both used with kind permission. All rights reserved.

CONTENTS

WHAT YOU'RE LOOKING FOR

Six inches of the finest West Virginia snow covered all the mailboxes on the road and the house numbering made no sense. Even and odd numbers jumped from one side of the road to the other almost at random, and houses being numbered in sequence was more of a suggestion than something done with consistency. Some mailboxes had the actual house number, above the family's name: "14053, McGill." Others had just a name. Still others had no name but the Rural PO Box number: "Box 18, County Road 337." To an outsider it was maddening. To have to wipe snow off of every mailbox for three miles, as he had done, was more so.

Jeff Everett had been here before, but not in many years. He'd been eight then, brought along to his great-grandfather's house by his parents and their parents over Christmas holiday under the implied threat of it possibly being the patriarch's last Christmas. His great-grandfather's idea of entertainment was a string of endless stories of wartime, 1917 and '18 in the French countryside, being bombed by the Germans left, right, and center, and of loose French mademoiselles though Jeff didn't really understand those stories then. The place bored Jeff: he'd had to leave his Atari at home, the only thing to do was read or play outside in the below-freezing weather, and there was still an outhouse even though the main house had running water installed when his grandfather was a boy. The upside was that the long, high hills were excellent for sledding, which Jeff and his brothers did often, as much to get themselves out of the house and away from the war stories as for fun.

The mailbox he cleared off was the wrong one, wrong address, wrong name, wrong everything. Jeff trudged back to the car, stepping in his own footsteps, and drove on to the next one. He'd been at it for forty-five minutes and was getting annoyed. No one in the nearby town of Mineral Wells seemed to know the road he was trying to find, and what directions his grandfather provided weren't all that good. He'd found the road by a combination of dumb luck and determination. Finding the address where he was headed would take more of the same.

Jeff's cellphone rang as he pulled up to the next mailbox. "Hello, dear. Oh, cold but good. There's six inches of snow on the ground here and I don't recognize anything. Well, I don't remember the actual drive up there. I was eight. I wasn't paying attention to where I was going. No, the GPS is useless. If

I don't find it soon I'll have to give up for the night. Well, I would have started sooner if anyone knew where I was going. Even the lawyer wasn't sure. Okay. Love you."

Jeff got out of the car and walked to the mailbox. For the first time that afternoon, the surroundings seemed familiar. A break in the barbed wire fence indicated where the dirt track driveway was, running off probably along a ridge that seemed just wide enough for it and eventually behind a copse. On either side the snow lay flat and undisturbed over wide expanses, raising up on one side into some trees and down the other toward a valley. He wiped the snow off the mailbox and found his own last name there. A mile away, up a drive along a snow-covered ridge, was the house he was here to find.

Jeff went back to his car, a little faster than he'd left it, and turned it up the drive. No one had driven it since the snowfall. More than once Jeff had to clear away a small drift so the car could get through. On the third such time he heard a shot. It echoed for a moment among the hills. Jeff crouched slightly and looked around. Right next to the tree line on the hill above was a small camper, big enough for one or two people to sleep in. Was someone here on his great-grandfather's land that wasn't supposed to be or—?

"Deer hunters."

His mother walked next to him, blowing into her hands and looking toward the tree line, concerned. He was eight again. Then he dropped prone onto the ground with his hands covering his head when he heard the report. His mother had come out to watch over her three sons as they tobogganed down one of the bigger hillsides, and had forgotten her gloves. Jeff's two brothers, Richie and Dave, laughed at his reaction to the shot, even as their mother sighed and helped him up out of the snow. One of them had pointed out the small camper, up on the ridge. The camper then was smaller, grey, and resembled a canned ham on its side. It didn't look like it had been used lately.

"Your great-grandfather lets hunters come up here during deer season. He's had a deer problem since I don't know when. They get into the crops and ruin them a little bit, and after a while if they go unchecked there can be too many running around."

"He lets people come and shoot Bambi?" Jeff said. His brothers chuckled again and would have mocked him had their mother not been around.

"Well," she said, "yes. He still goes out himself, although he's getting on in years and he hasn't hit anything since before your father and I got married, so he lets other people do it. He's out hunting with your father and grandfather now, actually. If we're very lucky, we'll get dinner out of it." She frowned. "But I thought shooting with a gun was illegal this time of year."

2

Jeff exhaled. His great-grandfather was "getting on in years" back then and only died week before last, outliving all but one of his children— Jeff's grandfather, as it happened—and even some of their children. He wondered who fired the shot and hoped they missed. Whoever they were certainly took after the old man, who didn't care about that particular state law either. Jeff kicked away more snow from in front of the car and kept going.

The house came into view as he rounded the copse. Lonely, white as the snow that surrounded it, the two-story farmhouse looked dark and almost neglected. His great-grandfather hadn't lived there for two years, residing instead at a senior facility in Parkersburg at the request of his remaining child and assorted nieces and nephews who still lived in the area. In the rapidly fading light, it looked forboding and lonely.

Jeff pulled the car behind the house and shut the motor off. In front of him, half under the snow, was a small wire fence surrounding what was the garden in warmer weather. Jeff had touched the wire once and received a small electric jolt; his brothers, who told him to touch it in the first place, told him to keep quiet about the jolt or there'd be trouble. To the left of that should have been the outhouse but it was gone. While Jeff was in high school the family insisted on installing an indoor toilet, far too late for Jeff to appreciate it, and saving anyone else the anxiety of stumbling across the backyard at three in the morning for an emergency pee. Behind him by sixty yards was the barn, massive then as now, which he'd been in only once, briefly.

With the engine off there was hardly any noise. The crunch he made when putting his foot through the snow died in the cool air, and the only other thing he could hear was his arms scraping against his sides in the bulky coat. He opened the back door with the key he'd gotten at the lawyer's that morning, stepped through, and closed the door behind him.

The sleigh bells on the back of the office door jingled for a moment and then rested. The noise of the traffic shushing its way through the slush and the still-falling snow outside vanished like it had never existed, replaced by the near-stillness of the lawyer's office. Just inside there was a cubicle intended for a receptionist, but judging from the lack of supplies and personal effects it had sat vacant for quite some time. An office door was ajar some feet beyond. A light was on inside, and Jeff thought he could faintly hear music playing. Jeff was about to call a hello when a voice came at him. "Have a seat. I'll be right up with you."

A handful of seconds later Jeff was joined by a gentleman of middling years, graying, and dressed well even though he was alone. "Paul Levens," he said, offering a hand. "You must be Mr. Everett. Glad you could make it in through the snow. Come on back to my office."

The office was cramped. Almost every surface was filled with books stacked sideways or collections of folders. Mr. Levens cleared a mound of such off a chair for Jeff before seating himself in a plush chair behind the desk. "Have to admit," he said. "The call from the family took me a bit by surprise. The estate's been settled, was done so a while back. So why are you coming to look at the house?"

Jeff sighed. "They didn't tell you, did they? What I do, I mean."

Mr. Levens shook his head.

"I'm a personal gravestone shopper."

There was a long silence while the lawyer took that in.

"Families hire me to design and acquire headstones that accurately represent the deceased, right down to the epitaph."

"First I've heard of something like that."

"First of my kind, so far as I'm aware. Anyway, I interview the family and friends, go through the personal effects, and use that information to design a custom-made tombstone."

The lawyer looked at Jeff like he'd just spoken Chinese. "Sounds kind of morbid."

Jeff shrugged. "Could be if I let it, I suppose. Really all I'm trying to do is help families honor their loved ones."

"And your family has hired you to do your grandfather's."

"Great-grandfather. And hired isn't the term I would use. Bullied, berated, badgered…"

The lawyer nodded. "So you're on to the personal effects phase. Well, good luck to you. Nobody's been out there since he was put in that home a couple years back. Probably dusty as all get out. Power may or may not be on, but the water was shut off to keep the pipes from bursting so you won't have that."

"I don't expect to be out there long. A couple of hours, maybe."

"Good enough. You can put the key through the mail slot when you're through." The lawyer stood and offered his hand again. "Hope you find what you're looking for. I'm headed home after this. Christmas is only two days away and the wife won't let me forget it."

The house—this house, his great-grandfather's house—had no idea it was nearly Christmas, or that its owner hadn't seen the inside of it in so long, or that everything was now under a heavy layer of dust. Someone had come and tidied the place, though. The kitchen, where Jeff found himself, was completely put away, the counters cleared, the sink emptied, the table devoid of anything but the tablecloth. Jeff thought for a moment about opening the refrigerator—a Westinghouse dating back to the Korean War from the look of it—but decided not to.

The dining room next door offered more of the same. Someone, probably the same someone that cleaned the kitchen, covered the furniture with sheets now greyed with two years accumulated dust. Jeff knew he'd have to lift the sheets on the side tables at some point and was thankful he'd thought to bring a surgical mask to keep the dust out of his lungs. The odd lumps running across the top of them indicated picture frames beneath, which could give a clue about interests or help fill in other gaps. The living room offered more of the same.

The master bedroom opened off of the living room; Jeff remembered that much from his childhood visit. Jeff and his brothers slept on air mattresses in the living room, while his parents and grandparents had the two bedrooms upstairs. It gave everything a sort of campground effect, but his great-grandfather rose at five o'clock on most days and his grandfather rose at the same time, the combined effect of being a farmer's son and serving in the second World War, so the days tended to start earlier than any of the boys liked.

Opening the door to the master bedroom, Jeff felt like he was venturing into forbidden land. The room was deemed off-limits to the boys growing up. Inside was nothing particularly special: a full-size bed, a tall dresser, a vanity, and nightstands with lamps on both sides of the bed. The someone who had thought to cover the dining and living rooms in sheets hadn't bothered in here, but the bed was made. The comforter looked handmade; Jeff couldn't see anyone going to a shop and purchasing anything with such a haphazard quality about it. The nightstand on the side nearest the door was empty save for the lamp and an alarm clock; the other had the lamp and an old rotary phone. Jeff picked up the receiver and got nothing. Partway under the phone base was a notepad with names and phone numbers in large print to accommodate the old man's failing eyesight. The first entry on the pad was "DOKTER." Jeff snorted at the misspelling. The next one down from that was "EUNICE."

Eunice was the oldest daughter of his grandfather's brother. Jeff had heard about her long before she turned up on his phone. Most of the family, his grandfather included, avoided dealing with her because of how she addressed people: like they were servants. "You have to come," she said on the phone call to Jeff, the words barked more than anything else.

"Yes, but I don't know that I can. It's Christmas, the kids are out of school—"

"Nonsense. You're needed. The family wants you to do the headstone. Your great-grandfather would have wanted you to."

"My great-grandfather met me once, thirty years ago, and I doubt he could pick me out of a line-up."

"Don't get snippy with me, young man." Jeff rolled his eyes at this; at thirty-eight, with three children in grade school, young was what he didn't feel. "I shall have to call your father."

"Have fun holding the séance, then," he said, and broke the connection. It was only when his grandfather called and made a plea of his own that Jeff consented to come.

"Stop," someone said from behind him. "Stop right there." Two metallic clicks followed. Jeff raised his arms slowly and stayed facing the nightstand. "Turn around," the voice said. "Nice and easy." He did, and found himself on the wrong end of a shotgun being aimed at him from the doorway. The woman holding it looked around his age, although the fur-lined cap and heavy winter coat made it difficult to tell.

"I can explain," he said.

"So can I. Might maybe you start by 'splaining how it is you're in my great-grandpappy's house."

"He's mine too. I'm Jeff Everett. I think your aunt hired me."

"Momma never did like Aunt Eunice."

Jeff sat at the kitchen table. The woman, Stella Mae Everett, opened up one of the cabinets, looked inside for a moment, then closed it again. They'd stared at each other in the bedroom door for a few seconds, then Jeff explained who he was and why he was there. Stella Mae apologized and brought him back into the kitchen. The shotgun, unloaded and broken, was on the counter.

"She talked to me like I was six," he said. "My grandfather had to step in to prevent a family incident."

"Don't know him," Stella Mae said. "Don't know hardly anyone from that branch of the family. Suppose that happens when they live clear the other side of Ohio." She opened another cabinet, pulled out two mugs, and blew the dust off them. "Hope you like your coffee black," she said, sitting down and unscrewing the top of a Thermos.

"Black's fine," he said. "Yeah, I can't say I know any of your branch either. Mom would mention some of you from time to time, but to me you were just people I'd never met."

Stella Mae passed him a mugful and sipped at her own. "So your grandpa and mine were brothers. What's that make us, then?"

"Second cousins."

She smiled. "Neat. Ain't never had any of them."

"Well, now you've got seven. Me, my two brothers, and our four cousins." They sat for a moment, saying nothing. "I take it you saw him regularly, our great-grandfather?"

"Often enough, I suppose. There was three or four of us made the trip up here every couple of days with food and such, and then out to visit him at the home when he went there. It was Aunt Eunice that found him when he fell and broke his hip in the first place, and put him in the nursing home."

Jeff looked at Stella Mae. He'd met her before, he was sure of it, back on that Christmas trip. He had an idea of her with a pageboy cut, blonde, still plump about the face, in a tee-shirt and jeans. And then he didn't.

"He was—kind of funny, actually." A smile came on Stella Mae's face as she swirled the coffee in her cup. "Up at the ass crack of dawn every day, liked everything just so. This was his chair, the one I'm in. No one else was allowed to sit here, not even—"

"Hey!" The voice came from the doorway into the dining room, reported more than spoken. Jeff turned in his chair; his great-grandfather stood there, hands on his hips, his face scowled. "Get up out of that chair!"

Jeff looked back at Stella Mae, maybe eight or nine. He was sitting in the same spot, his young face slack with surprise. Her face was flush. "I'm sorry." She scooted out of the chair and shuffled off to the counter.

"That's more like it," their great-grandfather said. His face was red. "Don't you sit in my chair ever again." He turned and went back into the dining room, not even bothering to sit in the now-vacant chair.

"You okay?" When he looked again, Stella Mae was back in the same hunting gear she'd been wearing.

"Yeah," he said. "I'm fine."

"Look like you've seen a ghost."

He shook his head. "I just— I never really cared for him much. He wasn't very friendly to us, my brother and my mother and me, even after—" Jeff fell silent then.

Stella Mae looked at him for a long moment. "That was your father, wasn't it? The one he shot."

Jeff nodded.

"I was here that day." She swirled her coffee around for a second.

7

Jeff said nothing. He remembered the day, the hour, the minute she was thinking of, and where he'd been.

"Where were you?" she said. "When you heard."

"Out in the barn."

"Show me." She stood up and put her gloves on. "'Sides, I like the smell out there."

Jeff hadn't intended on going back to the barn at all, if he could help it. The memory of that afternoon was clearer now he was at the house again.

"You comin'?" she said, her hand on the doorknob.

He looked at her for a moment. "Sure," he said.

They left the house and plodded across the snow toward the barn, their breath fogging the air before them. "I loved the big ol' tire swing that he hung from the center rafter," she said. "Used to come out here all the time and ride on that."

"I only went in there the one time," Jeff said. "I had this idea that he had cows and sheep and all that, and I'd been in barns before. I've never really cared for the smell of manure."

"Oh, it wasn't that bad."

"Well, no, but I didn't know that then. I didn't know the cows were in the fields most of the time, and how spotless they tried to keep it."

Stella Mae opened a small side door, leading into the lower level of the barn. "That was us, mostly, me and my cousins. They used to bring us over the week after Easter, do a big clean-out and scrub-down of the barn. Said it would build character." The two climbed up a ladder through an opening along the wall and emerged into the main area of the barn. "Don't know that it ever did, but it sure got us all used to the smell of that." She pointed up to the rafters, and the massive leaves of tobacco hanging down from them.

Jeff closed his eyes and inhaled long and deep.

"I thought there were bats up there, first time I was out here," his mother said.

He opened his eyes. His mother was standing beside him. In one hand, he was holding the sled they had used that morning. Jeff had asked his mother what was out here. His brothers had gone ahead into the house, disinterested. "Really?" he said.

"Oh, yeah. Your father, comedian that he is, said they would come out at night and fly all around the house. Said they went for women and children because they were easier to pick off. They'd swarm in and knock them down and drink their blood. Complete nonsense."

He marveled at the big tobacco leaves for a moment longer and was about to ask how large they grew when the sound of a door slamming came from the level below. Up through the opening came his oldest brother Richie. His face was red and tear-streaked, and his voice panicked. "Mom," he said. "It's Dad. And you've gotta come."

Jeff closed his eyes and was back in the present. "I'll be back in the house," he said, and went back down the ladder.

❖   ❖   ❖

Stella Mae found Jeff in one of the upstairs bedrooms. He was standing at the foot of the bed, hands in pockets, staring at the pillows. She took her gloves off and stuffed them into a coat pocket.

"They shuffled me home pretty quick after your Dad was brought in. Didn't say anything, just, 'Get on home now, Stella Mae.'"

The dust settled a little more around them.

"I'm sorry," she said.

Jeff shrugged. "Nothing to be sorry about."

"Must be hard, coming back to the place where your father died."

Jeff stared down at his shoes. His mother sobbed at the side of the bed, holding his father's hand as he coughed and shook. "They shouldn't be in here, Kevin," she said, barely able to be understood. "They shouldn't be seeing this."

"Shh," his father said. Jeff, Richie, and Dave were lined up at the foot of the bed, all unable to make eye contact with anything but the footboard. The sheets on their father's left side were a rich brown, the blood stain spreading inch by inch. "I want to see them."

From another room, the old man made himself heard. "Dammit, he's ruining all our sheets. You know how much new sheets cost? And us being on a fixed income and all. Damn waste of perfectly good sheets up there."

His mother was sobbing harder now.

His father coughed again, and shook harder than he had done. "My boys," he said. "My good sons." Another fit of coughing took him. "You take care of your mother. Richie. Dave. Jeff. You listen. You listen to her." He coughed a few more times, each weaker than the last, and shook a little more, and then he didn't.

Stella Mae slid her hands in her pants pockets. "I remember the funeral. Well, I remember going to the funeral. Had no real idea who it was for. Parents just told us to put on our Sunday best and we drove across Ohio."

"They had us there, in the front row, jackets and ties. We were supposed to cry but we didn't. And everyone kept saying how brave we all were, like that meant something. Watching him bleed out all over the sheets, knowing that was him up in the casket. Yeah. Brave."

Jeff rubbed a finger across the bottom of his nose.

"Damn fool took his gloves off. Fifteen degrees out and he takes his gloves off. Grandpa said he was muttering about fighting the Krauts at Cantigny and he didn't need any goddamned gloves then, never mind that it was the middle of May during that battle. So he's out there, gloves off, and of course he gets cold, doesn't he? Fingers freeze up, don't quite do what he wants them to do. They're on a trail moving from one blind to the other. Dad's in front, Grandpa behind him, great-grandpa behind him. Dad and Grandpa had bows and arrows, but great-grandpa's got a gun, never mind that it's illegal to hunt deer with a gun after the first of December. This is his land, and nobody was gonna tell him what he could and couldn't do on it. Deer jumps out onto the trail, great-grandpa raises his gun and tells them to get out of the way. Grandpa bails out, but before Dad can move the old man's fingers twitch from the cold—"

Stella Mae sniffed.

"They got him back here—Grandpa did, anyway—and all the old man can do is bitch. No apologies. No acts of contrition. Just wants him to stop bleeding onto the linens, because now they'll have to buy a new set and they're on a fixed income."

She stepped forward, took Jeff by the arm, and led him downstairs, back to the kitchen. They sat down in the chairs they had been at before and said nothing. Outside the light faded from grey.

"If you don't mind me asking," she said. "Why did you come back here? I mean, your grandfather, Aunt Eunice—you could have told them no."

Jeff shrugged. "You think there's a lot of call for a personal gravestone shopper?" He glanced sideways out a window and realized he couldn't see his car in the darkness. "I'd best be getting on. It'll be hard enough getting back down to the main road, and it's supposed to snow more tonight."

"You're welcome to stay with me in the camper. Might be safer."

"Can't, really. I've got to get back to Dayton. The kids expect me home for Christmas, and it'll take long enough to get back there through the snow as it is."

Neither one said anything for a moment. "You come up with your epitaph?" she said.

"'God Rest His Soul,' probably. I don't really care. Eunice can do it her damn self if she doesn't like it." They stood and went outside. When they were next to his car, they stopped. "You want a lift back to the camper?"

"Nah. Walking's good for me." Stella Mae smiled, and stepped forward and hugged him. "Good to see you again."

"You too. Stay in touch."

She started back towards the woods, putting a headband flashlight on as she went, but stopped and turned to face him after a dozen feet. "You're very brave, you know. Coming back." Stella Mae gave a small wave and continued her walk through the snow. A moment later the darkness swallowed her up.

Jeff drove back on the long driveway. As he reached the dirt road, and the mailbox he'd cleared off hours before, his cellphone rang: his wife, probably wanting an update. He pushed the button to send the call straight to voicemail, and all was silent as the grave again.

PERHAPS, PERHAPS, PERHAPS

The crowd, it seemed, spilled into every shop, every restaurant but this one. Outside, the Playa de Armas was filled with people, festive, giddy, boisterous. Some ate, some drank, some danced, some did all three. Weaving between them all were locals: small girls selling postcards and dolls; boys selling single-use cameras and CDs of native music; women of indeterminate ages selling belt pouches and shoulder slings to hold bottles of water. Every four steps they took they made a sale, their faces frozen in smiles as if each customer was Santa Claus come in June.

Inside, Mitch looked away from the window and the crowd beyond. It wasn't any use looking for Carmel anymore. He couldn't tell one face from another, and he wouldn't even see her until she was right there, just the other side of the glass. She was late, but that wasn't anything new. At every meeting, every rendez-vous there was something, a reason, an excuse, each one distinguishable from the last only by the date given. Mitch had learned to live with that. And he had to admit, even in the best of circumstances she, who saw this every year, who would know how to navigate the crowd, would have difficulty doing so. Still, two hours late was a bit much even for her. She would be along sooner or later, Mitch knew that, but each passing minute felt longer than the one before, and he wondered if he wasn't wearing out his welcome here in the restaurant.

A slightly balding man approached Mitch's table. "Are you ready to order, señor? If you're having difficulties, I can make suggestions, or—?"

"No," he said, staring into what was left of his coca tea. "Still waiting. If that's not a problem."

The man ran a finger along his pencil-thin moustache, nearly erasing it. "Of course," he said, and walked back into the bowels of the café.

Mitch swirled the leaves in his tea and took another sip. The locals swore by the tea as a remedy for outsiders not used to the high altitude and low oxygen of Cusco—"Trust me, señor, very reliable," the waiter had said as he left it—but Mitch found hardly anything redeeming about it. A memory of boiling bark in water and then drinking it on a dare by a friend when he was eight superimposed the taste of the coca, informed it. Carmel, who had lived in Cusco for a dozen years, swore by it, but then she liked a lot of things he didn't: ice in her coffee, rain in the sky, the lights low during lovemaking. After their affair in college was over, it seemed that all they'd ever had in common was the sex, but they remained in contact afterwards, frequently at first, then less and less over time.

The radio came then to the chorus of a song he only knew in English. He sang quietly over top of the Spanish, "And I don't want to wind up / Being parted, broken-hearted." Mitch put the cup of coca down and pushed the saucer away.

"Hey," a voice said behind him. He turned and saw Carmel standing just inside the door, sunglasses pushed up into her hair, a smile on her face that said how happy she was to be here, to see him.

Mitch stood and held his arms out. "Finally made it, I see."

"Would have been here twenty minutes ago, but the crowd—" She motioned out the window and rolled her eyes. The two hugged, and as they backed apart Carmel looked into his eyes with a penetrating stare that had always made Mitch a little nervous. "You look tired."

"I am tired. Air travel in Peru isn't everything it's cracked up to be."

She frowned. "You know what I mean."

The easy smile that had slid on his face a moment earlier slid off again. "Yes, well," he said, taking his seat.

Carmel sat opposite him. The waiter placed a cup of coca tea and a menu in front of her, assuring her that should she have any questions she needed but to ask. She added a packet of sugar to the tea and took a sip, staring at Mitch over the rim of the cup. "I'm glad you called. I'm sorry about—"

"It's okay." Mitch looked everywhere but at her. If he was honest with himself, really honest, he was happy to see her again. All of his memories of their relationship were filled with regret, that if he had said this or done that then they would still be together. Talking to her on the phone, getting a letter with a Peruvian postmark, even reading an e-mail from her was trying. All that ever came to him was a wave of nostalgia followed by a wave of nausea. He cast about for something to say to fill the growing silence. "Is the square usually that busy?"

She took an extra beat before glancing at the crowd. "Inti Raymi. Festival of the Sun. You managed to come on Winter Solstice."

The news confused him for a moment. It was a clear, sunny day in June, not the big snowy winter he was used to back in Detroit. Then it registered that he was below the equator, and the seasons were the other way around. "Oh."

"Biggest day of the year in Cusco. About half an hour from now the King of the Incas will come onto the Playa, make a speech, then walk up to the Saqsayhuaman ruins above the city and sacrifice a llama to the gods to get the sun to come out. It's pretty interesting, if you're interested. Locals can get in cheap."

"I'm, uh—no. Tired, actually. I haven't checked in yet, and I think I'm starting to feel the change in altitude. But if you want to come around for dinner, I understand there's a very nice restaurant in the hotel. I'm at the Monasterio."

She raised her eyebrows and gave a low whistle. "I suppose I don't need to tell you you're at the nicest hotel in town. How'd you swing that at this time of year?"

Mitch shrugged. "Friend lined it up for me. He's some upper suit in the company that owns it."

Carmel gave a small laugh. "You know everybody, don't you? Okay, how about nine, then? The locals tend to eat later here than you're used to." He nodded, and they both stood up. They said a few parting pleasantries before Carmel drifted out of the restaurant and back into the throbbing crowd. For a moment he could follow her as she weaved through the crowd, headed for nowhere special. Then he couldn't see her at all, and the only hint she'd ever been there was the half-drank cup of tea.

Mitch hardly touched his lunch during the conversation they didn't have. He had been looking forward to seeing her again ever since he called to see what she was doing for a couple of days, but now that he was here and in her company he was starting to think he'd made a mistake. The waiter asked if everything was alright with the lunch, was Mitch ill, he could recommend a couple of good remedies, but Mitch said no, paid and left.

Fifteen minutes later he was at the front desk of the Hotel Monasterio, winded and shaken. The crowd, spilled out beyond the Playa and into the approaching streets, was nearly impenetrable. He'd had to shout more than once to be let through and that, combined with the effort of pulling his very full suitcase uphill for two blocks at altitude, drained him. Then there were the vendors, charming from a distance but annoying and pushy upon experience. One, a teenage boy who called himself John Travolta, followed him for half a block trying to sell him artwork, and the children in general used pleading as a sales tactic. Mitch found them adorable for the first thirty seconds, but by the time he walked into the lobby he was happy they couldn't follow him anymore.

"Reservation for Brand, Mitchell," he said to the front desk clerk. Mitch confirmed his information, showed his credit card, "Oh, and there'll be someone joining me for dinner at around nine, a Miss Carmel Rogers. Would you be so kind as to set a reservation for two in the restaurant?"

"Very good, sir. We'll call you when she arrives. Oh, sir?" the clerk said as Mitch turned to go. "There's a package for you. The airline brought it over about half an hour ago." The clerk produced a box roughly a foot long and six inches to a side wrapped in brown paper. Mitch took the box and continued back to his room, more than ready for a shower and a nap.

The entertainment in the hotel restaurant was a two-man ensemble, one playing a guitar, the other tapping and thumping on a wooden crate, taking it in turns singing the songs. Mitch and Carmel were shown to a table across the room from the men, whose music was loud enough to be heard but not so loud as to preclude conversation. The restaurant seemed fairly large, looking like it could seat a hundred people, but theirs was one of only three tables occupied. Carmel commented on that after the hostess left them. "As many people as there are in town I thought this place would be fuller."

Mitch scanned the room. He'd found out, reading the informational brochure in his room, that the building had been a Franciscan monastery in the 1500's, back during the original Spanish occupation. The restaurant walls were of solid stone except on one side where arches opened onto a courtyard. The room lights were dimmed but not so low that the artwork, all of it of a religious nature, couldn't be admired. "So, how was the ritual sacrifice?"

Carmel shrugged. "Same as it is every year. Some chanting, some praying, llama gets stabbed, the sun comes out, everybody parties. Well, except the llama."

He shook his head.

"What?" she said.

"Amazed I ever thought that'd be fun to watch, that's all." Carmel once described the ceremony in one of her long, rambling letters. Mitch had expressed an interest in seeing it once some years earlier, but the idea was forgotten by the next exchange of mail.

"The needless killing of an animal to satisfy someone's god?" Carmel smirked. "You're getting old. Cautious."

Mitch sighed. If he had a nickel for every time someone accused him of being old he could cover the national debt. Everyone around him seemed to be young, vibrant, alive. He felt himself slowing down sometimes, becoming circumspect in his thoughts and responses. He missed being impulsive from time to time, usually when he heard co-workers describing their latest after-hours exploits. He missed it again now. "I'm just not sure I see the point is all," he said to fill the silence.

"You're joking." Carmel looked at him, eyes wide as anything, a smile barely contained on her face. "You can't see the point of ritual?"

"Well, yes, I—" His voice trailed off as he thought for a moment. There wasn't any real reason for the llama sacrifice. Incas five hundred years before believed the sacrifice held annually on the winter solstice would bring a fortuitous growing season. Crops would be plentiful, farm animals would be strong, and the sun would shine over them all day in and day out. Now almanacs and meteorologists could predict the weather without killing anything, and still the Incas carried on with the bloodletting. "I know it's what they have and I know it's what they do. I just wonder why they keep doing it."

Carmel smiled and shook her head.

"What?" he said.

"Nothing. It's—nothing."

The two-man band moved to a small alcove twenty feet from their table, and started playing another song. Carmel started singing along, her pleasant alto providing a contrast to the singer's smooth tenor. "Bésame, bésame mucho / Como si fuera esta noche la última vez."

"Stop," Mitch said. "Please."

She stopped singing and looked at him. "Oh. Sorry. I didn't—I forgot." The song had been one of Angela's favorites. Mitch serenaded her with it the night he proposed, and then again at the wedding reception. Her mother insisted on playing it before the funeral, something Mitch tried to stop from happening. Mitch's mother thought it unconscionable.

"Listen," Carmel said. "I'm sorry I didn't make it. To the funeral."

"It's okay."

"I tried. I couldn't get a flight out of Lima in time."

"It's alright. Really."

"I just—I should have been there for you."

Mitch remained silent. Angela's family would have wondered why this random person had flown ten hours one way for a funeral. When they found out who she was, that Carmel and Mitch had been an item in college, there would have been talk and anger that Mitch didn't need. He would have appreciated the gesture, but he couldn't bring himself to tell Carmel that it was probably for the best she couldn't make it.

"I keep meaning to visit. Every now and then I actually get as far as looking at airfares to Detroit, coming up and seeing how domestic bliss is treating you. I suppose that wouldn't have went over very well. Or possibly invited you down for a few days."

Mitch stared into the flickering candle centerpiece. He knew, on some level, that she was trying to be complacent. She had even mentioned in her letters once or twice the possibility of visiting, or having Angela and him down for a while. But the actions had never even come close to the words, not on his end and he doubted on hers, and he had no delusions that either would visit the other. He thought about responding, but the arrival of the food a moment later saved him from wondering further.

Dinner ended quietly without much more in the way of comment from either of them. Mitch could feel jet lag and the altitude change beginning to reassert themselves over dessert, and he'd had to stifle a yawn as he said goodnight to Carmel in the foyer. He'd only barely had the energy to strip out of his clothes once he'd reached his room, but now that he was horizontal sleep refused to claim him. Or maybe it had; the room was dark enough that he couldn't tell if any time had passed or how much, and he couldn't find the energy to reach out for the alarm clock. Outside the window some teenaged boys from the sound of it whooped and set off a string of firecrackers. One of them said something in Spanish and the rest laughed as their voices drifted away, leaving Mitch in silence again. There, in the dark with only the ceiling for company, every second lasted an hour, every minute a season.

Mitch's thoughts drifted back to his last visit here, on his honeymoon with Angela. They'd had to stay a night in Cusco before continuing on to Aguas Calientes, the small village at the foot of Machu Picchu. The hotel was over in what was called New Cusco, the more modern half of the city, lacking in any of the Spanish Colonial architectural touches. That night passed miserably. A party louder and longer-lasting than the one that had just left raged seemingly just outside their door, ensuring that they were up until the small hours of the morning. If the noise hadn't kept them up, the altitude sickness may have. Neither Mitch nor Angela had expected the difference in atmosphere to be quite so marked, the air quite so thin. Add to that the fleas that nipped at their ankles like playful pets and they were quite happy to leave. This experience was a vast improvement, Mitch thought, but it did not escape him that he wouldn't have returned were Angela still alive.

The years, though, had been good to Carmel. She looked almost the same as the last time Mitch had seen her—was it twelve years ago now, or perhaps longer? There were maybe a few crow's feet around her eyes, and perhaps her face was a little fuller than he remembered, but she still looked young, radiant, alive. She was flowering here in Peru, she had said at dinner, far more than she thought she ever could in the States. *She would have been here when we came through for the honeymoon*, Mitch thought. *She might even have been out with the revelers that night.* The thought of happening upon her that evening, with his new bride only paces away, didn't please him, each mental reconstruction of the possible scene ending worse than the one before.

He wondered what would have happened if Carmel and he had stayed together. Would they be here, high in the Peruvian Andes, enjoying life at sixteen revolutions per minute as opposed to everyone else's thirty three and a third? Would he look and feel as young as Carmel appeared to, enjoying life to its full? Or would they be back in Detroit, he successful in business but Carmel a shade of herself, the possibilities of her life going, going, gone in the wind? Would they still enjoy each other's company? His thoughts drifted to the package that was waiting for him when he arrived, already tucked into the backpack he'd be taking tomorrow, what it was and what he was about to do. He began to fall asleep at last, knowing that it would be finished the next day, and he could move on.

❖ ❖ ❖

They boarded the Hiram Bingham train at Poroy Station, twenty minutes outside of central Cusco. Though brunch was to be served during the first leg of the trip, between Poroy and Ollantaytambo, Mitch and Carmel partook of the breakfast buffet at the hotel. Carmel seemed to have one of nearly everything. She returned to the buffet thrice, leaving Mitch wondering where she stored it all. He, by contrast, ate very little. Although the buffet had been his idea, although he said he was ravenous, he managed only a banana and a glass of water. When Carmel asked him if anything was wrong he said no, everything's fine, but he suspected she knew he was lying.

The train pulled out of Poroy Station at nine precisely. According to the schedule they would arrive at Aguas Calientes at half past twelve, then take a bus two thousand feet up to the ruins atop Machu Picchu. A guide would lead them on a tour, offering explanations and assumption about the Inca who had lived there. Then there would be high tea offered at the Sanctuary Lodge just outside the main gates before boarding the return train. The entire trip, from departure to return, would last just over twelve hours. The train had but three cars, one dining and two bar cars. As the train left Poroy Station the complement of two dozen passengers, Mitch and Carmel among them, congregated in one of the bar cars and enjoyed the first complementary Pisco sour of the day.

"I usually don't drink this early, but," Mitch said, and downed half the glass in one go. He licked his lips appreciatively. "What is this again? Rum?"

"Brandy," Carmel said after taking a sip of her own. "Egg white, cinnamon, lemon juice, syrup, and local bitters."

"It's good." Mitch sighed and looked out the panorama windows. Some enterprising people had carved out various things in the mountainside scrub: football team logos, political party references, the odd Biblical chapter and verse. It was difficult to tell, but the words and pictures seemed hundreds of feet high. The planning required to remove certain batches of scrub, leaving the desired picture or phrase, must have been lengthy. Then there was the skill involved. Some of the mountainsides where the pictures were looked nearly sheer. Mitch couldn't imagine anything like it in the States, but here it seemed like it belonged. He was lost in the countryside, and it was a few seconds before he realized Carmel was talking to him.

"Did you sleep well?" she said.

"I suppose." In truth, he didn't feel like he'd slept well at all. Other than the party that had passed by his window, he'd woken a couple of times to use the bathroom. Nothing new there; he did that at home as well. But it took him longer here to fall back to sleep. It might have been the lower oxygen, he thought, or it might have been that he wasn't in his own bed. But he was fooling himself with those reasons and he knew it. His eyes went to the backpack, resting next to him on the floor.

"Listen," Carmel said after he'd been silent for a moment. "Listen. If you're going to be mopey and sulky all day, that's only going to make things worse."

He sighed. "I'll try and cheer up a little, if it'll make you happy."

"The point is for you to be happy. I'm fine." Carmel took another long gulp of her Pisco sour. "You could have stayed at my place, you know. Saved yourself the money."

"I thought about that. I appreciate the offer, really, but I find as I get older that I like my privacy more and more, my own space. And, you know, it would have just been awkward."

Carmel grinned. "And this isn't? An ex-girlfriend accompanying you on a pilgrimage for your late wife?"

"Point taken." He sipped his drink and looked out the window. Their side of the train gave a view of a vast open space, the Sacred Valley of the Incas. Farms arranged in patchworked tiles covered most of the flat spaces. Here and there he could see dots of people moving, tilling the fields by hand or by ox. "Why did you agree to come?"

She didn't say anything for a moment. "Because I know how important she was to you. You think I couldn't see that in all your letters? The way you talked about her, everything she did, how wonderful she was to you. It was impossible to miss. I used to want you to feel that way about me, a long time ago. And I won't lie, I got jealous at first when I read that in your letters."

A beat went by before Mitch responded. "I had no idea."

"Yeah, well. I grew out of it, I suppose. Focused on the good times. And I had a new life here, new friends, new lovers. And when you called and said you were coming, and what had happened, I felt a small tug again, hoping to reconnect, maybe answer an old question or two."

"And?"

Carmel took another drink of her Pisco sour, and smiled.

❖   ❖   ❖

The road from Aguas Calientes to Machu Picchu was barely two lanes wide in most places. Buses going in opposite directions only passed each other near the frequent switchbacks along the 2,000-foot ascent. Although the road was reasonably well used—a bus a minute each direction eight hours a day every day—it was never paved and was littered with rocks and stones, and in some places there were ruts deep enough to hang up posters. Mitch and Carmel's driver managed to find each and every rock and rut on the road, it seemed, and they felt like martinis but they time they reached the top.

The road came to a stop in front of the Sanctuary Lodge, the hotel outside the front gates of the ruins. The rest of the train passengers gathered in front of the hotel to wait for the complementary tour guide. Mitch and Carmel went to the entrance to the ruins, tickets in hand.

"You know where you're going?" Carmel said.

"Pretty sure. It's been a while, but I think I remember."

Mitch and Angela had spent two days wandering through the ruins where they were here. Mitch had enjoyed wandering along the top of them, making the hour and a half walk out to the Sun Gate high above the ruins, the last stop along the Inca Trail. Angela enjoyed looking in the caves that opened into the mountainside below, at the bottom of a steep and shallow stairway. She had taken him down to the caves at the end of the second day, led him inside one when the roving archaeologists weren't looking. He was only barely able to stand up straight inside. "The Incans believed the caves were the opening to the underworld," she had told him. "They would come here and communicate with the departed, hoping to receive guidance and knowledge." The words had rung in Mitch's mind since Angela died, had only gotten louder with each successive moment he'd been in Peru, and now, as he crossed through the ruins and spied the stairway down, her voice was overpowering in his mind.

They made their way down the stairway to the caves. Mitch stepped inside one, nearly scraping his head along the ceiling. Carmel came in behind him. "Well," she said, her voice echoing into the darkness before them. "Here we are."

Mitch looked around the cave. It looked vaguely familiar to him although he couldn't tell one cave from another. Some small rocks littered the floor, and the air felt damp and smelled faintly of mold. Outside, a light rain began to fall. "Yeah," he said, his voice flat. "Here we are." Neither of them moved for a moment, then Mitch slid the backpack off his shoulder, removed the package, and pulled from it the urn containing Angela's remains. He touched his forehead to the lid for a moment, then opened it, stepped further back into the cave, and scattered the ashes against one wall of the cave. *Just what you wanted, Angela*, he thought. "I want to be buried here, looking out onto this beautiful valley," you said. He put the urn away and stared at the spot where he'd spread the ashes. "And when you need to communicate with me, Mitch, I'll be here. I'll be right—"

"Hey," said a voice from outside the cave. Mitch and Carmel turned to see a man in a white jumpsuit peering at them. "You're not supposed to be in there."

Carmel looked at Mitch before turning to face the man. "Sorry. We were just curious, you know, how far back in the caves go." They climbed out of the cave and made their way back up the stair, the man gazing after them.

The next noon found them at the café on the Playa de Armas. The Playa today was not quite empty but it was nowhere near as full as it had been. All the tourists had already gone home, back to the States or Europe, or back to their small villages to wait for the tourism dollar to find them. The waiter, mustache hanging on by the follicles, breezed over when they sat down and took Mitch's suitcase out of the way, a mostly unnecessary gesture: Mitch and Carmel were again the only customers. "I feel foolish being the only customers in here," Mitch said. "Like we've come before opening."

"We almost have. Siesta isn't for an hour or so." Carmel looked out the window almost absently. "I love this town. All the cathedrals and architecture."

Mitch said nothing, scanning the walls instead.

"You should just come sometime. Here, I mean. Enjoy the town and scenery and—" Her voice trailed off.

"Yeah," Mitch said, trying to sound non-committal. "Sure."

Carmel looked at her watch. "I'd better go. I'm expected at the art studio in half an hour," she said, and stood up. "You're welcome to join me, wait for your flight there."

He rubbed the stubble on his chin. "Thought I might just poke around town. They'll hold my suitcase here if I ask them to, I think, and there's a couple of places I wanted to have a look at."

Carmel nodded. "Well, call when you get home, okay?"

Mitch stopped rubbing his chin. "Yeah, I'll—be in touch, I suppose."

Carmel turned and left the restaurant. As Mitch watched her walk across the Playa he wondered if they would ever meet again. He shook his head and a moment later heard a discreet cough behind him. The waiter had come back with a Pisco sour.

"Pardon me, señor," he said. "I couldn't help but hear. You intended to spend the afternoon looking around our wonderful city. I'm very familiar with everything around here. Maybe I could help you find something."

Mitch stared at the man for a moment, then took the Pisco sour and drank it down. In the background, the same song that had greeted him two days earlier was playing again. He could hear Angela singing in his head, "If you can't make your mind up / We'll never get started."

"Direction," he said then. "I seem to have lost mine. Could you help me find that?"

The waiter's mustache vanished into nothing.

LIBERTY BELL

The entire point of the Project, as I outlined it in my annual Mayor's Open Forum to Liberty, was to revitalize the town's economy. Before the tower was built—and let's not kid ourselves—there was no reason to come here. There wasn't a shopping center or a fancy restaurant, or even a miniature golf center within the township limits. The buildings around the town square were half empty, all of them in varying states of decay. About the only reason anybody would actually want to live here is because of the decent school system, which only gets the high marks it does because the class sizes are so small. A destination Liberty was not. Now we actually have some tourism. The general public beyond Union County wants to know what that big spire right in the center of Liberty is. There may have been some problems between conception and realization, but I am here to tell you that the end result makes the problems we had during the construction phase laughable.

To begin with, the excitement generated by the mere announcement of the Project was palpable. When I went into Ted's Barber Shop that same afternoon for my bi-weekly haircut, all of the other patrons couldn't stop talking about it. It'll revitalize the community, they said. It's sad to see half the shops on the town square vacant, all the work and all the money gone to the cities a hundred miles away. At Sunday services that weekend there were a half a dozen prayer requests that the Project did was it was supposed to do, and that was just at the Presbyterian Church. The Catholics across town had a special mass, and the Shriners started rehearsing in the event a parade broke out. Everywhere I went, people patted me on the back and said that it was the best thing they'd heard of in who knew how long, and keep up the good work and such.

The Project began in earnest when we announced that ideas and input on what exactly the final product should look like would be welcomed, and the ideas began pouring in, not just from the residents of Liberty but also from surrounding communities, most of which were in monetary crunches of their own. Somebody put our call for assistance out on the Internet, and for whatever reason people who lived as far away as New York and San Francisco sent drawings. We received something like 150 designs a day for the next six weeks. The Post Office was so backed up with the envelopes and boxes that contained entries that they had to bring in a temporary just to handle the extra traffic. We piled the lot of them in one of the vacant classrooms at the high school, and the Monday following the deadline the City Council and I began the tedious and daunting task of sifting through the deluge of entries to find the one that would, in fact, be the financial salvation of Liberty.

The design we finally settled on was a carillon bell tower, two hundred and fifty feet high at its summit, dwarfing every other structure in Union County. It would be built directly in the center of the town square, at the cost of a portion of the playground therein, and every year we would hold a festival at which the carillon would be rung, bringing joy and money to the hearts and wallets of Liberty. The town's founding fathers would have been pleased.

Now, I will be the first to admit that the designer and contractor we settled on may not have been totally in tune with the personality of the area. Dix Handfield came very highly recommended by one of the cousins of one of the Council members, and the sketches and photographs he sent along, while possibly suggestive (shall we say) in places, there was nothing that the Mothers League of Liberty would object to. It was only after the project was completed that Mr. Handfield's career in the adult film industry was discovered, and though the cousin of the aforementioned Councilmember was found to be one of the often-featured performers in Mr. Handfield's films, I understand that the family feud this discovery triggered has since settled into a calm acceptance. The Councilmember is still expecting to be re-elected in November.

Once he was hired, Mr. Handfield was placed in control of the Project and given a deadline of Labor Day of the following year. He began taking bids immediately for the construction of both the bell tower itself and for the bells. The companies that were eventually awarded the contracts came well-referenced, and the Council and I visited some of their other structures to examine the quality thereof. We were not advised until after Mr. Handfield returned to New York that ranking influential executives at the winning companies were, in fact, relatives of his. Specifically, his uncle owned the company that built the tower, and no less than three cousins worked at the bell factory. In the larger sense this should not have been of issue. After all, Mr. Handfield's uncle did not himself build the tower, nor did any of his three cousins do any work on the bells themselves. We did, however, find these "coincidences," as Mr. Handfield put it, to be on the curious side.

Having spent this amount of time calling Mr. Handfield's general character into question, I feel we should give him some benefit of the doubt. The construction delays that occurred during the building of the tower were not his fault. There were, of course, the two separate tornados that tore through Liberty less than ten days apart, both of which leveled the construction site and most of the town square, and the second of which is the cause of our high school classes now being conducted in circus tents, courtesy of the governor's Emergency Relief Fund.

It was shortly after construction recommenced on the tower two weeks after the second tornado hit that the first graffiti of "Liberty is Cursed" showed up, although since there wasn't much in the way of standing structures at the time, the vandals spray-painted the streets. The tower was burned down three times in short order after that: once by a lightning strike; once by the Liberty's Curse vandals (they left their autograph on the construction office); and once when a construction worker failed to notice the No Smoking sign next to the still-unexplained containers of highly explosive liquids. One can make an argument that the latter case is more an example of it blowing up as opposed to burning down, but I believe that to be a moot point.

(I would be remiss if I did not mention the number of injuries that occurred on the work site. Sixteen workers managed to fall from various heights and break between them some twenty-five limbs, twenty ribs, and a handful of vertebrae. Although there were no human fatalities, at least one raccoon did manage to fall fifty feet to its death, but again, Mr. Handfield cannot be held to blame for this.)

During this time, as you'll recall, Liberty's public image suffered greatly. The Liberty is Cursed" graffiti was filmed by television crews from as far away as Dayton, under the guise of documenting the double tornado disaster. The things shown on the evening news on the subject were somewhat less than enthusiastic. Someone in town told one of the reporters about Old Man Millard who lives out on County Road 25 a couple of miles south of town, and they got an interview with him. He said something during the interview along the lines of, "I don't think Liberty is cursed. Just in an unlucky stretch is all. We need that carillon more than ever." When the interview aired that night, all they showed of it was, "Liberty is cursed." Then the anchor lady rambled on for another minute about how the whole town agreed with him, which was a complete lie. After that when we saw newsfolk coming we just ignored them, pretended like they weren't there, and nobody gave any more interviews.

The bells were shipped from the foundry in New Jersey the first week of August. When the train carrying the bells pulled in at the station just outside of town, half the population turned up to watch them unload the massive crates. The crates were five feet to a side at least, with some of the straw packaging filtering out like the last stray hairs on an otherwise bald head. The crates were loaded into a couple of flatbed trucks rented special for transporting the bells the one mile from the station to the tower, and the townspeople followed behind the first of them as if they were in a big parade. I half expected the Shriners to turn up, but they didn't.

The crates were undone at the base of the tower, the bells unpacked with a crowd marveling at each one like they'd all been given a second Christmas in the middle of August. There were forty-nine bells in all of varying sizes to give the carillon a four-octave range. The clangers would be operated by a small piano keyboard in a room built into the base of the tower. A scaffold structure was set up on the one side of the tower with ropes and pulleys and whatnot for the actual hoisting of the bells. They were big and heavy enough that only four or five of them could be hoisted up the tower every day. While only one bell was dropped during the lifting process, there were a few tense moments immediately thereafter when it was discovered that one of the workers was trapped beneath the bell. Fortunately, it landed open side down, and avoided making contact with the man cupped (as it were) beneath it. The rescue operation took six hours—many of the ropes in the pulley system needed to be replaced, requiring a drive into Richmond—which was long enough for a charity benefit to be organized. The captive, a Mr. Hector Gonzales, has written a book detailing his ordeal, which he has called "My Terror Under Middle C." (There are rumors that Martin Sheen will portray Mr. Gonzales in a Movie-of-the-Week, but those are unsubstantiated at this point.)

Despite all the setbacks, the tower was still on schedule to be finished by the prescribed Labor Day. We began advertising its premiere in not only the local communities but on television newscasts as far away as South Bend. The problem was that the last bell would be installed the day before, so there would be no trial run of any sort. (And how would we do a trial run anyway? Everybody would hear it then, which would defeat the purpose of a big show.) The City Council organized a festival around it, which, in truth, Liberty was in no condition to hold. Most of the downtown buildings were still rubble thanks to the two tornadoes. Most of the citizens who stayed to brave out the reconstruction were living in tents, or in the elementary school gym, so the famed "Open Arms of Liberty" had been closed for repairs for a few months. Still, the city needed the revenue, so the festival went ahead as planned.

The grand unveiling of the carillon was the main event. The high school marching band and orchestra rehearsed several songs, and the last one scheduled to be played was "Edelweiss," with the main melody provided by the carillon. After the song concluded there would be a fireworks display and an announcement of the winner of the Name the Carillon contest. (Grand prize: two nights in Detroit and tickets to a Tigers game.)

I will admit that security the night before the event was a little lax. We didn't think we needed any. Was someone going to run off with the carillon? No. Would another tornado tear through town, destroying the carillon before it had even been rung? We certainly hoped not. What we had failed to consider was: would the tower be spray-painted in big black letters with "Liberty is Cursed," to which the answer was an unfortunate yes. The news cameras, which arrived at eight the next morning to set up camera locations for that night's big event, took pictures of the graffiti for the midday newscasts, which used the pictures as the lead story. I am happy to report that we did manage to remove the graffiti before most of the festival crowd turned up.

The unveiling event came off without a hitch until the rainstorm came. The band played their songs, and then got to "Edelweiss," and let me tell you there wasn't a dry eye to be seen. The carillon, the last bastion of hope of the little nowhere town of Liberty, was a big hit. Every note shimmered through the town, and even the orchestra members were having trouble not being awed by the sound of the bells. When it started to rain after the song ended, no one cared. When there were lightning flashes seen during the fireworks, no one paid them any attention.

I need not give the precise details of what happened next; most of you saw it during the live broadcast of the fireworks. The lightning strike on the carillon caught nearly everyone by surprise, as did the bits of brick from the tower that rained down on the marching band and orchestra members below like the sitting ducks they were. Had Dix Handfield not started running around and screaming, "My erection! My beautiful erection!" the riot may not have happened at all. There was no further damage to the carillon, and other than a few bruises to a few arms and heads the only thing damaged in the band was a tuba dented by the falling debris.

In the end, the carillon was a success. Little Mary Whitfield, a fifth grader at the elementary school, came up with the winning name: The Liberty Bell. A few people didn't like it—something about the other one being cracked—until they were reminded that the tower had been cracked by the lightning and wasn't likely to be repaired. Enough money came into the town during the festival that most of the buildings are being constructed again, and plans are underway for another festival next year. At least four of the national fast food chains have expressed interest in putting a franchise here, not to mention Starbucks. People want to come to our little town again, and really—isn't that the important thing?

Ghost

South of Piqua there's a rest stop. One building has the restrooms, another has the vending machines, and behind them, behind the lot for cars and vans, down a small slope is a picnic grove. Two dozen picnic tables are dotted across the area, some shaded by maples with canopies high enough to not be in the way. Near half of them are charcoal grills with smaller tables thoughtfully placed next to them as a set-up and preparation area. The rest stop a hundred miles back, near Bowling Green, doesn't have the grills. A dog-walking path winds its way through the grove, starting and ending back at the parking lot.

When I pulled into the rest stop there were only three other cars in the lot. The area where the trucks parking was mostly empty. I went in to the building where the bathrooms were. The men's was closed for cleaning. That's okay, I thought. I'm only twenty miles from my brother's house. I can get that far, and I don't need it that badly. But it was a fine day and the drive had been a long one, so I crossed the parking lot and walked through the grove.

The sound of the freeway faded as I descended the slope. A small wind came through the trees as I idly wandered over to a grill. It was empty, no remains of a stray cigarette butt let alone ashes from a cookout long over to be found. Not too far away was a trash can: empty. I drifted over to another grill which had coals in it that didn't look like they'd even been lit. Did the person put them there and then—what, realize they'd forgotten some crucial ingredient, like the hamburger? The accompanying trash can wasn't quite empty, some shredded and torn papers covering the bottom of the can, but the amount of ants crawling over them told me they'd been there for some time.

I looked around me in the grove then and realized that I was probably it for the day, the only person that would wander down here and see what there was to see. Long past were the days when families passing through would pull off and stop here, occupying one of the picnic tables instead of finding the nearest fast food place. Cold cuts would have been packed, chips and drinks acquired before getting on the freeway that morning or, if someone was feeling adventur-ous, a grill would be used, the children throwing a Frisbee while waiting for the coals to be ready. Instead of a ten-minute restroom break, families would be at these places for an hour or more, stopping and resting as the name suggested.

I climbed back up the hill to the parking lot. Two of the cars had gone. Leaning against the trunk of the third, a teenage girl applied her thumbs to her cellphone without once looking up at what was across the parking lot from her. I looked again at the picnic grove. From above it looked even lonelier. I tried to envision what it would have looked like, fully in use, families at all of the picnic tables, but the sound of the freeway kept my mind from fleshing out this fantasy. I could see, though, the one grill where I'd found the unlit coals, and envisioned myself there being the one to put this place to the use it was designed for, stopping here on my next trip through with a bag of coals, a roll of tin foil, and a pound of ground chuck. Then people would come and see what I was doing, and maybe remember, for a while, to just stop. The image faded then, the ghost of a future rest stop disappeared, and I too turned my back and walked away.

SWEET

We were under attack again. It had only been seven hours since the last shelling, gummy bears and jelly beans dropping onto our huts. The Chieftain of the other tribe explained during one of the rounds of parlays that using actual bombs would look bad to the Global Tribal Community, inviting scorn and possible sanctions upon them. Bombs, bad, gumdrops—fine, apparently. Our Chieftain at the time relayed this to the tribe and was pelted for his troubles with the gold-foil-wrapped chocolate coins we'd been deluged with only that morning, causing him some minor bruises and abrasions and hastening the resignation some of us thought overdue. The Council of Elders issued a statement saying that the party responsible for starting the coin throwing would be punished. But I never was.

Anyway, we were being shelled again, not with explosive shells, but plastic egg shells. Some of them were mercifully empty, but others were filled with candy—toffees, mostly, but some nougat and more of the chocolate coins. The empty ones were not all that big a deal; they broke into little harmless pieces of plastic. The full ones, though, could do some damage if one was to hit somebody about the head or shoulders. Our newest Chieftain, George, had been hit on the head with three such candy-filled eggs and was only now regaining consciousness. "This has to stop," he said.

We had all been saying that since the bombings began, but seldom out loud. Glen the Blacksmith grunted an acknowledgement, but what he was thinking was probably much ruder. Geof the Builder tapped his foot while Glenn the Baker ate some jelly beans that had come in the attack.

"With all due respect," I said, "this we know. Only yesterday my daughter was hit with a ball of cookie dough. We need to make a decision about our retaliation."

"Patience, Greg of Nothing." Chieftain George tried to sit up, unsuccessfully. "Retaliation may not be the wisest course of action."

"Not the wisest course of action? We've been shelled twice daily for the last two hundred days. Not only is the collateral damage such that our huts are barely standing but our children are now obese and have, on average, six cavities each. It's only through great luck that our corn fields remain undamaged. We must do something." I would have slammed my fist on the table but we were under it, owing to the ongoing egg barrage and the numerous holes in the ceiling.

Chieftain George sighed, having managed to bring himself upright enough to lean against a table leg. "Their Chieftain is coming to parlay again tomorrow at the meeting place. Perhaps then we can get the shelling stopped and our lives back to normal.

I counted no less than three scoffs at this, not including my own. It is worth noting at this point that the only reason George was Chieftain was because he could not step backward fast enough. As per our custom, all able-bodied village men line up shoulder to shoulder every seventh midday in the Central Square for what is known as the Big Question, posed by the Council of Elders. The first person to step forward is given the task outlined in the Question. Sometimes the Big Question is operational—"Who will oversee the construction of the new town barber shop?"—and sometimes it is personal—"Which of you will offer your hand in marriage to the lovely Jackie the Vintner? No, not you, John the Farmer, you're already married."—but it caught us all by surprise when, two days after the last Chieftain was pelted with the chocolate coins, the Big Question was, "Which of you will be the new Chieftain?" The job, we all knew, came with no real perks except for the privilege of fielding everyone's complaints. George was picking his ear as the Big Question was asked and didn't realize it had ended until he looked around and saw that everyone else had stepped backward.

From a corner of the room came a cough and all heads turned toward the source. Phill the Elder, was sitting crosslegged under an end table idly stacking candy bricks. "We have parlayed many times with them. Always it has failed. Sometimes it has been our fault, sometimes theirs, sometimes both and neither, but the end result has always been the same. Perhaps this time the end result will be different. I do not know. But we must put faith in our Chieftain, or else he will surely fail."

Chieftain George smirked in my general direction. He knew I did not approve of his performance as Chieftain, and he suspected it was me that painted a large red bullseye on the roof of his hut following a particularly unsuccessful parlay. What happened the next day is remembered as the Gummy Worm Incident, which involved directed enemy fire of three tons of the gelatinous treats at the indicated target. No one was hurt, the attack having come at midday while everyone was working the corn fields, but the roof collapsed and the hut is still unusable. I maintain to this day that the three dozen people that saw me atop his hut with a can of red paint were mistaken.

"So that's it?" I said. I knew I was being rude, but I didn't care. "Let's go and do the same thing over again and maybe we'll get a different result? Tell me, Chieftain, Elder, do either of you know the definition of insanity?"

"Enough," Chieftain George said, harder than anyone thought he could. "This time, instead of going with a group of Elders I will go alone, as a show of good intention." He looked around, waiting for another scoff. None came. "That's the end of it," he said then. "I will parlay."

Word made it around the village about the following day's parlay. Most of the townspeople thought the idea of going alone was at once fantastically brave and exceptionally stupid. A few people whispered that it was a machismo thing, a response of sorts for taking three candy-filled eggs to the head, but also for having his hut bombarded. I was confronted during our tribal evening meal by four townspeople led by one particularly angry woman whose name I did not know insisting that all of it, from Chieftain George's rise to power right through to that day's bombing, was my fault. There was no point in responding; she wouldn't have believed me.

The next morning all of the townspeople gathered in the Central Square to see Chieftain George off on his parlay mission. He would walk the entire way, and would reach the meeting place sometime in mid-afternoon. The Council of Elders blessed him and said a few other words. No sooner had he turned to leave the Square and the throng of people behind than a scream came from a far corner. About half the crowd shouted, "Air raid! Incoming!" and all two thousand of us scrambled for cover. Chieftain George had not reached the edge of the crowd. Once the shouting and the running started there was no getting out for him. Less than half the crowd managed to leave the square before the miniature chocolate bars really started to hit.

An hour later, after the shelling stopped, I was in the large hospital hut helping tend to the wounded. Most suffered only minor injuries, slight concussions from the candy or bumps and bruises from the stampede, and nothing more serious than a broken arm. Glen the Blacksmith and I were at adjacent workstations. "You're not helping any, you know," he said, wrapping a bandage around a small girl's head.

"You don't seriously think that was my fault, do you?"

He shrugged. "The shelling? No, although we're very lucky they left the chocolate in wrappers. We've got another hot day coming. No, the whole parlay thing, Chieftain George going alone."

"I didn't make him do that."

"You've been chipping away at his ego since he became Chieftain. A rude comment here, a smirk there, the bullseye on his hut—oh, stop denying it. Everyone knows it was you."

I applied some ointment to an older gentleman's arm and started bandaging it. "I think there are questions that need to be asked, that's all. Why are we being shelled in the first place? How is it they've hit the town but not even tried to hit our corn fields? Wouldn't it be more effective to cut off our food sup—"

Glen the Blacksmith shushed me. "Not everyone needs to hear that." He gave the girl he was helping a banana and told her to rest for the remainder of the day. She skipped off, holding the banana like it was a prize. "Look, nobody cares about the corn field. We can eat, and it employs three quarters of the town. If it's destroyed, the town will fall, but so long as it's unharmed nobody wants to ask why. What matters more is why we're being shelled."

I asked the old man if I'd wrapped the bandage too tight. He said no and I told him he was done and he left. "So?"

"Were you not listening to Phill the Elder yesterday? This is what the parlay is supposed to accomplish, the parlay Chieftain George went to alone because you goaded him into it."

"He's a weak leader."

"I know that. You know that. Pretty much everyone in town knows that. And I'm sure he reminds himself of that every day when he wakes up. But you sure as the Maker didn't step forward when the Big Question came. Everybody knows that, too, including Chieftain George. Don't be surprised if that comes back on you."

His point about the Big Question was both correct and unfair. Nobody else, including him, had stepped forward either. And I had no desire to lead. Chieftain George's predecessor was a good friend of mine who noted to anyone who would listen that no matter what he did at least one townsperson called him an idiot for doing it, and our friendship didn't stop me from pelting him with chocolate coins. Still, I didn't feel like arguing the point with Glen the Blacksmith. It had been a long day already, what with the shelling and the wounded, and I wanted more than anything a lie down, so I went back to my hut to have one, stepping around the piles of miniature chocolate bars as best I could.

The sun was already down when a pounding on the side of my hut woke me. "Wake up." Glen the Blacksmith's voice came through the walls at top volume. "Council of Elders have called for a Big Question in the Central Square."

"What?"

"Council of Elders, Big Question, Central Square." His voice was already drifting away with his footsteps.

I dressed at top speed. There wasn't any precedent for a Big Question being called in the middle of the night. It was usually done at midday. Sometimes people would bring lunches to the Central Square and make a picnic of it. I arrived in a dead heat with the other stragglers. The line of men had already started to form. I took a place next to Glen the Blacksmith. A moment later, Phill the Elder stepped to the center of the Square, next to the Great Communal Fire, and everyone fell silent. Dead quiet though it was, no one was sleeping through the tension.

"Chieftain George has been taken hostage," he said. Sharp intakes of breath punctuated the crowd. "They have made but one demand: that we do not attempt a rescue. Though he is not—" here he stopped to stare around at the crowd before fixing me with a hard gaze, "—particularly beloved, he is still our Chieftain. Another parlay has been arranged for tomorrow midday. Who will go to negotiate for his release? Ah, we have a volunteer."

I had been too put off by his gaze to bother stepping backward.

I knew the sun was up because licorice was falling from the sky, black as opposed to the red that everyone favors. The last time we were shelled with licorice the sewers were backed up for a week and the whole town stank like a teenaged boy's armpit. I could feel the complaining begin already.

I had no plan. I knew where I was going and when I had to be there, and had a good idea what was expected of me, but that was about it. The rest I still didn't know. I was more concerned about the immediate future, specifically getting out of town. My popularity, which was low to begin with, took another dip after the Big Question. The group of four townspeople who had accosted me before started booing as soon as Phill the Elder stopped talking. Most of the rest of the crowd joined a moment later, and I found myself running for cover amidst a hailstorm of jawbreakers left over from a highly destructive shelling three days earlier.

I was dressing when someone knocked at my hut. A moment later Phill the Elder entered. He sat at the foot of my bed while I finished dressing.

"This is unfortunate," he said. "Necessary, but unfortunate."

I said nothing.

"He's not hurt, thank the Maker," he went on. "They assure us of that much. They have agreed to release him following a successful parlay."

I kept dressing. He paused, expecting an answer, but he wouldn't like what I had to say.

"Had he not gone alone, Chieftain George would not be in this predicament, and the town with him."

I had had enough. "You can't blame that on me."

"Everyone already does. Whether or not they can is not the point."

"He's unfit to lead. His plan of action had been to follow what everyone else has done before him. You'll notice that hasn't gotten us much of anywhere, as I said yesterday. There's been nothing new, nothing that shows any sign of stopping this. And if he's that strong of a leader, he wouldn't have felt needled into going alone. Tell me I'm wrong."

The silence lingered like one of Glen the Blacksmith's anvils. Half a minute passed before he responded. "You're not."

I pulled my shoes on, one foot at a time, and stared into Phill the Elder eyes. A tranquility shone there, and I wanted to shake him from it. "Why haven't they bombed our corn fields?" I said.

It worked. He was unable to hide the surprise from his eyes for the briefest of moments before the tranquil replaced itself. It was obvious he knew the answer, but I opted not to press. Instead I smiled and left the hut. No one stopped me on my way out of town. Everyone was too busy trying to keep the licorice from overwhelming the town again.

The path to the meeting place isn't too bad. Most of it is relatively level after the first large hill right outside of the village. If you turn and look down from the top of the hill, as I did, you can see most of the village below, or what remains of it. I figured—correctly, as I eventually found out—that it was from here or somewhere nearby that the attacks on our village were launched. They had done it all with gilders, using colored cloth that matched the sky, swooping out over our village, dropping the sweets, and swooping back.

I reached the meeting space just after midday. It was a large plateau atop one of the many hills in the area, with large stumps for everyone to sit on. I took the one nearest where I had entered, and a few minutes later was joined by four men, I only recognized one of them: Chieftain George, who was bound at the wrists and gagged. No one in the village outside of the Elders and the Chieftain had ever met or described the tribespeople who were shelling us. They were not especially tall, a little shorter than I, but undeniably larger around the middle. If our children continued on their current dietary trend, they would eventually look like this. Chieftain George looked surprised that it was me that had come, alone as he had, or possibly he was just afraid.

"You have come alone," said one of the others, slightly taller and portlier and sitting between the other two. I took him to be their Chieftain.

There was a long silence. I felt like I was missing a protocol.

I spoke next. "What has our tribesman done to warrant being held hostage?"

The three men looked at each other for a second, and then back at me. "Your Elders have not told you?"

Had Phill the Elder been there at that moment I would have slapped him, arthritic joints and all. "No."

"He threatened action against us."

I pursed my lips and looked over at Chieftain George. He had a defiant look about his face. "Go on," I said.

"Open warfare," the Chieftain said. "He became quite— demonstrative. He said something I choose not to repeat involving our family trees. This was why we subdued him."

The combative look remained in Chieftain George's eyes. I had figured they took him captive merely for coming alone, instead of with a party of Elders, and they were finally pressing an advantage. But he had tried to fight. A twinkling of respect for him came to me, but rather than let anyone else see it, I merely nodded my head, and turned back to their Chieftain. "I am in no position to make such threats, as I am sure you well know. Also, please accept my apology on behalf of my people for our Chieftain's outrage. Well-intentioned though it may have been, we do not dispute how misguided it was."

The Chieftain nodded in acquiescence. "Accepted. We will not release him, however."

I knew the next line was mine to say, that I was supposed to determine the terms of Chieftain George's release, but now that I was here there were other things that needed to be told. Chieftain George could wait. Before I spoke, I let the silence linger, perhaps an extra moment or two longer than was necessary. "If I may, sir. Why do you not attack our corn fields?"

It was a moment after I spoke before the three of them started laughing. I chanced a glance at Chieftain George but he was looking at them too. "They really haven't told you anything, have they?" the Chieftain said in between chuckles.

I shook my head, knowing I would not like what came next.

"Because we couldn't then use your corn to make corn syrup after we take over your village."

My mind reeled. The bombing got us, or at least the children, addicted to candy—corn sugar, more or less. The takeover, when it came, would be a peaceful one; we would already be singing the praises of their products. They would be our saviors, and our great corn fields would be given over to their purpose. Worse, time was not an issue; if anything, the longer the bombings went on, the easier things would be. I was impressed, if somewhat angry at being bombarded with sweets twice a day.

My eyes flickered from one point on the ground to another. I had no particular love for the village leadership, but the thought of the village itself becoming something else was something I could not bear. I had grown up in the village. I had found love and lost it again a few times there. Now I was left to wonder what would have happened if we had responded sooner. The village was in no condition to repel them now. Our strategy, parlay after endless parlay, was a losing one. Sitting there, now, I searched my mind for a long moment for a means of ending the invasion, to preserve our village, sooner rather than later. I saw only one way.

I stood up then and went to leave, to go back to the village. "Excuse me," their Chieftain said, then gestured to Chieftain George. "Your compatriot?"

I thought for a moment, then look at Chieftain George, his eyes pleading. His willingness to stand up to our invaders was truly worthy. Would that it had happened sooner, that it hadn't taken someone like me yelling at him. "I have some things to discuss with my Tribal Elders," I said. "Tomorrow, perhaps?" I walked away then. They'd be there the next day or not. That would be an issue for Phill the Elder.

It was well past dark by the time I got back to the village. I had stopped a few times on the way to consider everything I had heard and seen, to reassess what our options were, what my options were. They couldn't use real bombs. Our old Chieftain had said that. If they did, they would in turn be sanctioned. So what would drive them to use real bombs? The same thing that would save our village, the same thing I had to do. Right outside the village I found a hunk of wood a few inches thick and about as long as my forearm. I took it.

The village was silent. The Great Communal Fire in the Central Square burned as ever. The attending guard had fallen asleep. He didn't see me approach, take my tunic off, wrap it around the end of the piece of wood, and stick it into the fire. The tunic lit almost immediately. My torch was ready.

"I can't let you do that," Phill the Elder said from somewhere behind me.

I turned to face him. The tranquility was gone from his eyes, replaced with—was it fear? "How long ago did you surrender?" I said.

His chest collapsed a little. "A few days after the first shelling."

I took a step forward. "You betrayed us."

"We had nothing to fight back with. Nothing. You remember those days. We were all desperate, trying to figure out what was happening to us. We've always been peaceful—"

"Admirable, I'm sure. But as I said yesterday, where has it gotten us?"

"We've survived for this long." There was a hint of anger in his voice. "You know this. We have nothing with which to fight back. We never have. They could have swarmed in and decimated us anytime they felt like. It was my policy that kept us alive."

"Better to fall on our virtues than have them used against us so ruthlessly, and so willingly." I held the torch higher above me. "You betrayed us. Chieftain George was supposed to tell them everything was fine at the parlay. It was a good thing I rode him so hard. Instead he threatened them. Had he not, I wouldn't have gone. Now maybe I can save this village from a future of domination by high blood pressure and tooth decay."

"By burning it to the ground?" Phill the Elder spread his arms wide. "Who will that save?"

I stepped to one side to go around him. "Burn the village?" I smiled at him. "No. Burn the corn fields."

LITTLE BLACK DOTS

Everywhere he looked: sand. Golden, blinding in the midday sun, small clouds of it blowing in the breeze, and he was buried to his neck in it. He could tell he was closer to the ground than usual; the dunes looked different than they would have were he standing up, and he could feel the sand prickling the underside of his chin. The real clue came when he tried to stretch his arms, bend at the knees, and wiggle his toes. Nothing. He cried for help, help, could anybody hear him, he was stuck in the sand, and it was during these cries that he woke up screaming for his wife Laney. She wasn't there, wasn't going to be there, and he didn't know what to do.

Jack Trundle sat up in bed. The writhing he'd done before waking scattered the sheets half off the bed. He'd gotten used to the small layer of sweat, the tears he felt coursing down his face. He looked at his bedside clock: half past one. That dawn was still hours away only made him feel worse. The following day was supposed to be his first back on the job after a sabbatical to clear up Laney's affairs, and to grieve, and to get his life back together. He'd been hoping to get a full night's sleep, but that hadn't happened in weeks. Now he would turn up feeling like a blunted pencil. On the set, at least, he had the help of make-up. The hairdresser made his hair neat, Wardrobe put him in a smart suit—never the same one twice, except for that nice one he wore every Christmas—and when the red light came on, the city got the Jack Trundle it knew and loved. Detroit's favorite morning anchorperson having nightmares? Impossible!

Trundle made his way to the master bathroom that opened off the bedroom. His foot hit an unexpected obstacle, a carton of sympathy mail he'd forgotten in his exhaustion. The day after Laney died, his co-anchor on the show (the attractive younger woman to his educated older man) made an impassioned plea for support, and the public had responded with letters of well-wishing too numerous to count or adequately store in his townhouse. Trundle hadn't read most of the letters. The one time he'd tried, he teared up after three letters, and after that he wanted to avoid them altogether. Despite that the mail cartons were cramping the floor space, Trundle found he couldn't throw the letters out either. To do so, he felt, would imply that he didn't care about the public's concern, even if no one but he knew he'd not read the letters before tossing them.

As soon as Trundle turned on the bathroom light he turned it off again. The bright light reminded him of the desert sun he was trapped beneath on a nightly basis. Besides, he knew where everything was, knew where all the fixtures were, knew what was what by touch. Trundle turned on the cold water tap and splashed some on his face. It brought him back to where he was and who he was, and once upon a time that would have been enough to push a dream out of his head. This time, it did nothing: Jack Trundle was being buried to the neck in a desert on a nightly basis by his subconscious.

Three hours later, he was shivering. He agreed to come back on two days notice to do a remote location shoot even though it meant standing outside at dawn on Woodward in below freezing temperatures, because the story was too big to ignore. The station provided him with a heavy winter coat, thick wool gloves, and a fur-lined hat left over from the last Soviet Army, and still the three-degree windchill managed to find its way through these and every other layer Trundle was wearing.

"We're here live at the Detroit Institute of Arts, where tonight an unprecedented display of undiscovered artistic talent will be exhibited." This he said with a popular Trundleism, the knowing right index finger pointed upward, the uncapped black pen gripped in the web of the hand, forming a V with the finger. "Former Senator Brent Hawkins is displaying what he calls his real life's work, art and sculptures that he has created over his lifetime, here tonight."

The museum was closed, off limits to everyone except Hawkins, the curator, and a guard, all of whom were unavailable for interviews. Hawkins had hinted in press releases for weeks that he would take one member of the press on a personally guided tour of the exhibit. The identity of the reporter hadn't been announced yet, but at the moment the only thing on Trundle's mind was the next commercial break and the warm cup of coffee that would be waiting in the van.

Trundle recited the rest of his speech, prompted the weather person to give the day's forecast, and another reporter to run down the national and international news (gas prices up, unemployment down, war on the other side of the world, and quick sports highlights) before some playful banter with his co-host back in the studio, and the commercial break. After that, nothing for twenty minutes while the co-host did an exposé piece about corrupt government officials.

The red light on the camera went dark and Trundle stopped pretending to try to smile. The cameraman—Hugh, who had gloves that covered his fingertips—relaxed the shoulder holding the camera as Trundle stepped closer. "How you holding up?" Hugh said.

"Fine, I guess."

Hugh looked him up and down for a moment then said, "Let's get you back in the van."

A minute later, Trundle was pulling the door shut on the passenger side. Hugh handed him a Thermos full of coffee and lit a cigarette. "Didn't get much sleep last night, huh?"

Trundle poured some coffee into a styrofoam cup and stirred in some sugar. "Some. More than I have been."

"Buried in the sand again?"

Trundle had told Hugh about the dreams a few weeks before. "Yeah." He put the cup down on the table and started to rub his eyes. Hugh rolled down the window half an inch and tipped the ash from his cigarette onto the street.

"I don't mind so much, you know. The dream. If I could sleep, if I knew what the dream meant."

"Something to do with your wife, maybe."

Trundle didn't respond right away. If there was a connection between Laney and the desertscape, he couldn't see it. They'd never been to a tropical climate together, no places with sand that didn't have a large body of water nearby. "Maybe," he said. "I don't know."

Hugh took another long drag on his cigarette, flipped the butt out the window, and motioned for the Thermos. "You'll figure it out. I know you will."

"Yeah," Trundle said. "Yeah."

Almost as soon as Hugh opened the Thermos, his cellphone rang. He checked the number before answering, but Trundle didn't see who it was. "Yeah, what's up? Uh huh. Uh huh. Yeah. I'll tell him." Hugh closed the phone and sighed. "Hawkins picked you. Twelve thirty, front entrance."

The last time he brought Laney to this museum was for the opening of a group of local women artists that she'd wanted to see. Trundle went more out of a sense of husbandly duty than anything else. His appreciation of art was uninformed. He could recognize a fine painting when he saw it, and the paintings and sculptures were fine, to be sure, but after four rooms one painting seemed very much like another. The truly artistic eye belonged to Laney, who was at one museum or another every other week it seemed. She was on her way to developing a fine collection of her own, displaying new acquisitions in places of prominence in their townhouse. People complimented Trundle on the art during parties, and he gently deflected each commendation toward Laney.

Three months later, Trundle found himself outside the doors to that same museum, peering inside to see if he could get the attention of a security guard.

He was presenting himself at the prescribed hour, ready to get his interview, and very much wanting to be somewhere else, anywhere else but there. Trundle hadn't been back to the museum since, hadn't had the inclination to go. It had been bad enough out at the curb that morning during the live broadcast, but now that he was up close to the thing Trundle desperately didn't want to be there. Thoughts of Laney here and the art event bounded through his head like rampaging cattle.

Trundle looked toward the street where the van was still parked from the morning shoot, students from the adjacent university dotting the sidewalk in packs of twos and threes, ants in a colony. The sun peeked through the clouds and bathed the entire street in a wash of light. Trundle shielded his eyes and blinked, and opened to see the street covered in sand, the buildings gone, the ants going about their business in the open desert. He rubbed his eyes and blinked again, and the city was back.

A guard pushed open one of the front doors from the inside. "Mr. Trundle?"

Trundle turned. "Yes?"

"You can come in." The guard stood to one side as Trundle entered the building. "He's waiting for you in the gallery," the guard said, and resumed his position to one side of the main doors.

Trundle looked around the main foyer. The entrance to the gallery with Hawkins's installation beyond was on one wall. Trundle could see a few walls, but nothing in the way of actual artwork. After a moment he turned back toward the guard. "What's this all about?"

"Sir?"

"Why the secrecy? What's he got going on back there that he's not letting us in on?"

"Can't say. I'm not much on art. All's I was told to do was to let you in the front door at twelve thirty sharp, and no one else until six." The guard shifted on his stool.

Trundle chewed on that for another second, then said, "My cameraman. He's getting his gear together. We thought we might do a sit down interview with Hawkins. Let him in, will you? He won't come any further than the lobby." The guard nodded and Trundle went off to explore the gallery. Even the doorframe was decorated special, everything in merlot. For two dozen rooms that twisted and turned through the complex, paintings and sculptures of varying quality lined the walls. One of the paintings jumped out at him. It was almost entirely of sky blue, putting it into stark contrast with the wall behind it. Thoughts of the last event here with Laney, of the painting she'd tried so hard to get him to understand, came flooding back into his mind. Laney tried to educate him at every turn. She knew he was something of a lost cause, but she wanted to share her appreciation. "See this piece," she said that night, gesturing at one of the paintings. "Look at the brush strokes there and there, soft, trailing off into the horizon. It seems like an unfinished thought, but it's all over the canvas. It's meant to convey distance, how vast the world is at ground level."

"Uh huh," Trundle said, and leaned in close to the painting as if to examine the portion she was talking about. To him, it was a large light blue area toward the top and a large beige area at the bottom, with some little black dots where the two areas met. He didn't give her the chance to explain the picture more fully, as she'd moved on to the next piece. Six days after that she was gone. Trundle turned his attention to a nearby sculpture to stem the flow of memories. He studied it, lost in thought, until he could sense someone standing behind him.

There was a minute's worth of silence before the other person spoke. "You've found my attempt at a Venus. Not very good, I'm afraid. I've never been great at sculpting. This one took half a dozen tries to get right. I kept over-sculpting. Typical. I'd be going along just fine for a bit, get the ears done or something like that, and then whoops, I've accidentally chopped off her nose. Ah, well. Gotta break some eggs. But you should see the scrap pile. What a mess that is."

Through all this Trundle had been standing with his back to the man, but he knew the voice. "I'm sure it's not so bad as all that, Senator."

"Take my word for it, Mr. Trundle, it is. Do you like what you see?"

Trundle shrugged. "Art was never my thing."

The pause that followed suggested a handful of things to Trundle: annoyance, amusement, a decision to redirect the conversation. "Pity. Do you have any questions?"

Trundle turned around to face the Senator. "Several. My cameraman's setting up in the lobby."

"In due course. First I want to ask your opinion on something. Come into the next room and look at something for me."

Hawkins exited into a short hallway that emptied into a room with nothing in it save for a life-sized stuffed camel. Trundle entered the room, saw the camel, and stopped. Two walls were painted a dusk blue, a fading sun was portrayed on a third, a city wall exterior painted on the wall the camel was facing, a small opening in the center of that wall to a fifty-foot long tunnel, five feet to a side, painted in complete black. The floor under the camel, under Hawkins, and under Trundle, was covered in sand.

"This room took me three weeks to complete, most of it doing the city wall there. The hard part was the texture. Go ahead up and feel it. I had some rocks from Egypt shipped in special for the wall. I was trying to make it as real as possible, give whoever sees this the feeling they're actually in the desert with the camel."

Trundle looked around the room, not moving from the doorway. For a moment, he thought he was buried to the neck again, trapped by sand on all sides and tortured by his own mind. "What— How—?"

Hawkins stroked the neck of the stuffed camel. "I just wanted to see if you got the reference."

Trundle was still trying to wrap his mind around what was in front of him. He couldn't shake the feeling of being restrained. The spotlights in the room burned his face as if he was back under the sun, back in the desert.

"No? 'And again I say unto you, it is easier for a camel to go through the eye of a needle, than it is for a rich man to enter the Kingdom of God.' Book of Matthew. This is the popular version of what they were talking about, though. This tunnel here—which wasn't quite so long at the time—was referred to as the Needle's Eye. A lot of biblical era cities had them. After the city gates closed for the evening, the only way in or out of the city was through one of these. As you can see, it's hardly big enough for a fully loaded camel to pass through." Hawkins motioned to the tunnel.

Trundle bent double and went through. On the other end was a room, twenty by twenty by twenty, completely black except for some stars, little glowing dots on the walls, floor, and ceiling. He felt almost weightless then, as if someone had pulled the ground out from under him but he'd forgotten to fall, forgotten how to.

"Do you know what this is, Mr. Trundle?" Hawkins had quietly entered behind him.

He wanted to say something, but his mind was still trying to wrap itself around what he'd seen in the last room, and now in this one. "No."

"What most people see when they close their eyes. Certainly no artistic rendering will ever do it justice, but something like this."

Trundle stared at the dots, slackjawed.

Hawkins ducked back into the tunnel. "That's what I wondered. Thank you very much, Mr. Trundle."

After a moment, Trundle went back through the tunnel to the room with the camel, unnerved by the floating sensation the room with the stars gave him. Hawkins was nowhere to be found. The feeling of being enclosed in the sane came on him again, and he left the room quickly and headed back to the museum foyer, his disbelief hanging over him like a shroud.

The formal opening of the Hawkins exhibit was strictly a black-tie affair. Only four hundred of the nation's elite and their spouses, all dressed to the nines, were extended invitations; power lobbyists, Congressmen, and three former Presidents had run the tight security brigade in support of one of their own. To the surprise of some, the invitees were not party-specific, but those that knew him best knew that half of Hawkins's Wednesday golfing foursome sat on the other side of the aisle. The main entrance hall had been made over in the course of the afternoon, gold and white balloons lining the ceilings and the balustrades, a full course buffet flanked by ice sculptures, garcons and garconettes wandering this way and that with their trays of hors d'oeuvres.

"So, this is how the other half lives," Hugh said, taking it all in. "I've never hadda wear a tuxedo to do my job." He wriggled his bow tie for effect.

The station had known about Trundle's invitation to the opening before he had, and sent Hugh duly armed to get some shots of the interior that the other networks wouldn't have for another day. Still, though, when Jack Trundle walked into a party, no matter how formal or informal, he was used to being recognized by at least a few of his fellow partygoers. Tonight, nothing. A concierge showed no sign of recognizing who he was as his coat was taken in exchange for a ticket, or possibly didn't want to admit it. Trundle looked around the room again, hoping someone would break from the pack, come over, shake his hand, welcome him, but no one did. Hawkins himself was nowhere to be seen. Suddenly, Trundle felt like he didn't want to be recognized, didn't even want to be here.

"Relax," Trundle told Hugh. "Try to look like you belong here. Come find me in half an hour and we'll tape the bit they asked you to."

Hugh nodded and the two went their separate ways. Most of the crowd was gathered in the general area of the entrance to Hawkins's exhibit, some queued up awaiting entrance to the rooms beyond, others chatting in groups of two and three as they absently ate hors d'oeuvres and drank champagne. Trundle went instead to another smaller open space further back in the museum, where the exhibit of the local women artists was still set up. Every step he took echoed off the hardwood floor and marble walls like Trundle was in a cave. Almost by accident, he found himself on a bench in front of the painting Laney had explained to him, with the brush strokes that led off to nowhere. Trundle sat there, stared at the painting, and Laney's explanation played over and over again in his head. It's meant to convey distance, how vast the world is at ground level.

"Strange, isn't it?" said a voice from beside him. It was Hawkins. "Room full of people all looking for conversation, all looking to make an impression on me on the one night I'm trying to be something other than what they're used to seeing. Suddenly I wish I'd done this in a more low-key sort of way, maybe even used a pseudonym or something."

Trundle didn't jump at the sound of the voice. He'd almost been expecting it.

"I heard about your wife. I'm sorry."

Trundle didn't know what to say. He was shocked that Hawkins had taken the time and effort to find out anything about him. Surely the Senator had greater concerns than Trundle's personal well-being.

"Good woman, I take it," Hawkins said.

Trundle nodded.

"I'm told she enjoyed art. Came here often."

Trundle shifted his head slightly toward Hawkins, wondering how he would have known something so trivial as that.

"I play poker once a month with your boss. That's strictly on the QT, of course. If the media found out a Senator and a local news executive played poker every month, they'd have a field day with it. You won't tell, will you?" The smile on Hawkins's face was evident in every word.

"She liked this one," Trundle said, and lifted a limp arm toward the painting. "Tried to tell me about it, what was going on, what the brushstrokes of it meant and all that."

"Think about her a lot?"

"Every day. Every—every minute. I still think of her in the present tense, still expect her to come through the door sometime in mid-evening. And eight, nine o'clock comes and goes, and I remember Laney isn't coming home and why, and that just makes everything worse."

Trundle ran his hands through his hair and looked at the beige of the painting, the little black dots sitting atop it like so many afterthoughts. His waking and dream lives had started bleeding into each other, and it was difficult to tell the difference. Was this painting before him real, or the room he'd been in earlier, or Hawkins? He searched his mind for reasons why this would happen, signs that it was or wasn't, and came up nil. *Maybe I'm meant to work it out for myself*, he thought.

"It occurred to me, last night, that I'd forgotten what that sounded like, Laney coming home. She'd done it every night for twenty years, and now she doesn't." And yet I saw your painting today and it reminded me of this one, and what Laney said. I hadn't thought about that day since it happened—barely thought about it while it was happening—but I can see that moment clear as anything in my head. I can't remember the sound of her coming home, but I can remember that one little nothing moment."

"It's like that, sometimes. You get older and find yourself remembering things about your loved one that you'd forgotten, little scraps that were so much flotsam at the time, and something in the now calls it back up. And maybe you're remembering it wrong, but you're remembering something." Hawkins sat on the bench next to Trundle and considered the painting before them.

"Every night since Laney died, I've had this dream I'm buried to my neck in the desert." Trundle lifted his arm at the painting. "That one. And your full-room one too. Just me and the sand and the sun. And something my wife said when she was talking about this painting. 'How vast the world is at ground level.' And I feel so small and helpless. And alone. And when I wake up it takes me a minute to remember who I am, and where I am, and why there isn't anyone next to me in bed. And I saw your rooms today— I saw—" He shook his head, trying to find the words. Trundle looked at the painting again. "I don't want Laney to fade away, but I want to hope again."

Hawkins said nothing for a long minute. "Someday the stars will come back." Around them there was only silence.

Everywhere he looked: sand. Same as it had been before, except now he was buried to his waist. Trundle swiveled, trying to determine what else had changed. No, that dune had always been in front of him, and the wind was still blowing little sand clouds around.

Trundle tried to leverage himself out but the sand was packed too tightly around his legs. He began to scoop sand away from himself, fling it as far away as he could so it didn't roll back into place. But the surrounding area caved into what he had just emptied out, and the sand would blow along and level it out again. Trundle began taking bigger handfuls, tried throwing them farther, and the hole began to grow, slowly at first, then more steadily. Soon he could shift his knees, at which point he tried muscling himself out again. This time it worked.

Trundle stood a few feet away from the hole and looked at the landscape around him. There were three dunes behind where he'd been buried, one situated between and beyond the other two. And what was that on it? A person? A camel? From this distance it was impossible to tell. All it looked like was a little black dot upon the sand. What it was exactly Trundle didn't know and didn't care, but he started walking toward it. Whatever it was, it was a sign of life.

LAMENT

During the day it's a series of hyperventilations: he wants fed, he wants burped, he's got a dirty diaper, he wants held. That's the one his father has the most problems with, the holding, and probably that's because his father didn't hold him very much or maybe because that self-same father was not the most expressive with his emotions like a lot of fathers then weren't. The little one, the toddler, the baby, doesn't care. He wants held or burped or changed or fed, and so he gets held or burped or changed or fed.

But at night it's different. At night the baby sleeps, peacefully, breathing in and out like somebody who's been doing that a lot longer than he has, nice and even, unhurried. He takes up real estate between his mother and father in the bed, and when his parents wake up bruised in the ribs from his random kicks his mother doesn't seem to mind too much. The father, though, still objects although he knows enough to know there's no point in objecting. He doesn't want the baby in the bed. He would like the extra real estate back. He would like to not suffer a mysterious middle-of-the-night injury.

One night the father is home late. He's been out; the where doesn't matter. Mother and baby are already asleep. He lies down quietly, trying not to disturb either one. No sooner does he hit the mattress than his son the baby starts wiggling but it's only a small change in position. In this moment he wants to hold his son, look into his eyes, and become someone else entirely, but he doesn't. He knows what sort of crying and fussing picking him up would cause. And as he drifts off to sleep he wonders if he'll ever be that man that can hold his son without thinking, "How did this happen?"

At Chichén Itzá

As he stood in the long, winding line of people waiting to clear customs at Cancún International, Nick wondered why the designers hadn't made the room air conditioned. A thousand people an hour went through the room, all anxious to have their passports stamped as quickly as possible so they could begin shopping or drinking or sunning themselves. The bulk fans that had been installed weren't up to the task of keeping that many people cool. Even though there was no direct sunlight, the room reeked of the humid Cancún heat. Nick's wife, Kate, didn't seem to be much affected by the heat. Their friends Tommy and Gina were just as sweaty as Nick.

When they reached the concourse forty-five minutes later, Nick grabbed the first taxi wrangler who wasn't already trying to sell himself to someone else and gave him the name of a hotel. The wrangler led the group outside to the parking lot, Nick and Kate following closely behind, Tommy and Gina trying to keep up, confused looks on their faces, to a van with a driver looking onto the plague of cars with a disinterest only a local could manage. They were all slightly panicked now, even Kate, who only showed it with a widening of the eyes just big enough that only Nick noticed.

Only one car at a time could fit through the parking lot exit. The scrum of cars and vans in the plaza moved through the opening on wheels of molasses, horns blaring, drivers beckoning to one another in a near-futile gambit to inch closer to freedom. By the time the van cleared everyone was unsticking their shirts from their chests, except for the driver, who didn't seem to need the air conditioning. When the van reached cruising speed, which seemed to alternate between thirty-five and seventy depending on how thick the traffic was, Nick and Tommy opened every window and the group cooled in the artificial breeze.

Nick looked over at Kate, who had eyes for nothing but the sea that loomed just beyond the buildings on one side of the road, and put a hand on her shoulder. "You okay, honey?" She took his hand and placed it back on the seat between them without a glance. Tommy and Gina didn't seem to notice as they marveled at a car rental place where for two hundred pesos you could rent an old model Volkswagen Beetle for the day.

The hotel lobby bustled with activity. People in casualwear drifted in the direction of the hotel's restaurant, eager to get a start on the evening's relaxation. The two couples checked in and parted company, agreeing to meet in the lobby in half an hour for dinner. No sooner had Nick closed the room door behind them and set the luggage down with a grunt than Kate collapsed onto the bed. He fiddled with the thermostat controls, trying to set the air conditioning to a reasonable temperature, then sat on the bed next to her. He could see out onto the beach and the Caribbean beyond. The waves rolled in and rolled out again, advertising the sea beyond, uncaring whether or not people ventured in. Sunbathing women slept on chaise lounges dragged from poolside, but no children could be seen. The husbands were probably at the bar, Nick guessed, watching the sports channel, looking for tones of home.

"So?" he said.

Kate didn't say anything for a few seconds. "So?"

"When are we going to tell them?"

Kate didn't respond. In the mirror hanging on the wall opposite the bed Nick watched her chest rise and fall with her breathing.

"Look," she said. "It's been a long day. I'm tired, I'm hungry, and I'm grimy. Do we have to do this now?" She stood up and walked toward the bathroom.

"You never want to talk about it," he said, but the bathroom door snapped shut before he finished.

The restaurant opened onto the beach, a waist-high brick wall the only thing separating the surf from the tile. A live mariachi band occupied one corner, playing music loud enough to make people shout to be heard three feet away from each other. Tommy and Gina arrived first. "You've gotta have a margarita, Nick, I'm telling you," he said, signaling the nearest garçon who emitted the same sort of detached ambivalence the taxi driver had. "Pitcher of margaritas," Tommy said, louder than he needed to even with the mariachi at top volume.

The women started talking about their careers, Kate in mid-level management, Gina as a retail manager; about their common friends, people they knew from high school that they ran into at the grocery or the mall; about their husbands, how Tommy was a lipless wonder and Nick had the sensitivity of a sea cucumber. Tommy interjected from time to time to make a snarky comment, but mostly he watched the mariachi band, clapped louder than anyone else in the restaurant, refilling his margarita glass twice for each one of everyone else's. Nick's chair offered a view of the beach. As the wives talked and Tommy drank, Nick lost himself in watching the moonlit surf. The bit nearest the sea was smooth, the water washing up on to the beach every few seconds and clearing away as soon as it arrived.

"Snap out of it," Kate said, slapping his arm. "We're gonna rent a car tomorrow, go over to Chichén Itzá, climb the Castle."

"You want to drive to Chichén Itzá?" Nick said. Visions of everything that could go wrong flashed through his mind like a blooper reel: the car stalled out at the side of the highway, the sun as high as it could get, Tommy banging on the trunk like it would help jumpstart the dead motor inside, the wives off to one side crying, Nick with his shirt off and one thumb extended, waiting for assistance that might never come.

"Come on, it'll be a blast," Tommy said. His cheeks glowed red in the half-light of the restaurant. "We'll load up a cooler with some ice and some drinks. You know, make a day of it."

Nick planned to visit Chichén Itzá at some point over the trip. He knew touring companies went there every day, gathering up at some central point then heading out on a converted Greyhound. There'd be a stop at a sacred cenoté, and maybe a quick spin through Valladolid, the only town worthy of the name between Cancún and the ruins. "We could take a tour group out. Be simpler, easier."

"Nah. Nowhere near as much fun. Not as independent." Tommy had a gleam in his eye that might have been enthusiasm and might have been tequila.

"Well?" Kate said.

Nick looked around the group. He didn't like the idea, but he could tell from the look in everyone's eyes that they wanted to go. Kate was staring at him more intently than the other two. Every fight they'd ever had, every argument, every time she'd accused him of being no fun at all, burned on her face like a dare.

"Yeah, all right," he said. Kate's eyes widened in surprise. "But I get to drive."

At just past seven the next morning Nick went down to the restaurant in search of breakfast. Gina was already there, sipping a glass of water and staring out at the ocean. The sunlight reflected off the water backlit her, making her hair seem afire. She didn't notice Nick approaching. "Good morning," he said.

Gina made a noise somewhere between a cough and a laugh; she was sipping her coffee when he spoke. The people at the next table over glanced in their direction at the sound, and looked away when it became apparent Gina wasn't choking. "You shouldn't sneak up on a girl," she said, hand to her chest, and offered Nick the other chair with a regal motion. "Kate's not up, I take it?"

"No, she's still asleep. Probably will be for another few hours yet. Tommy?"

"Out cold. He's like that every time he—" She left the sentence there, but Nick couldn't miss the resentment in her voice.

"Everything all right?"

She bit at one of her nails and looked out onto the ocean. "I just wish he'd drink a little less, that's all." The rest of breakfast passed without further comment.

Tommy rented one of the Beetles they'd seen by the road the day before. It seemed like it was in reasonably good shape, though the eggshell white paint did nothing to hide the rust spots creeping in at odd corners. The interior was the black plastic vinyl kind that sticks to bare thighs in temperatures over seventy; the day's forecast was sunny and ninety-five on the coast, hotter still in the interior of the country where the group was headed. The car had no air conditioning, which Tommy felt could be relieved by a full case of longnecks, stowed in a pair of styrofoam coolers in the front storage. "We'll have to pull over every now and then for refills, but no worries," he said. Nick's reservations about whether or not the car would start again if stopped went unspoken.

The women came out side by side, sunglasses and other accoutrements at hand, and looked at the car. The expression on her face said quite clearly Gina wanted to turn around and go back into the hotel. Kate, though, started laughing. "Oh, this is wonderful. I've always wanted to ride in one of these."

Tommy tossed the keys to Nick from where he was standing in front of the car. "Have at it, Jeeves." With two bottles of beer cradled in his other arm, Tommy walked to the other car door. "The ancient Mayans await."

By ten the temperature had climbed into three digits. They hoped the wind whipping in through the car windows would help, but it didn't; it cooled, but was dry and fell short of refreshing. Nick discovered less than a mile outside of Cancún proper that the car shuddered above fifty miles an hour. Tommy laughed and did a voice that sounded like it was being shaken like a martini. He stopped after a couple of sentences when Kate slapped him on the arm. The two of them laughed and started singing something that sounded like a mariachi leftover from the night before. Nick exchanged a glance with Gina, who was riding shotgun, and kept the speedometer low. Between the heat and the bad singing, he was miserable before the trip really got going, and wished he'd ignored Kate's unspoken dare and insisted on the tour bus.

Two hours and four stops to get more beers from the cooler (which Tommy and Kate drank in the backseat, coaxing Gina to join them on the third round), they arrived at the small town of Valladolid. At the center of town was a square, itself a park with a fountain at the center, picnic tables scattered beneath trees, benches lining the paths leading to the fountain from the four corners. Kids ran in every direction, making it impossible to tell which children were with which parents. The shops lining the square were almost all open air, the merchants or their helpers on the pavement outside trying to pull in passers-by. Nick took a parking spot on the square, easier to find than he'd thought given how many people were about. Tommy and Gina went off toward a convenience store in search of snacks, while he and Kate took one of the few shaded benches in the park, one of the few in the shade. Nick glanced around the square and noticed with a combination of alarm and amazement that they were two of perhaps a dozen non-Mexicans in sight.

"Jesus, it's hot," Kate said. She fanned herself with her floppy hat.

A large tour bus entered the square. Nick could see the people inside looking out at the scene like it was a zoo display, the townspeople—and him, by extension—nothing more than a curiosity, animals, subhuman. On a few faces he saw revulsion: how could people live like this? The bus drove all four sides of the square and left on the same road it had come in on, without showing any sign of stopping to let passengers off. "Lucky them," he said without meaning to.

Kate heard him. "That's your problem, you know. No sense of adventure."

Nick knew this argument well, having heard it before more times than he could count. Their conversations ended more and more frequently with her criticizing him, saying he was too lazy or too bumbling or "duller than a pencil." In return he said she was overly critical, needlessly hurtful, as if she only said or did things to spite him. There'd been little playful fights, without venom, as long as they had been together. Now every word was meant to sting.

They sat in silence for a few moments more. A woman passed in front of them carrying a baby in one arm and leading a child with the other. The child stared at Nick as she walked by, one finger stuck in her mouth, her face with the look of amazement children have when seeing something new and unique. Then the mother said andale and their pace quickened, and were part of the landscape again as fast as they'd come from it.

"It's too late for us, isn't it?" Nick said.

Kate didn't answer right away. "I don't know. Maybe. If only—" She made a shrugging gesture with her hands and started crowd-watching again.

"What?"

She looked down at the pavement for a moment before turning to him. "If only you weren't so uptight all the time, afraid to take chances, afraid to have fun."

Nick started to protest, but she shushed him with a motion.

"You are, Nick. You know you are, deep down. Take today. Sure, we could have taken a tour bus, but everyone does that. It's the tourist thing to do, the safe thing to do. Who rents a car and drives halfway into the Mexican mainland?"

"It hasn't occurred to you that we might get lost or break down?"

"And what if we do? We stop, we get directions. Someone will help us. Or they won't. But we're seeing this country in a way most people don't: up close, unafraid. Once upon a time ago, you would have been all over this idea. You might even have suggested it yourself. Now—" Kate sighed.

Nick felt defeated. He wanted to tell her that he was trying. He had agreed to this drive, after all, and felt that should have counted for something. *Maybe I should have pointed that out*, he thought. *Maybe she would concede that I was making an effort at least.* Their relationship seemed like it was getting away from him. He struggled to find the right thing to say, the right way to show Kate that he wanted to be everything she wanted him to be, but Tommy and Gina came back before he said anything. Tommy skipped across the street like a teenager, Gina following behind apologizing to the cars that had screeched to a halt to avoid them. There was a cenoté, a sacred water hole, not too far away that they wanted to see. Kate stood up and walked toward the car. Nick sighed and followed the three of them, disappointed that he couldn't find the words.

They located the cenoté with little difficulty. An enterprising soul had cleared out a parking area large enough to house several tour buses, and had put up a small botanical gardens and a building with bathroom facilities, vending machines, and a gift shop. A pamphlet Nick found in the shop gave some history on the cenoté. It was a sacred site to the Mayans when they lived in the area. They dropped trinkets and the occasional virgin to her death in the drink in an attempt to appease their gods and bring some rain. There was no way out of the hole until the late Seventies, when a stairway was carved into the earth and a small viewing platform created just above water level. Now tourists use the cenoté as a makeshift swimming pool, frolicking for a few moments in the crystal blue waters to escape from the heat above. Nick had no intention of getting in. They hadn't thought to bring a towel, and the idea of walking through the ruins wearing wet shorts didn't appeal to him. Gina and Kate jumped in anyway, street clothes and all. Tommy, who didn't know how to swim, sat on the platform with Nick, watching their wives frolic in the sapphire blue water. Nick's attention shifted to the foliage hanging down into the cavern, roots from the trees above growing down into the cavern in search of water, sustenance. Water, here, was life. The surface didn't have much of either. The topsoil was thin in most places, not ideal for growth except by the hardiest of plants, and hardly any rain comes. But down below water can be found. Life can be found.

Tommy slapped Nick on the arm to get his attention. "I said are you having fun yet?"

"Oh, I'm okay," Nick said. "Just daydreaming."

He nodded. Nick and Tommy hadn't spoken to each other much during the trip. The few times they had had been strained and, Nick thought, a little forced. Sitting on the platform, Nick realized they didn't really have anything to say to each other. Tommy was loud, excitable, outgoing. *Everything Kate wants me to be*, he thought. *And he and Gina seem like they're happy.*

"I think Gina's leaving me," Tommy said, his voice low. He took a drink from the beer he'd brought down with him.

Tommy's tone startled Nick. There was a ring of sadness there that he didn't quite think Tommy capable of feeling. Gina climbed out of the water before Nick could respond. Tommy gave him a look that indicated quite clearly that he shouldn't say anything and then went over to her. "Good?"

"Good, hell. Great! Haven't enjoyed a swim like that in forever." She slivered slightly. "You okay, Nick? You look like you've seen a ghost."

Nick realized his mouth was open slightly, and he'd been unable to hide the surprise from his face. Every moment of the trip now he'd have to reevaluate, see if he missed a sign that the union wasn't as good as he thought it was. Gina had said something at breakfast, that she didn't like Tommy's drinking. Was that coming between them? If it was, they seemed to be hiding it well otherwise.

"Let's get you up into the sun," Tommy said to Gina. "You can warm up, dry off a little."

As they started up the long winding stair Gina gave the bottle of beer a sour look that Tommy didn't see. A moment later her face cleared and they were talking again in a light conversational tone. *Is this Kate and me?* Nick thought. *Do they have the same problems as we do? Or are they just better at hiding it?* He looked down at Kate, floating on her back out in the center, staring up at the light above, and wondered if she knew about Tommy and Gina.

They pulled into Chichén Itzá a couple of minutes before two. There was another stop at the side of the highway so Tommy could get more beers, but he was drinking alone. Kate was asleep in the passenger seat, and every time he checked the rear view mirror Nick saw Gina staring at the scenery without really seeing it. Both of the women squished for a few minutes after their swim in the cenoté, but the combination of the arid heat and the breeze running through the car dried all of their clothes except their shorts. Tommy asked Nick to turn on the radio at one point, but all stations were static, and the rest of the trip passed mostly in silence.

There was no issue finding a parking spot at Chichén Itzá. The portion of the lot given over to cars was barely a quarter full, while the area reserved for buses was packed to overflowing. Nick thought one of them might have been the one that went through Valladolid. They all looked the same, even the ones that didn't.

The entrance building to the complex had a small movie theater showing a film that explained how the ruins were found and what all the buildings were supposed to mean. They went in at Kate and Gina's urging, at least long enough to enjoy the air conditioning. There was no one else inside. Tommy took a seat and reclined, neck resting on the back of the chair, face to the ceiling, eyes closed. Nick watched the movie but wasn't taking any of it in, happy for the relative comfort.

They'd come in toward the end of the picture. The narrator talked about climbing the central structure of the ruins, the Temple of Kukulcán, or "El Castillo," the Castle. Even though the feet of the Mayans were small by modern standards, a fully dressed Mayan priest could not go straight up the stairs. The only way to climb them was at an angle. The pattern of the both ascent and descent was serpentine, and in this way the priest would pay homage to Kukulcán, God of Serpents.

"Whatever," Tommy said. "We ready?" He got up and went out the door back into the main building. Gina and Kate followed. A moment later, lips pursed, so did Nick.

They exited out the back of the building and walked down a path wide enough for cars to pass each other on until they reached a large clearing, in the center of which was the Castle. Other buildings were scattered around the edges. People flitted on and around them, some following tour guides explaining things, some walking around trying to find that one good shot, that one good angle from which to take a picture of the Castle. All of the other buildings and structures between them didn't attract half the crowd that the Castle did.

The stair on the west side was equipped with a rope running down the center. Along it were people in varying states of ascent and descent. As the group watched, two people headed in opposite directions using the rope met in the middle. The person descending took a very tentative step to one side, letting the climber through before scurrying back to the rope and continuing downward.

"Right," Tommy said. "Who wants to climb up with me?" His face was pale and his eyes slightly unfocused, but Nick could hear the robustness in his voice, like nothing was going to stop Tommy from going up.

"I'll come," Kate said.

Nick looked up at the top. He didn't like heights. Kate knew this, but he also wondered if by not climbing she would accuse him of being dull again. "Maybe when you come back down," he said.

"Go on ahead," Gina said. "I'll be up in a minute."

Tommy and Kate climbed the stair on the north side. There was no rope, but less traffic. Kate weaved back and forth as we'd seen in the movie. Tommy went straight up, the heels of his feet hanging over the edge of each step, climbing much slower than Kate. When Kate reached the top she immediately went to rest against the small building there. Nick could barely see her. She seemed like an ant atop a dirt hill, small and far away. *You're already gone, aren't you?* Nick thought. *You're already gone.*

"She's leaving me, you know," Nick said. "Kate is." He turned from watching Tommy struggle with his climb still a third of the way from the summit, to look at Gina. She was watching them as well, her hand shielding her eyes from the fierce sun.

"I know," she said.

Nick looked back up at Kate, so far above, and raised his hand to let her know he could see her. Then Tommy lost his footing, fell face front to the stair, and in the million seconds afterwards he failed to get a handhold, someone screamed, and the world fell to pieces around the lot of them.

Nick started shouting for the medics the moment Tommy hit the ground. The ambulance was at the northern base in seconds, Tommy loaded moments after that. Gina was sedated at Nick's insistence before being placed on another gurney. She was wheeled in next to her husband, and the ambulance left at top speed for Cancún. Nick had overheard one of the paramedics say hardly a day passes in summer where someone doesn't collapse from heat prostration, not enough of the right fluids and so forth.

Nick and Kate were interviewed under a tree in the central area, three hundred feet from the base of the Castle by the park director and a policeman. A squad car took Kate and Nick back. Don't worry about the rental, the police said. Everything can be explained at the other end; someone will come along and get it in a couple days. The nurses at the hospital where Tommy and Gina were taken asked few questions. Two folding chairs were placed in the hall outside Gina and Tommy's room. Kate was inside trying to talk to the doctors.

Nick replayed the police interview in his head: what had Tommy eaten, what had he drank, did he have any health problems, any sort of a history? Had he ever passed out before, ever vomited as a result of over-drinking? Had there been anything out of the ordinary in his behavior, had there been any problems at work or at home? He sighed. He told the police he hadn't known of any. No good reason to tell them there were problems. No good reason not to. Maybe Tommy and Gina are working things out on their own. Maybe they've given up already.

Gina was twenty feet away from Tommy when he landed. Her screams echoed through Nick's head, preparing to haunt him like a banshee. She started screaming the second Tommy slipped and not stopped until after she was sedated.

Kate came out of the room and sat in the other chair. "Still sedated?" Nick said.

She nodded.

"How you holding up?" Nick said.

Kate said little during the police interview, and nothing since. Nick thought she was seeing it again and again in her head, perhaps the slip, the tumble, the landing, or perhaps what Tommy looked like there on the ground, bloody and broken. "You did the right thing. For Gina. Sedating her."

He looked at Kate, defeated, dirty and tired, and realized how small the issue had become. "I am trying," he said.

"You weren't ever going to climb the Castle, were you?" she said.

"I—" he said, and thought for a moment. There was nothing to be gained by false bravery. Not anymore. "No."

"That's you. Mister Dependable."

"Yes. Well." Nick placed a hand on her shoulder.

Kate sniffed, and left it there.

LAYOVER

The concourse had become his second home, he knew it that well. His fellow passengers were the houseguests he couldn't get rid of, the workers at the restaurants and gift shops a personal wait staff that was starting to learn his peculiarities. All this may have been well and good, except that it meant being stranded in the Detroit airport for three days. The food supply was rapidly declining, toilet paper was being portioned out at every restroom door, and garbage cans were full to overflowing again within half an hour of being emptied. Adam stank just like everyone else not lucky enough to have a room at the connected airport hotel, from not having a hot shower for two days and he knew it.

The piped-in muzak started playing "Don't Cry For Me, Argentina." Adam sighed. This was the first time he'd been snowed in during a layover, on his way home to Miami from a three-day talkfest in Seattle, and after two days all he wanted was to be back in the comfort of his own home. His emotions were worn down, and the sound of the song only made him feel haunted. Hearing it made him think of his failed marriage, of everything that had gone wrong, everything that hadn't been said, and how much lonelier he felt with every passing day.

Adam stood at a sink in the men's room nearest to his gate now, splashing his face with the coldest water the faucet would give him. The stubble was getting darker and more prominent, as were the black rings under his eyes. If he had known when he left Denver that there'd be eighteen inches of snow waiting at his layover in Detroit—if only he'd looked at the forecasts—he would have loaded a change of clothes in his carry-on, but as it was he was dressed for Miami, and he was stuck with the damned Hawaiian print shirt and khaki shorts and sandals he was wearing when he boarded his flight three days earlier.

Adam returned to the seat he called home and found his bag still there, leaning against the metal legs like a support strut. Leaving unattended baggage was advised against, yes, but where would the thief go? Into the six-foot snowdrifts and the subzero weather? They wouldn't have gotten much anyway, his last maybe twenty dollars. The seat, though, was now occupied, which ordinarily he wouldn't have minded except that every other seat was taken, and had been for two days. *So much for the aid of my fellow passengers*, he thought. There was supposed to be an unspoken agreement, everybody looked out for everybody else's bags and seats, they were all in this together, except that this woman had violated the agreement. As he approached, his sense of chivalry did battle with his bad knees. Under different circumstances, he would have been more than happy to let the woman sitting there now stay seated. It was, after all, only a seat. But for the last two days, it had been his seat. His body had conformed itself to the contours of the chair. It pretty well had to; the chair was made of that hard-shell plastic that doesn't bend except under the hottest of heats.

He came around the end of the row, still thinking about what he would say to this woman, how he would say it, if he would say it. She was reading a magazine thick enough to be a phone book, and it didn't even look like she was reading it all that closely. Even from the side, her eyes had a glazed over look that suggested she wasn't reading the magazine so much as holding it in front of her. The rings under her eyes looked as dark as his own, Adam noticed, maybe darker. Her hair, a shade of auburn he found attractive in general, looked clean and fresh in comparison to everyone else in the terminal. The diamond studs in her earlobes were just large enough to spot in the right light but otherwise understated. The woman might have been appealing under other circumstances. Now she looked as tired as he felt. He came to a full stop in front of the chair next to the one that had been his own and tried to think of the politest way to ask her to move.

Jane wasn't in much better condition. Her flight from Boston to Detroit three days earlier hadn't gone very well. Her plane had no sooner been pushed back from the gate than it was pulling in again. One of the engines was malfunctioning, and the delay in waiting for another plane to become available guaranteed that Jane would miss her connection to Seattle. When the replacement plane finally landed in Detroit, Jane was told that there would be no flights to Seattle that night or even to anyplace closer to it than Denver on any carrier. She had little choice but to take a hotel room. The snow had only just started falling when she checked in, but she fell asleep that first night without looking out of the window or turning on the television. The appearance of a foot of snow by daybreak came as a shock, trampling what little desire she had left to ever fly again. She'd wanted to get home, back to her life, but with all that snow on the ground she wasn't going anywhere anytime soon.

Her time in Boston hadn't been much better. A funeral she hadn't wanted to attend but did and an argument with her daughter Cynthia cast a dark pall on the entire visit, and Jane was more than ready to go. Now here she was, neither here nor there. The upside was that, unlike the fifteen hundred or so stuck without a room, she did have a bed to sleep in, a shower to get clean in, a laundry room which she'd already made use of, and privacy. Not actually sleeping in the airport proper meant that if she'd wanted to be anywhere near her gate during the day, she'd have to stand; all of the chairs were claimed by those less fortunate than she was. She kept her eyes peeled when she was around, looking for that one single passenger to step away for a little, and she could claim the seat, rest her feet for a stretch, give it back courteously upon his or her return. She had only just sat down in an empty chair at the gate across the concourse from her own and opened her reading material, a magazine irrelevant to her everyday life except for an article on why teenage girls are so hard to manage, when above her and to her right someone said, "Pardon me, ma'am, but—"

The words died there. He had meant to say, "That's my bag there next to you," and then take the bag. One arm was extended in the general direction of the bag in anticipation of the act. What stopped him was the woman's eyes. They reminded Adam of Leslie's, the slight bloodshot in the corners and the bags beneath them, signs of someone not sleeping well. In the last years of their marriage, Leslie's eyes looked exactly as this woman's did. Leslie worked, always worked, always moving, always somewhere else, and when Adam was with her, Leslie's eyes showed little but her exhaustion. This woman's eyes had that too, that exhausted look, like her mind had shut off and her body was running on whatever was left over. She looked up at him, and he received the full-on effect of the vacant stare for the briefest of moments. He watched as the look on her face went from empty to surprise to guilt to resignation so effortlessly it was impossible to tell where one look ended and the next began.

She let the magazine close. "I'm sorry," she said. "This is your seat."

"No, please," Adam said. He became aware just then that his arm was still extended. He brought it back to his side under the pretense of scratching his other wrist. "I mean, yeah, but you can – I don't need it just now." Adam wondered why he couldn't finish a sentence. He was tired, certainly, not thinking straight – that had to be it. This stuttering was just another manifestation of that. "You look tired."

The woman gave a half-smile, and what power there was behind her eyes shone a little brighter. "Haven't been sleeping too well. I keep thinking how miserable it is to be stuck here, how much I'd rather be home right now."

"I'm ready to never fly again. Drive everywhere instead. At least that way you can control where you stop and for how long."

The woman nodded. "Would've if I could've."

"It isn't all bad here. I mean, hey, complimentary pretzels anytime we'd like them. Oh, wait. They ran out yesterday." Adam shook his head. "Which flight are you, then?"

She pointed to the gate across the concourse. "Seattle. Boston to Detroit to Seattle. I had the option of stopping in New York, but no, it was cheaper to stop here. And what's it doing in New York? Nothing. No snow, no closures. I could've been home by now."

Adam looked across to the waiting area for her gate. A group of half a dozen girls, ages (he guessed) somewhere between five and nine, had taken over most of the space with a game that might have been tag or might have been rugby. They were giggling and shouting as if on the other end of a soccer pitch from one another. "I can see why you're not sitting over there."

"Bit loud. Last night I had a dream that my daughter had multiplied and grown into a gaggle of six-year-olds. They were all complaining that they didn't have enough food, they didn't like the candy bars anymore, could they have a square meal please? When my daughter was six, all she wanted was junk food. I think my subconscious is trying to tell me that if I don't have something resembling real food soon I'll go crazy."

"Well," Adam said, scratching his chin, "the Tex-Mex place at the other end of the airport still has food. I heard a guy in the men's room say so, and I was thinking of going and checking it out. You wanna—?" He stopped mid-question. There was no intention to ask her to dinner when he opened his mouth, but he found he didn't mind. This brief conversation was the best he'd had since becoming stranded. "I'm getting tired of eating alone," he said, trying to fill in the odd pause he'd started. "Gets depressing after a bit."

She smiled and stood up. "Sure. My name's Jane, by the way."

"Adam." He reached down and picked up his bag.

"What about your seat?"

"Don't worry. It isn't going anywhere."

They were seated after a pair of squatters were asked to leave. A seat was a seat, after all, and people were staying in the Tex-Mex place for upwards of two hours after they'd finished their meals, sipping their waters as long as management would tolerate it.

Adam stirred the ice in his water and looked the laminate-card menu up and down. Most of the selections were marked through with a grease pencil. What was left over—one entrée, three margaritas, and the sweetened iced tea—were clearly the least popular options of what was usually available. Still, it was more than could be had at the stalls in the concourse, which had only sunflower seeds and energy drinks left in stock.

"The thing is," Jane said after a few moments silence, "I don't even like Tex-Mex. But then it's either this or whatever's left over in the concourse." She put the menu down and ran a finger through her hair. That sentence didn't come out quite right, she thought. Certainly it was true: she didn't much care for the style of food, but given the choice between it and sunflower seeds, she would take the Tex-Mex. But she'd completely left Adam out of the equation, and he was why she was here to begin with. Their brief conversation back at the gate was the longest she'd had with a fellow passenger since becoming stranded. And he'd seemed genuine in saying she should keep the seat she'd taken from him.

This wasn't like her, going for meals with complete strangers. Her friends back home would have said taking any dinner dates was out of character. But then she was very seldom approached. She looked ten or fifteen years younger than she was, but she wasn't outgoing, wasn't a conversationalist, hadn't been since the waning years of her marriage when it was clear her husband wasn't listening to her anymore, and if he wasn't why bother, right? Just shut up and look pretty when we're out, that was Jack's underlying message, and she had for a while, before discovering there was somebody else and all the grief that brought her—

"Jane?"

A lock of hair was wrapped six times around her right index finger and a waiter was standing at the table, poised and ready to "Ma'am" her until he got what he was after.

"The quesadillas, I guess," she said. "And a peach margarita, please." The waiter jotted it down and went away.

"Something wrong?" Adam asked. This wasn't the usual reaction he got from women. The hair twirling was new. The quiet indifference he was used to.

"This isn't like me, is all, dining with someone I hardly know," she said, looking at the tablecloth.

Adam didn't follow up on the statement. After Leslie had bundled up every-thing but the front lawn six years earlier, Adam shut himself off from women. He didn't think himself very attractive. He had a five o'clock shadow by lunchtime on a good day, and forever looked as if he was working on two hours sleep, ready to collapse at a moment's notice into a snoring mass of Jell-o. The few friends that stayed in contact after the divorce seldom tried to match him up with anybody.

The restaurant sound system started playing "Don't Cry For Me, Argentina" just then. Adam rubbed his eyes with one hand, pinching until he came to the bridge of his nose.

"Are you okay?" Jane asked.

Adam blinked and pondered the water. "I haven't done this in six years."

The gift shops were half empty. "This is ridiculous. All I wanted was a bottle of soda," she said. The coolers were part of the half that was empty.

"They ran out yesterday. It took five security guards to keep the duty-free from getting overrun. They were the only ones left with anything to drink, even if it was only Perrier. Even the booze was gone."

Jane smiled. "That had to have been funny."

"It was, considering the guards lost. I don't think the five Japanese in there knew what hit 'em." He looked over at the magazine rack; all that was left was gardening magazines. "So much for getting something to read. All I've got in my bag is training materials."

"Oh?"

Adam opened his bag and pulled out a spiral-bound volume with the title "You, Too, Can Be a Better Salesperson" in large friendly letters across the front. "I do seminars for my company. Here for three days, there for three days, somewhere else for four days, home for three days, lather, rinse, repeat. Sounded neat in the beginning, but really it's just seeing the insides of different hotels."

"You can have my magazine if you want it."

Adam looked down at her magazine. It was one devoted to parenting issues. "Tempting, but no. Thanks, though. The bar up there may have something left," Adam said, pointing farther down the concourse. "If you're interested."

"One margarita a day is my limit," she said, turning to go. "But you can buy me a soda, if there's any to be had."

"Okay." He followed Jane. She hadn't rejected him yet, wished him good night, sent him on his way, back to his chair if it was even still empty. They took a bar-height table that had just opened up. There were no barstools in sight. Adam tried to keep the conversation going. "How long have you lived in Seattle?"

"Five years," she said. "Cleveland before that."

"So why Seattle?"

Jane took a long breath to give herself a moment to think, not about how to phrase her answer, but whether or not to give the correct one. She was outside her comfort zone far enough already, not only striking up a conversation with a complete stranger, but taking an invitation to dinner as well. The question had been innocently asked; her reason could have been as innocuous as taking a new job. Adam seemed nice enough, but she wasn't sure about telling him something as personal as the precise reason she'd moved so far away. She decided to take another chance, though, and hope for the best. "To get away," she said.

Adam nodded. "Other side of the country is away. That's why I moved to Miami," he said, ordering a beer for each of them, hoping she wouldn't notice the change in her beverage. "It's not L.A. I mean, nothing is. But Leslie's not in Miami, which is fine with me."

"Ex-wife?"

He hadn't meant to say Leslie's name, hadn't even meant to bring her up, but now the topic was out there, and he thought a change of topic would only serve to end the connection between them. "We grew up together, had the same group of friends, got married right out of high school before we went to UCLA. Majored in the same thing. A few years after college, things just fell to crap. I mean, there wasn't just one moment you can point to and say, 'That's when my marriage fell apart.' It was a bunch of little things. She decided she wanted to explore her creative side. I ended up doing longer hours at my workplace. It all just drifted us further apart. We tried to reconnect, tried to do things together. We took up ballroom dancing, couples therapy, tried romantic getaway weekends. None of it worked. She went her way, I went mine."

"Mine cheated on me. Took up with a college sophomore. Had a heart attack while screwing her last Saturday. The funeral was three days ago. I only went because Cynthia wanted me to. She said it'd look funny if I didn't, never mind that I live on the other side of the country." She said it without thinking, the words spilling out of her mouth like a dirty secret. Jane looked at Adam, whose face had the same tired look as it had when they first met, no trace of judgment on it. To her surprise, now that she'd said it, she was glad she had.

Adam raised his glass in a toast. "To getting away."

Jane toasted and swallowed before realizing she wasn't having soda.

Adam could tell from fifty feet down the concourse that the seat he'd been calling his own was again occupied.

"Sorry about that," Jane said.

"What's to be sorry about?" Adam shrugged. "It was a seat. I'll make do. Besides, we're not going anywhere, and after two nights sleeping in those chairs, I'll take my chances that the floor's more comfortable."

"Still, you know, I feel guilty. You wouldn't have this problem if I hadn't taken your seat."

He knew what she meant, that he'd still have his seat and, therefore, somewhere to sleep if she hadn't sat there. He also wouldn't have had the dinner and the conversation that had come with it had she chosen a different seat, to say nothing of the small attraction he felt for her. Adam tried not to give away any hint that were the situation a little different he would express an interest in her, romantic, sexual. To him, all that could be was problematic.

"Don't worry about it," he said after a few seconds. Adam looked toward Jane's gate. A few of the girls were still playing. Two were splayed every which way on a couple of chairs. "What about you? Think you can find a spot where the kids won't trample you?"

"No. Well," Jane chewed her lower lip for a second. "I have a room."

Visions ran through his head: pictures of him succumbing to eight to ten hours of sleep on a mattress, of getting up in the middle of the night to use a toilet that didn't auto-flush, of shaving and brushing his teeth at a sink that didn't have motion sensors and that ran both hot and cold water. As quickly as these thoughts came, they left. It was Jane's room, her bed, her toilet, her sink. He couldn't impose, and he doubted she'd invite him of her own accord. They barely knew each other. "Come on. I'll walk you home."

"You don't have to. If you leave again, you'll have a harder time finding a spot."

Adam glanced around the waiting area, at the people, disheveled, dirty, angry, restless, bored. "I'll make do," he said.

They turned and walked slowly back toward the main hall which connected all the concourses. The hallway to the hotel was at the end of their concourse.

"I haven't been walked home in a long time."

"I haven't walked anyone home in a long time. It works out." Adam scratched his chin. "Did he ever do that for you?"

"Walk me home? A couple of times, in the beginning. He was very romantic during the courtship phase, but it didn't last."

"It never does. Romance, I mean. Mine didn't, mine and Leslie's. It was – you know how it is. You start out all expressive and whatnot, and then as you get to know each other you get a little more comfortable, a little less showy. There are couples who still express their fondness for each other, but most of them—most of us—don't. And romance fades and love wilts and it's over."

Jane looked over at him. She wanted to touch him on the arm, gently, and tell him, "You will go on."

They came to a stop at the tunnel to the hotel. "Well," she said, "it's been a marvelous evening. Thank you for dinner."

"My pleasure. Sleep well, Jane." He gave a half-bow, took a couple of steps backward, turned, and started walking away.

"Wait," she said.

Adam turned back toward her.

"My—there's two beds in the room. You can sleep on the other one, if you'd like."

He took a few steps back toward her. She looked sincerely sorry his chair was taken, but inviting him to share her room seemed like she was overcompensating. A little corner of his mind wondered if there wasn't something else behind the invitation. She hadn't seemed interested in a romantic sort of way, but he might have misread any signals she'd been sending out. *And yet*, he thought, *she doesn't seem nearly this brazen*. "Are you sure?"

Jane nodded. "It's the least I can do."

What am I doing? she asked herself as Adam's shower started in the next room. Why have I brought him here? What if he tries something? She knew—she hoped she knew—he wouldn't in the back of her head, but she wondered.

As the shower ran, Jane made herself comfortable. She changed into her pajamas, took her contacts out, and put her glasses on intending to read, but she didn't get that far. She put her head down on the pillow and dozed off before opening her book.

She was standing in the front entry to the house she and Jack shared. Through the windows she could see nothing but darkness, and the sound of crickets chirping could be heard from outside. There was a suitcase on either side of her, thick and overstuffed. This was the night she had left, a couple of hours after walking in on Jack and a co-ed naked and entwined in their bed. She could hear someone approaching, soft footfalls on the stairway to the upper floor, and a moment later. Cynthia appeared then, a girl of six, young and clueless as to what was happening between her parents. "Mommy," she said, "will you read me a bedtime story?" A thunderclap came from outside, close enough to shake the house, and the shockwave flung Jane to the ground, the soft ground, like a mattress and pillows, and the room light was on, and Adam was covering her with the comforter.

"Didn't mean to wake you," he said. "Thought you might be more comfortable under the covers."

She propped herself up and looked around the room. Nothing. No thunderstorm. No picnic basket. No proportionately accurate shrunken children in formalwear. Jane pursed her lips.

"Bad dream?" Adam said.

Jane took a moment in answering, still waiting for a version of her daughter to run into the room. "No. Not really. Not bad." She pulled herself up to a sitting position. "Did your parents ever read bedtime stories to you?"

Adam sat down on his bed and peeled the covers back from the pillows. "They weren't the type. My grandmother did whenever my brother and I went over to stay the night. She had a way of telling a story just so, and I would fall asleep somewhere in the middle."

"Would you read to your child, if you had one?"

Adam folded his hands in his lap. "I don't know. I don't exactly think of myself as an affectionate person. Did you ever read to Cynthia?"

"Never really got the chance. I spent a lot of nights working late when she was young. Most of the time Cynthia was already asleep when I got home. Jack did, I think. She's always been a lot closer to him than me, and when we split up she didn't take it well. Well, with Jack dying last month, it's just gotten worse. So I get to Boston for the funeral and Cynthia's giving me this attitude, like Jack dying is my fault. She blames me for our marriage falling apart, so, you know, why not this too? And I'm sitting there during the service, and I can just feel everyone staring at me, or glancing out of the corners of their eyes. What's the ex-wife doing here, gloating? Then on the way out to the airport Cynthia and I argued again, about Jack, about whose fault the divorce was, things she can never understand."

Adam didn't say a word. He heard the resentment in her voice, laden across every word like a wet blanket.

"Anyway, the magazine there," she said, "has an article that says children don't feel connected to their parents due to lack of family activities. They list bedtime reading as one of the better activities. And I can't help but wonder, you know, what if."

The silence lay there between them for a long minute.

"Leslie's favorite musical is 'Evita.' I had no idea when I married Leslie how much a fan she was of Andrew Lloyd Webber. She played a recording of it quite often. Saw the movie four times the weekend it opened. She knew all the words, sang along, and Leslie's got a pretty fair voice. There were a few times she had the opportunity to see it live. She would take one of her girlfriends, somebody she knew would genuinely enjoy herself. I think she thought if I ever agreed to go, it would be to placate her. Which, you know, she wasn't entirely wrong. Since the divorce, though, every now and then I'll hear the one song, 'Don't Cry For Me, Argentina,' runs through my head, and it'll just bring me down. There was a time when I'd never heard of the song, much less the musical. Six years later and it's like I can't get away from it."

Jane looked at Adam. In the half-light of the hotel room, his eyes looked darker, his face older than in the bright of the concourse. "What if."

"Something like that."

Outside the snow had stopped falling and the plows were being warmed up, but neither of them noticed.

Adam woke at nine o'clock. It took him a few moments to remember where he was, how he'd gotten there. It didn't really start to gel until he rolled over and saw Jane asleep on the other bed. The events of the evening before drifted back into his head in bits and pieces, the things he said mingling with the things he hadn't. He knew he hadn't thanked her properly for inviting him up to the room, not that he had any idea how to.

He looked down and realized he'd fallen asleep in the complimentary robe he'd put on after the shower. As quietly as he could manage, Adam gathered up his clothes and went into the bathroom to dress. He thought about how to get out of the room without waking or offending Jane. A thank you note, maybe, but that seemed to him like something a one-night stand would do. The best thing was to wait for Jane to wake up. Adam finished dressing, hung the robe on the hook fixed to the back of the bathroom door, and went back out into the room.

Jane was awake. "Hey."

"Hey."

"You been up long?"

"Only a couple minutes. You?"

"Oh, for a while now. I don't really do so well on hotel beds. Too stiff for my tastes."

"May I?" he said, pointing to a space next to her on the bed. She didn't say anything so he sat down. "Listen, Jane, I wanted to thank you—"

"Don't."

Adam opened his mouth to reply, then closed it again.

"You won't let me apologize for taking your seat, I won't let you thank me for the bed."

"You brought me up here because of the seat thing?"

"No," she said. "Well, yeah, that had something to do with it. And it was the right thing to do. But I brought you up here because—" Here she paused. There wasn't any one reason why, nothing she could put into words. She liked his company. She could talk to him without feeling embarrassed. Jane had told Adam things she didn't dare tell anyone else, things about her relationship with her daughter, how she truly felt about her late ex-husband. It hit her, then, what she liked about him. "I like talking to you," she said. "And I wanted to keep on talking."

Adam could see in her face that she'd only told half the truth. "If it makes you feel any better, I haven't told a lot of people about how Leslie and I fell apart either."

Jane blushed slightly. "I was worried, bringing you up here. A little part of me was afraid you would try something."

"I thought about it. I'd be lying if I said I hadn't."

"Why didn't you?"

Adam ran his fingers through what was left of his hair. "Because I like you too much."

They walked back down the concourse, toward their gates, side by side. Even above the general murmur of people talking, they could hear the group of young girls playing. "They don't ever tire out, do they?" Adam said.

"I suppose not. It's amazing, though. I don't remember having that much energy when I was that young. I mean, I guess I did. Cynthia did. My parents said I did. But even so—" She stopped and listened to the announcement on the public address system. "Oh God, my plane is boarding." She sped up, and Adam quickened his pace to match hers.

They covered the last hundred feet to her gate as quick as they could, weaving through the crowd like they were so many potholes. The announcement that all rows were boarding came just as they arrived, and a queue had already formed.

Jane turned toward Adam. "Well," she said. "This is more abrupt than I would have liked."

"Yeah, I—" He stopped. He wanted to tell her how much he had enjoyed the night before, how nice it had been to just talk to someone. He knew he'd said it already, back in the hotel room, but this was a more final moment. Adam adjusted the strap of the carry-on he had slung over his shoulder as Jane fished through her purse for her boarding pass. She found it and straightened up to look at him.

"What do we do now?" Adam asked.

"Promise each other we'll write, we'll call. Not do it," she said.

Adam nodded. They were busy people with their own jobs, their own lives. Not that there wasn't room for each other, but their front doors were a continent apart. Dating would be problematic under the best of circumstances, but with Adam's travel schedule being what it was, just maintaining contact would be difficult.

Adam pulled a business card out of his wallet and gave it to her. "My home number's on the back. If you ever make it down to Miami, my door is always open."

Jane pulled a folded-over cocktail napkin out of her pocket. "If you ever come up to Seattle. You know." She pressed it into his hands. "Well—"

"Well," he said.

She smiled and turned to join the boarding queue. He headed back across the concourse to his seat. It was empty again.

GREAT HORNY TOADS

The first one landed on the Fenton house. Eight thirty at night, Alan was in his living room watching television. His wife Lorraine, who hosted a garden social every June, was in the kitchen cleaning up after dinner. The kids were in their rooms, doing homework and screwing off online. And then they weren't. Then they were under a frog the size of a filling station, just like that. No goodbyes, no farewell garden parties, nothing.

I was sent to talk to the media. There's nothing in any book about being a small-town Mayor's spokesperson that covers the contingency of a giant frog landing on and crushing a house, or even anything on giant frogs in general. But someone called one of the Dayton television stations and told them, and a reported and crew were sent. I didn't see what good a statement would do—a giant frog on the rubble of a house spoke for itself, I thought—but the Mayor insisted I go and meet the TV crew there anyway.

When I got there, coffee in hand, there was already a crowd. The TV crew was already there setting up shop across the street from the frog because everyone forgot about the frog's tongue. Apparently the Fenton's dog, which was outside when the frog landed, was running around the front yard yapping away and in about a heartbeat the frog's tongue came out, wrapped around the dog, and sucked it in. So I went to the TV people, introduced myself—"Phil Davis, Spokesperson for the Mayor of Liberty"—and offered to make a statement. They weren't going to say no.

"This is a tragedy," I said. "The Fentons were kind and generous people, loved by everyone in the community. What they could have done to warrant this I do not know. Rest assured, however, that the Mayor's Office is going to launch a full investigation and will work around the clock until this situation is resolved. Thank you very much. No further comment at this time." It worked for the moment. The TV people did whatever it is TV people do and left me alone.

I walked over to the sheriff and we looked up at the frog. It was just sitting there, all quiet like. The area smelled like a pond. "So," I said. "Where'd it come from?"

He chewed something for a second. "The sky."

I sipped my coffee and thought of Exodus.

"We got four eyewitnesses say they saw it come down. Got their statements already. One second a house, next second a crash and a big damn frog where the house had been."

The frog might have exhaled and it might not have. "Any ideas on getting the frog out of here without hurting anything else?"

He chewed something again for a second. "Might maybe just let it leave when it wants to."

"It's a thought," I said. "Evacuate the street, give it all the space it wants."

So the neighborhood was emptied. Got everybody out who could get out by nine thirty and the rest by ten. The town went quiet then for the night. By morning the frog was gone.

Overnight the second one hit. Nobody's quite sure when exactly, other than it was after two in the morning. Jack Johnson, who owns a thousand acres and some out south of town, had some guys come in from Richmond and lay down some crop circles in one of his corn fields so he could see himself on the evening news. The crop circle guys left at two in the morning. By the time Old Man Johnson woke up at half past five the frog was already there, smack in the center of the formation, with no way it could've gotten there except from above. When the frog left that afternoon it knocked over some more corn stalks, so it wasn't so much a crop circle as a crop Rorschach ink blot. Still, Old Man Johnson got his TV coverage, so he was happy. The Mayor said he'd fax over a statement to the news people, but I don't know that he ever did.

No sooner had the second one hopped off for who-knows-where than the third one dropped, right smack on the playground at Hempstead Elementary. It was getting on time for the kids to leave for the day so everyone was inside, but the playscape that had gone in not two years earlier was destroyed. Kids scrambled from their desks to look out the windows when they heard the crash. Twenty seconds later they were greeted with a deafening croak from the frog, which is when the shouting and the running for cover started.

The news vans pulled up ten minutes later to the sight of the frog sitting atop a pile of aluminum and hard plastic that would no longer provide the school children an outlet for releasing their energy. City Hall is only two blocks away from the school so the police had the street barricaded fairly quickly, and it being a nice day I just walked over, coffee in hand like it was something I did all the time. The news people saw me coming and asked for a statement.

"This is a tragedy," I said. "Just a tragedy. And rest assured that the Mayor and the City Council will be launching a full investigation into what has happened here today, both here and out at Old Man Johnson's farm."

"Mr. Davis, Mr. Davis," one of them said. "Does the Mayor believe that a plague of biblical proportions may be about to befall the town?"

Well, if they didn't before they will now you've brought it up, I thought. A couple of cameras went click, click, click in the few seconds it took me to form a suitable response. "The Mayor is, as I said, preparing to launch a full investigation into the circumstances of today, and that question will be a part of it. Now if you'll excuse me." I walked away from the cameras and microphones and joined the sheriff back behind the security tape.

He was chewing something, and regarding the frog when I approached. "Glad the press is enjoying this," he said.

I nodded. "So?" I raised my pitch as I said it, hoping he'd get the idea.

"Still no clue. And now we got how many schoolkids saying it just fell from the sky."

I sipped my coffee for something to do. "I wonder where they hop off to."

The sheriff looked over at me with an odd look on his face. "Wrong question."

I looked back at the frog. "Yeah, I suppose it is."

From there it was two or three frogs a day. Some hit buildings, some hit crops. A few cars were crushed too, along with a semi trailer parked in one of those overnight truck lots outside of town. The driver was asleep in his cab when the frog hit and apparently a little bit after too. How he could sleep through what must have been a horrible racket I have no idea but he did.

The town was on full alert after that. The Community Watch people wanted to institute a curfew but other people said, "How will that help? The frogs fall night and day," and the idea was dropped. Children were escorted from point to point, even inside school, as if under military guard. Some people painted bullseyes on top of their houses, hoping to maybe get a few minutes of fame and an insurance payout. The only one lucky enough to have that work was Old Man Johnson who painted the target on an outhouse he didn't want anymore. As it turned out, he was the only one to be hit twice by the frogs.

A month to the day after the first one hit, the last one did. It landed on a gas station which was having its tanks filled. Somehow the metal canopies scraped together enough for sparks to fly, all the gasoline fumes in the air caught fire, and everything went boom. Thankfully nobody was hurt except for the frog, who didn't survive.

The TV crews turned up again to try and get some footage but they had to shoot around the frog, whose carcass was still in the flames. One leg was sticking straight up in the air like a flagpole, and the air for three blocks in every direction smelled of gasoline and charred amphibian.

I gave the TV people a statement anyway, on the sidewalk running past the gas station. "It is unfortunate that this has happened here today," I said, gesturing with the coffee I'd stopped along the way to pick up. "A local business has suffered great damage and a frog has been incinerated. The mayor is pleased that no one was injured in today's tragic, tragic accident, and vows to not rest until the deluge is over. Thank you very much. If you'll excuse me."

I joined the sheriff, who was leaning against an ambulance that turned up because someone thought it should. "Worst one yet," he said, chewing something.

"Looks like. How's the attendant?"

He gestured over to a young girl in a blue smock, shaking and being comforted by family and EMTs. "About that good."

I sipped my coffee. "We can't stop this, can we?"

He spit; a brown glob of something appeared on the pavement a few feet in front of us. "I should quit. Wife hates tasting it."

The press had a field day. "Frog Legs, Anyone?" was the headline of the Richmond newspaper the next morning, right above a picture of the blaze complete with charbroiling frog. The paper got sued a bunch for printing such an offensive picture, and they went under. The late night comedians were having fun with the frogs before, but this incident dominated their monologues for three nights.

The good news was that over the same stretch of time, tourism jumped. For whatever reason, people thought Liberty was a good place to be for that month. Folks from wherever came in to see both the novelty of an outsized frog as well as all the damage that had been wrought. A few enterprising people started putting together tours of all the damaged buildings, and Old Man Johnson charged people to have a look at the crop destruction. One of the restaurants in town started serving frog legs, but nobody thought that was in good taste and a week later they stopped. Still, for four glorious weeks, hotel rooms in town were hard to come by, and the sidewalks of Liberty were filled with locals who feared another frog falling, and tourists who hoped for it.

And then it stopped. The frogs didn't fall, the jokes weren't made, tourists started staying away again. Folks in town slept a little easier, a little deeper into the night. It was still talked about in the bars, but over time the stories changed. Buildings were smashed that hadn't been. People were crushed and miraculously survived to tell the tale. It became the stuff of fable.

Years later, when I retired after a lengthy career as a public defender, the town's paper sent a journalist to my office for an interview. In turn we came to my time as Spokesperson for the Mayor, and the crisis of the frogs.

"You pulled up in your car to the frog that landed on the first house, the—" He checked his notes briefly. "—Fentons. What was the first thing that went through your mind?"

I smiled. "Great horny toads," I said, trying to sound cartoonish.

The journalist chuckled. "It carried on for a month."

"Yes."

"Do you ever ask yourself why? What the town did to earn having giant frogs dropped on it, I mean."

I thought for a moment. "All the time," I said, and sipped my coffee.

THE GUY WHO MAKES THE COFFEE

The deejays had a name for him: El Disco Loco. Not that anyone ever called him that to his face. He was too good for business. He went out dancing six nights a week during the school year, and whatever bar he went to, so went the college girls, and behind them went the college guys who were trying to figure out what the fuss was over. Was it his look, perhaps, the shirt unbuttoned to just below the pectorals in a pattern that hinted at tiger striping, the pants that were tight in all the right places, the hair slicked back just so, the sparkling teeth, the puckish glint in his eye? Or was it the dancing, exuberant, louder than the music, expertly suggestive, gyrating from shoulders to knees, drawing the prospective partners in like a neon sign spelling out that this, ladies, is where the action is tonight? Either way, enrollment in dance classes at the university meant a two semester stay on a waiting list, and whatever bar he was at on a given night would sell out of the cheap beer and the plastic six-ounce cups it was served in, all in the name of getting close to the spectacle of Fernando.

When he wasn't on the dance floor, Fernando waited tables at the Mexican place uptown. He would have looked out of place at the only other sit-down restaurant in town, the Szechuan one a block further up High Street, and his liberal arts degree qualified him to be either a waiter or a telemarketer, or so he felt. That was where I met him, the Mexican place, but I knew who he was well before then. I was one of those college boys once, a pathetic hanger-on, hoping that the cute girl at the other end of the bar would ditch the scrub she was with and come over after I sent her a drink. I wasted a helluva lot of money that way, ended up drinking one of whatever they were having whether or not I wanted it. But drinking and romancing costs money, so I took the waiter job. I guess I was okay at it. I didn't spill the food on people or anything like that. Fernando, though. It started with the smile, always the smile. His teeth had a hypnotic effect after prolonged exposure, or perhaps the women were trying to figure out how they got that white. Then the accent helped. Not quite overdone, enough to convince you that he was from Cuba (with a hard "u"), in a low baritone guaranteed to get your attention. And he ended every exchange with a wink and a señorita that seemed genuine every time.

One night not long after I started working there, I was still figuring out how things went and all, in walks this group of four college girls, seniors maybe, and one of them was a complete knockout. The hostess put them in Fernando's area. He and I were standing at the bar, killing time 'cause the place was half empty.

77

"Nice looking table," I said.

Fernando looked over at them and shrugged. "Eh."

"Are you kidding? Look at the one there. The blonde."

He looked again. "She's okay."

Okay didn't begin to cover it. She was well out of my league, I knew that. If I'd had Fernando's hair, voice, and teeth, then I might stand a chance. As it was, all I had was a passing resemblance to Peter Noone, which meant nothing in my generation.

"The others, though," he said and reached over, grabbed a cocktail napkin, and started writing on it. "Five dollars says by the end of their meal I'll have at least one of their phone numbers."

About an hour later the table of girls left. I was back at the bar keeping one eye on my one table of customers and the other on the TV, and Fernando slid the cocktail napkin in front of me on the bar. "Open it."

I did. It belonged to someone named Linda. I looked at him, stunned that this incredibly average looking guy could so easily get a phone number. "How'd you do that?" I asked.

He gave me the shrug again, adding the smile. "Did you see the one of them leave the table for a minute?"

That would have been the knockout. "Yeah, I thought she went to the bathroom."

"She did," he said, "but not alone."

As he walked away, feeling of anger and awe toward Fernando stirred inside me, anger because he got the phone number of the one I thought most attractive at the table, the one he thought inferior to the others, and awe because he could get it in the first place. He was attractive enough to women that they would give him their numbers. And, as he came back to remind me a moment later, I was out five bucks.

Fernando needed a roommate, he said. What little he made as a salary wasn't enough to cover the bills. I wanted to get out of the dorms, so I took his offer to move in. The first night I was there he had a girl come home with him. Then the next, and the next, and the next. A different one every night. I saw them for the first time the morning after. I would come out to the living/dining room, beckoned from my bed by the smell of coffee already brewing thanks to the auto-timer setting, and I'd only just get my own mug poured when out they'd come. They would just saunter by, pretending I wasn't there. Some tried to fix their clothes or their hair or whatever, try and look respectable. It didn't always work. After I'd been there a month, the girl that came out of his bedroom was Linda. I was stirring my coffee when she wandered out in one of his shirts. On her it hung halfway down her thighs. "Smells good," she said. "Any for me?"

I poured her a mug and watched her dump cream and sugar into the coffee before taking a sip. "Fernando good to you?"

She didn't say anything for a long minute, instead pushing her hair out of her eyes and staring into the mug. "He's a sweet man. Very gentle."

Given the sounds that came from his room, "gentle" would not have been the word I used. The walls were thin; I knew more about his sex life than any man should. "You going to see him again?" Linda was the first one to stop to chat, have some coffee, and I'd been wondering anyway if, given the chance, any of them would care to repeat the experience.

"I might," she said. "I might not. That all depends."

"On?"

"Whether or not he calls me back."

Then you won't be here again, I thought. I hadn't seen Fernando call one back yet. Until now, but something told me he hadn't called Linda.

I didn't ask about the dancing for another week. I knew he went out and did whatever and came home with a girl, but usually I'd come home from the restaurant and he'd already be gone. Our nights off from the Mexican place finally coincided, and he announced that he was going out. "I'd like to come," I said.

He looked at me sideways, measuring me. I could see the wherefores floating through his mind, but instead he settled on a simpler question. "Do you dance?"

"Yeah, I can dance." I didn't sound very convincing.

Fernando arched an eyebrow. "Do you understand the meaning of the dance?" he demanded. "Do you know the dance in your heart and your soul? Do you feel the rhythm of the music in your heartbeat? Do you—do you dance?" By this last question his face was three inches from mine. His breath smelled of guacamole and cola, and his eyes had taken on a crispness I hadn't seen in them before. If I'd had the time, I could have counted the hairs in his barely-there goatee, he was that close to me.

I folded like a pup tent. "No. Not like that."

"Then you cannot dance," he said, turning and leaving. "Not with Fernando." I stayed in and the next morning, just like always, the girl came out in search of the coffee she was smelling.

A couple of days later I was at home, enjoying a day off. Linda showed up. She didn't call first to find out if Fernando would be there. She just came, looking for him. I told her he was at work, and her eyes lost what spark they had. "I have some coffee on," I told her. "You can wait for him here, if you like."

"No, I—" Her voice trailed off, her eyes darted from side to side, avoiding contact and committal. "I couldn't," she said.

"No, please. I insist," I said, and held the door open further. "Come in. Have some coffee. Relax a little."

She came in, sat down at the counter, clutched her purse with both hands like it was a lifeline. "This is awful nice of you. Was nice smelling it that morning when I was—" I put a full mug in front of her and got the cream from the fridge. She added some sugar and some cream, stirred, blew, sipped. "Do you know when he'll be back?"

"His shift at the restaurant ends at six. He should be back after that for a few hours before heading up to dance wherever."

"The Uptown Grill," she said, blew, sipped again. "I'll see him there." She stood up and walked to the door.

"Wait," I said. She stopped and turned back to me. "What is it? What is it about Fernando?"

Linda took a step back towards me. "He's so—alive. He radiates it, how happy he is to be who he is, where he is, doing what he's doing. And it's like he wants to share that joy with anyone, everyone he can. Just—when he dances, when he smiles." Linda gazed off into space for a moment. "He's not afraid of who he is. What else is there?" She left. I put the cream away.

Fernando got home at six fifteen and walked straight through the apartment to his bedroom, slamming both doors behind him. It was that way every day. Outside of his romancing he was not a socialite. I knocked on his door all the same and hoped for the best. He shouted for me to come in on the second try. I found him staring at himself in the mirror in his private bathroom. "I want to learn," I said.

He stared me in the eye. "You want to learn?"

"To dance. Like you."

His eyes shone with mirth. "You? Dance?" I nodded anxiously. "You cannot dance."

"I know. That's why I want to learn how. From you. I want to learn everything. I want to know how you— you—"

"How I get the chicks." He laughed. "There is more to it than just the dance, Paul. It is the clothes. It is the hair. It is the attitude you radiate to others. It is in understanding what your soul is made of. I can teach you every step I know, but that doesn't mean you'll be able to dance."

"It's a start," I said.

"Come with me tonight, then, and see what it is you aspire to." Then he showed me out of his room.

I was at the Uptown Grill at ten thirty. The beer'd been flowing for a while already. Students in assorted states of inebriation littered the pool tables and the bar like so many moths around a tiki torch. I had a corner table removed from the action a little, and an understanding with my waitress to keep the diet colas coming. I wanted as much of my senses as possible. The deejay'd been playing songs for a while, and girls mostly were on the dance floor. There were a few guys trying to wiggle and squirm their ways next to the attractive ones, but there was this pervading attitude of nothing doing. They were expecting their Fernando anytime now, and until then there'd be no action. The guys knew not to go too far away, though, to catch the ones Fernando didn't choose.

He turned up a few minutes short of midnight. It was like watching the Red Sea part, how fast the people cleared a path to the center of the dance floor. His entrance was timed to the ending of one song as if he'd meant it to happen that way, and then it was on with the techno-salsa. There was some shoving on the fringes, jockeying for position to be noticed and danced with, even from the girls who'd already had a turn that night. After about five minutes, I noticed Linda in the crowd of girls. She was actively pushing other girls aside, frantically trying to get to the center. She made it a minute later and waited her turn; Fernando would at least get to them all once before making his selection. Her turn came after another minute or so, and I saw her lips moving and her leaning into him so she could be heard over the music, but if Fernando replied at all I couldn't tell. She got her three or four spins before he twirled her back to the edge of the circle and moved on. Linda did manage to stay in the center of the circle but got no other turns with Fernando. She walked off the dance floor, out the front door, and away. I'd seen what I needed to see by then, and Linda looked genuinely upset. I caught up to her after half a block. "Linda? You okay?"

She stopped and looked at me. "I just wanted to talk to him. That's all. He wouldn't even do that much. He didn't say a word."

I didn't have a ready response to that. I couldn't tell her she was a one-night stand. She was working that out on her own as it was. What I could tell her I wasn't sure, but I knew she had something on her mind, and I wanted to hear what that was. "You wanna go somewhere? Talk? Get some coffee or something?"

We ended up at the fast food place three blocks away. I ordered some coffee for the two of us, and we took a booth in the back corner of the restaurant, removed from the action of slightly drunk co-eds marveling at the mediocre food. "You fell for him pretty bad, huh?"

Linda shrugged and smirked. "I guess I did. He made me feel—I don't know. Special."

I knew the feeling she was thinking of. She felt like the only girl in the world when she was with Fernando. A lot of girls came out of his bedroom the next morning wearing his shirts and saying the same thing.

"I mean," she said, "the son of a bitch approached me—not the other way around—in that stinking restaurant. I thought he was actually interested in me."

"He said he followed you into the ladies room."

This look of disgusted surprise came on her face, like somebody had just passed gas. "Hardly. He caught me on my cellphone outside the ladies room. I didn't even go in, let alone with him. He told me I was the definition of stunning, and to give him my number, maybe we could go dancing sometime. I thought it was funny and cute of him, so I did. He never called."

I turned that over for a moment in my mind, and even then I ducked behind a cliché. "He's a pig. For that, I apologize."

"That's rare," she said. "A man apologizing." A smile slid on to her face, a small smile, just big enough to let me know she appreciated the gesture, but before I could enjoy it more she took another sip of coffee, and it was gone. "I never see you out on the floor dancing."

"I don't—I mean, next to Fernando, I'm not much of a dancer."

"Nobody is, if you hadn't noticed."

This was true. Most of the girls who danced with Fernando weren't all that great, and hardly any of the guys were.

"On the other hand," she said and stopped, looking down into her coffee. "What?"

A long moment passed, then she said, "Nothing. Let's go."

I insisted on seeing her as far as her apartment. Not that I don't think she couldn't handle herself, but rather I was hoping that she would finish that thought. We got to her front door, and I wanted to kiss her goodnight, but instead she said, "Dance with me."

I didn't say anything for a moment. "What?"

"Dance with me."

"I don't—here?" I looked around. She had a third floor apartment, her door opening onto a walkway overlooking the parking lot. The only light was from the security lights at either end of the building, just bright enough to put everything into half-shadow.

"Why not?" she said. "Give me one good reason why not."

"I just—I can't. Someone might see." I knew they wouldn't, knew we were barely visible in the half-light, but I said it all the same. I took two steps backward and gave her a half-bow. "Goodnight, Linda."

Fernando and I worked the same shift the next day, and I gave him a lift into work. "So, you saw the dance?" he said.

I nodded. That I had.

"Do you feel, in your heart of hearts, you can dance like that?"

No. No, I certainly didn't.

"Bueno. I didn't want to say anything, but I had a feeling. You, my friend— you are too much the intellectual to dance like that."

That night I was in the same booth as the night before, same waitress, same standing order for diet cola. I watched the crowd, trying to figure out who was with whom, match this person to that, deduce who the roommates were just from the social patterns. It wasn't as hard as I thought it would be. People tended to stay in the same small group of friends that they came in with, the mingling between parties limited to a "How you doin'?" in passing. I looked around, trying to figure out who Fernando would take tonight. No one jumped out of the crowd, but then Fernando was himself not fickle with his choices. Some of the women were blonde, some brunette. Some had short hair, some long. Some were skinny, some weren't. What they all had in common was that they were young and impressionable, and Fernando was someone larger than life willing to swoop down and give them one night in heaven. I suspect.

"I don't get it," someone said from behind me. I turned and saw Linda standing there. Her arms were crossed and she had a look on her face that could have been disappointment and could have been heartburn.

"It's not what you think."

"Oh, it couldn't possibly be what I think, could it? It couldn't be you being so pathetic that you had to come and watch Fernando again. What, are you trying to learn from him? Do you want to be Fernando 2.0?" She looked at the people crowded at the bar. "Oh, I get it. Hoping for a little best friend action. Well, I hope she's cute."

Linda turned to go, but I grabbed her arm. "I'm here for you."

She just looked at me, her mouth slightly open. "What?"

"I'm here—I wanted to see whether or—whether or not you'd dance with Fernando again. I wanted to see whether or not you'd come back."

Her look didn't change. "Why on Earth did you think I would?"

"You did. You have. You came back last night. You're here tonight."

Linda shook her head and left. Had I been thinking I would have followed her, apologized for my lack of trust, for thinking she was every bit as shallow as the rest of them. I let her go, let her be mad at me, at Fernando, at whomever.

Almost a minute after Linda left, Fernando arrived. The deejay put on a nice upbeat tango-sounding dance mix and the circle of girls formed around him magically. Largely it was the same as I'd watched him do the night before with the steps rearranged to fit what was playing. The first few girls he danced with didn't last long, maybe ten seconds each, all looking stunned first to be dancing with Fernando, then to not be. One actually looked like she was a better dancer than Fernando, or at least more willing to shake her ass in a direction other than his, so she didn't last either. He settled eventually on a redhead I wasn't sure I'd seen in the crowd earlier, or if I had I couldn't remember what her roommate looked like. After a few minutes of gazing at the crowd and trying to figure out who was one person less, I left and started walking nowhere in particular.

After a while, I found myself in the parking lot outside Linda's apartment. From street level it looked even darker than it had the night before, the wattage of the security lights barely enough to reach the ground. I could see someone climbing the stairwell headed toward the top floor. From the back, the person looked vaguely familiar. "Linda?"

She stopped, turned around, and headed down to the nearest landing, some fifteen feet above me. "Paul."

"I thought I wanted to be Fernando," I said. "I thought he had it all worked out. He's so smooth, easy to approach, easy to talk to, so laid back. He gets his choice of women every night, and I saw that, and I thought, 'Here's a guy who's got it figured out. Here's a guy who's got the answers.' I can't approach women—hell, I can't approach people in general. I can't even take their food orders without being embarrassed. I'm just Paul, the quiet guy in the corner seat, the perennial best friend. And Fernando gets your number easy as pie, you who I noticed the second you walked into the restaurant, and you came out of Fernando's room that morning and I thought, 'Well, Paul, there's another one that got away. If you'd been more like Fernando this wouldn't have happened. You wouldn't be just the guy who makes the coffee anymore.'" The wind kicked up just then. I could see Linda hold herself to keep warm. "I—would you dance with me?"

She looked down at me. I couldn't tell, but she might have been squinting. "You sure you can handle it?" she said.

"No."

She came down the rest of the steps and stopped in front of me. "Give yourself a little credit," she said, taking my left hand in her right. "Just for once."

I put my other arm around her waist. We swayed back and forth for a little while, then we went up to her apartment and did it again. It didn't occur to me until hours later, well after the sun had come up, that I hadn't set the timer on the coffee maker back at my place, that Linda probably hadn't made any, but then she rolled over, and the smile on her face let me not care.

POSTER

You've bought a tube, a little cardboard one. Three bucks at the post office. Caps on both ends. Remind yourself to tape those down before you send it.

The poster's been haunting you for a while. It has a nice picture on it, and a poem written by an old flame. The poem was published by a literary journal somewhere out west—you know where, it's on the poster but you can't be bothered to look. The poet, the old flame, sent the poem to that journal on your advice. That was your relationship: you both wrote, but the poet had no idea how to get things out into the world. Once the poet started getting published, you both started writing more. You enchanted each other. The journal accepted and published the poem, created the poster and sent the poet two copies of everything. One was forwarded to you, "in appreciation for a job well done." You put it in your office at work, framed.

Then there was fighting. Words were said because words weren't said. The poet moved on, became involved with someone else, became engaged to someone else. That should have been me, you think. That should have been me. The poster came down later. And then nothing was said. There was nothing left to say that wasn't laced with anger and jealousy. The poster was buried away in a drawer.

You moved on too. Kind of. Always there, at the back of your mind, is the poet. Always wondering what things would have been like had the words been said. Would there still be anger? What would that look like? Would there still be communication? What is the poet doing now? And though you love the person you are now with, the poet comes back to you at odd moments, little things in the street or on TV that remind you, idle conversations on-line involving common friends when the poet chimes in. You try not to mind when you see this, when the poet is forced back into your life for a moment, but you do.

And you remember the poster. You hadn't forgotten about it, but just now it throbs at you from the filing cabinet you've hidden it in, frame and all. It has to go. This ghost has to be exorcised. So you've bought a tube. You know the address, as if you could forget. You weren't the one to walk away from the relationship. If it were up to you—but it isn't.

As you undo the clasps on the back of the frame, you think, Do I send a note? Do I say I'm doing fine? Do I say something angry? You roll the poster up, carefully—you're above damaging it, at least you think you are—and put it in the tube. You get a blank sheet of paper from the printer, take up a pen, and stare at the page for a minute, two minutes, three minutes. The words do not come. You cannot bring yourself to end the silence, mend the friendship. There's no space for you in each other's lives and you know it. You put the cap on the tube. Later, as you hand the tube to the postal agent, you say a silent prayer that the haunting will end, even though you know it won't.

THE MATCH

The matches were sold out again, as they had been every third Friday for four years. That night, the deadliest match ever attempted, the exploding barbed wire electrified cage metal mat match, would be fought between Killer Karl and his latest foe, Dashing Dan. I was covering the event on behalf of Prime Wrestling Action, a minor industry website with a subscription list of 300. I contacted the promoter two weeks ahead of time to get a pass into the show. Grateful for the exposure that he wasn't getting with some of the larger websites, he offered me a backstage pass so I could sit around and chat with the guys before the show. I accepted, because this meant I might possibly get the interview of a lifetime: I might get to talk to Killer Karl.

Killer Karl had been wrestling for a little more than ten years. How he'd managed to last that long was a mystery, considering he'd been working the bloodbath death matches for the last seven, each match more insane than the one before. Probably the only weapon that hadn't been used in any of his matches was a kitchen sink, although there was talk that his next big match would be a "Blow Up The House" match, in which Killer Karl and some other poor guy would fight in a house until one guy pinned the other, and then both guys and the referee would have sixty seconds to vacate the house and achieve a safe distance; the house would then, as the match title implied, blow up, whether or not anybody was in it. The house would be fully furnished, complete with cutlery, and everything would be legal as long as both competitors stayed inside the house.

During these ten years, Killer Karl had never once talked to the press. After bad knees forced him to do gimmick matches if he wanted to stay in the business, the only time most people heard him speak was during his post-match rant sessions while the smoke was clearing from the ring, during which he expressed no real joy at having won the day. Even the people who shared the card with him, including his opponent for the night, seldom heard him talk. He was his own person who valued his privacy (or so people figured), leaving others to create the underground icon persona which he was left to fulfill.

Only a handful of things are known about his pre-wrestling days, and by only a few people scattered across the country. The popular belief is that his real name is Carlton Jones; some sources have variants on that, like Johnson instead of Jones, but always something close. Further research revealed that a Carlton Jones who attended high school in nowhere, Ohio, resembled what a younger Killer Karl might have looked like, before the scars on his face. Some math, based on the date on the yearbook and a reasonable guess at what his age would have been then, made him about thirty-five years old. After his graduation, and before his first documented in-ring appearance some eight years later, there was nothing. Nobody knew who he'd trained with, and the person who promoted the first show he'd appeared on was five years dead. Of the people who worked that show, only two were still in the business and they couldn't remember the show, much less the person. None of the rest of the guys on that card I contacted knew anything either. No sources for the eight missing years came forward, no matter how deep I dug. For all intents and purposes, Killer Karl was for eight years a non-person.

The card wasn't supposed to start until eight, which in wrestling circles means about eight fifteen. People generally showed up three hours before that to get a spot in line for tickets. The arena these shows were held in only seated some twenty five hundred people, and the line for tickets even by the time I showed up that night was down the street, around the corner, and then a block down that street. Even in a recession they sold out every show. The only thing keeping this little group from challenging the bigs was its nature; brawls and blood and general mayhem had been in the mainstream and gone again like a one-hit wonder boy band. But there was a niche group of fans, and they turned up for every show.

I parked my car some blocks from the arena, and found myself at the back door a little past four thirty. The promoter let me in. The only other person already there was Killer Karl; the rest of the guys usually didn't start turning up until just after six. Karl had been at the arena since early in the morning, supervising the installation of the explosives that a pyrotechnic expert friend of his set up and supplied every time the match required them. Karl was, I was told, sitting in the arena, in the ring, meditating. I lit a cigarette and headed out to see him.

The undercard was an afterthought. The matches were hot and action-filled, but people don't go to a wrestling show to watch the preliminaries. Certainly the crowd paid attention to the first few matches, but each was no more special or exciting than the one before, and yet the crowd grew more excited and volatile with each passing match. Everybody just wanted to see the cage blow up. Karl winning was a given; he always did.

I watched the proceedings from the emergency medical station set up on a stage fifty feet from the ring. The promoter had gone to some expense to ensure the safety of both Killer Karl and Dashing Dan. He had both men go under the knife and have installed a special medical transmitter that would send the necessary statistics via low band radio to the medical station, where they would be monitored by qualified personnel. If at any time either man was in severe danger of sustaining permanent injury, the match was to be stopped then and there. It was among the myriad of machinery that I watched the show. I was as anxious to see the cage go up as anyone else. The preliminaries no more held my attention than anyone else's.

I watched the medical personnel fine-tuning the machinery. The sensors were already on, activated, and fully operative. There were two main monitors, one for each man, labeled with black marker on masking tape. The heartbeats pounded across the screen, the blood pressure numbers rolled up and down, the brain wave scans fluxing to infinity.

Nobody in the arena knew exactly what all that equipment on the stage was all about. Not yet. The promoter informed me that it would be explained to the fans prior to the ring introductions. I doubted the fans would be happy with a medical stoppage; wasn't the entire point of an exploding barbed wire electrified cage match to see one man injure the other? I said as much to the promoter; he shrugged, saying that nobody wants to see either man killed.

Before the card started but after the fans started swarming inside, I went backstage to chat with some of the workers. I wanted to get a word with Dashing Dan, get his thoughts for posterity's sake before he stepped inside the cage. When I managed to find him, he had just come from attempting to discuss the match with Killer Karl. Apparently, Karl had little to say for himself; Dan had done most of the talking, suggested a series of spots, while Karl had said nothing before sending him away, telling him to prepare himself, what happens happens, and saying no more. The promoter, who was nearby, shrugged. This was nothing new for Killer Karl. He had demanded his own dressing room, separate from the rest of the boys, and he very seldom interacted with anyone. Dan walked away. The promoter asked me if I wanted to sit in the emergency medical section that evening, watch the lines go up and down during the match and keep me out of the madding crowd that would riot if Karl lost.

I looked again at the screens. The monitors were alive. Dashing Dan's heart rate was higher than a kite. Killer Karl's was normal. The meditation was doing what it was supposed to do: relax him.

I pushed aside the curtain that hid the backstage area from the arena. Killer Karl was kneeling with his back to the curtain in the center of the ring. His arms were at his side, his thumb and middle fingers joined at the tips forming a circle on each hand. He didn't notice me stepping through the curtain, or hear it swish back into place. I stood in front of the curtain for nearly a minute, puffing from my cigarette. Quietly so as not to disturb the process, I walked behind the last row of folding chairs around the ring, moving clockwise, until I stood facing Killer Karl directly. During the minute or so I was walking Karl had not shown any indication that he was even aware of my presence. He looked peaceful.

My cigarette burned on. Still Killer Karl did not move. His breathing was barely noticeable. His eyes were tightly closed, his face unreadable. Was he just meditating, or planning the high spots of his forthcoming match out? From where I stood, it was impossible to tell.

Then a metal folding chair at ringside began to levitate without the aid of any hidden strings or attachments, and the last of my cigarette fell to the floor.

The card that night was only six matches deep, counting the main event. The promoter had opted to run the first five matches straight through, and then have a fifteen minute intermission to set up the barbed wire and the cage, which was not a simple operation. With the metal mat attached directly to the metal ring structure, the entire ring would theoretically be able to conduct the electricity in the cage if the cage, in any way, touched the ring; it was a theory no one was willing to attempt to disprove, especially the promoter, financially concerned about such things. The cage, then, was set on eight three-foot poles set so that there was a pole in each corner and a pole in the center of each side, and built large enough so that each side of the cage would be about ten inches from the edge of the ring apron, leaving a gap just large enough for the wrestlers and the referee to weasel in and out of the ring for the match; also, the cage would be attached to the ceiling by a series of cables, specially designed not to conduct electricity, to prevent the cage from toppling onto the crowd. From here, the promoter hoped that the ring wouldn't slip and slide into the cage and test the theory, but then slipping and sliding wasn't really likely, as the ropes would be wrapped in barbed wire, and the wrestlers would avoid being whipped into them.

By the time intermission ended, and the cage and all the gimmickry had been set up, the average IQ of the crowd had dropped forty points, and some members of the crowd were drooling openly. The mere anticipation of the match had successfully returned the fans to the savage state from which they had originated. They wanted to see one guy finish the other, beat him within an inch of his life and then let him live, only to do it all over again in the "Blow Up The House" match. The fans were also hoping that Killer Karl would make it through in one piece, because his survival was essential to blood and gore wrestling fans; nobody else could quite do it like he could.

Dashing Dan's entrance music played over the public address system, and the fans erupted into boos and jeers. Tonight was the first time he'd ever been booed during a match, he told me years later, and he had no idea how to handle it. He walked out from behind the curtain, stood startled for a moment, then walked on to the ring, contorted himself so he could get in the cage, and then jumped around to keep himself warm and ready, the crowd out of his thoughts. A few thrown objects bounced harmlessly off the cage. Then the music changed, the crowd roared louder than at rock concerts, and Killer Karl appeared from behind the curtain and walked to the ring, not even acknowledging the fans. He shifted himself to get into the cage, stood up in the ring, and ran across and attacked Dashing Dan, and just like that the match to end all matches began.

During the opening exchange, another well armored person, the referee, made his way inside the cage. The referee was covered in thick padding so that if he was accidentally pushed into the barbed wire ropes they wouldn't hurt him. He also wore a large helmet on his head, also for protection, if he found himself in the ring when it blew up, which had been the case the last time Killer Karl had done an exploding ring match. The match rules worked like this: basically, the objective was to survive. Exactly fifteen minutes after the start of the match, the ring and the cage would explode, regardless of whether or not anyone was in it. In order to escape from the cage, first you had to pin your opponent. If you got pinned, you had to stay inside the cage, but that rule was never adhered to closely; Karl had a reputation of helping his victims out of the ring before it exploded. The four sides of the ring had special explosives attached to them that went off every time one guy or the other (or the referee) went into the ropes on that side, but these were mostly for show, and seldom if ever did any damage to the wrestlers themselves, but did serious damage to the refs (the refs are wimps; that's how wrestling works), and thus the padding (which was seldom helpful in these cases; again, that's wrestling).

That the ring announcements had been skipped altogether was not a loss to anyone. Everyone in the arena knew who was who, and what the match was, and what the rules were, so anything the announcer could have said would have been redundant. The ring announcer had been standing at ringside prepared to identify the combatants, but when Karl started beating on Dan he sat back down in his seat.

The ringside bell joined the metal folding chair in mid-air. My jaw made an attempt to join the cigarette butt on the floor. I looked at Killer Karl, and was frightened by what I saw. His forehead and temples were throbbing. He slowly moved his hands to his temples and gritted his teeth. A table and another couple chairs began to levitate. Then Karl tilted his head backward, opened his mouth as wide as humanly possible, and screamed, high, out of the vocal range of most sopranos, barely audible yet distinct, piercing, unavoidable. Another dozen chairs began to rise, along with any small object not otherwise tied down and even a few that were. After a moment, I covered my ears to lessen the pain it brought me but it didn't help. My eardrums cried in pain. I wanted to react, scream myself, but something held me frozen.

And then it stopped. Killer Karl snapped himself back to the position I had originally found him in. The pain in my ears vanished as quickly as it came, and the levitating objects returned to the floor and assumed rest position as if they'd never been five feet off the ground without physical help. Karl's breathing was more pronounced now. He had hardly moved at all, yet he looked completely exhausted. Over the space of a minute, Karl regained control of himself, returning to his normal breathing pattern, until he was once again at complete calm, as I had found him five minutes earlier.

Then his eyes opened.

The way wrestling works is: the bad guy gets the initial advantage, then the good guy gets the advantage for a while, then there's a period of even exchanges back and forth, and then either the good guy scores a clean win or the bad guy scores some sort of screwjob win. There's more to it than that, and certainly not every match follows this formula, but that's the basic concept behind most matches. Knowing that, even the most casual of fans would have a better than average chance of guessing that Karl would be the first one sent into the barbed wire, even if they know nothing else about professional wrestling.

Karl got in the first few shots but Dan rallied quickly, blocking a punch and then scoring a few of his own. Karl went down after the fourth, and as he got back up Dan leveled him with a dropkick that sent him back to the mat. Dan picked Karl up and tried to whip him into the ropes, but Karl stopped himself, not wanting to run into the barbed wire. Dan threw another dropkick to the back of his head, and into the barbed wire Karl went. The explosives went off, and the crowd erupted into cheers. A few small cuts opened themselves up and down Karl's body but the only thing seriously damaged was his pride, the face he'd lost by having had first blood drawn on him. Now he was angry. As Karl tilted his head down to look at his body, Dan tried for another dropkick. Karl saw him coming and wisely stepped a foot to his left as Dan's feet were leaving the ground, past the point where Dan could effectively stop himself. Dan crumpled to the mat; the tide had turned. As Dan came full to his feet Karl nailed him with a right, staggering him. Then Karl grabbed Dan's hair, ran him across the ring and threw him headlong into the barbed wire and cage, and the explosives went off again, and the crowd cheered again.

The next eight minutes were even. Both men were bloodied, having had their foreheads raked cruelly across the barbed wire covered ropes. Both were exhausted from the high loss of blood mixed with the physical output. And yet neither was ready to be pinned. Even though both wanted to leave the cage, neither one was quite ready to admit defeat, leaving the other glorious in victory no matter what the script said. They had left pretext behind for the legitimate anger each one now felt for the other. This was the realism wrestling had been striving for for years and the crowd sensed it, allowed themselves to be caught up in it, and they wanted more.

And then, with ten minutes gone in the match and five minutes remaining, the first of the alarm sirens began to go off.

Our eyes met from a hundred feet apart. With the same power that had allowed the chairs to levitate he held me with his gaze as he stood. I was in terrified, wondering what my penalty would be for having witnessed what had just happened. Was I the first to have seen it? If not, what had happened to the others who had also seen?

Killer Karl began to move. I remained still, held by the immense power in his gaze. Somehow I knew that he could catch me before I got a hundred feet away. Karl stepped through the ropes, jumped down to the arena floor, and began walking toward me. His gaze never moved from me, and yet he navigated the chair set-up without even a first glance. After a small eternity, Karl was standing not a foot in front of me. We stood there for a minute, him holding me in place with his stare, me standing there like a deer in headlights.

Then he said, "Let's talk."

The fans saw this as an incentive to begin cheering louder, urging both men to lie down so that a pin could be made, and both could leave the cage, but that wasn't going to happen. Both men were tired, bloody, exhausted beyond reason, yet neither was ready to concede.

Dashing Dan and the referee began arguing over a disputed two-count; Dan shouted that the referee was counting slow on purpose; the referee maintained his innocence. All the while, Killer Karl was recovering. He rose to his feet, got a running start, and drove a knee high into Dan's back. Dan pitched forward into the referee, and both stumbled into the ropes and the cage, and despite all the safety measures taken to protect him, the referee collapsed like a rag doll. So did Dan, and to the delight of the crowd, Karl had the true upper hand at last. Karl looked around at them, disgusted, then turned, pulled Dan to his knees, then picked him up and slammed him into the metal mat. And again. And again. As he did this, the monitors beeped madly. Karl's heart rate and blood pressure were through the roof and climbing still. Karl covered Dan and the semi-conscious referee managed to get a three count before passing out completely. The fans erupted into cheers, drowning out the siren. Karl's heart rate went faster still. He went to where the referee lay prone and rolled him under the bottom rope and off the apron. The referee fell past the cage and crumpled to the arena floor as emergency medical personnel moved to tend to him. Karl watched this, and then turned his attention to Dan. Dan had regained his sense, and while Karl's back was turned, he reached down into his tights and pulled out a bag of white powder. As Karl turned back, Dan took some of the powder and threw it into Karl's eyes, blinding him. The fans booed as Dan climbed to his feet and watched Karl struggle, flailing at thin air. Dan took Karl by the hair and threw him into the ropes. Karl cleared them and went into the cage, and his heartbeat monitor flatlined. He continued to flop around, clawing at his eyes trying to get the powder out. Dan gave the audience the finger as he slid under the ropes and out of the cage.

Killer Karl was alone. He clawed at his eyes, still trying to get the powder out, and the machines still showed no heartbeat. The emergency medical station personnel began chattering nervously amongst themselves; was there a malfunction or had his heart really stopped beating? The second siren began going off; the ring and cage would explode in one minute, and Karl was still inside the structure, swinging at nothing. Was this in the script? No one in the crowd, including myself, was certain.

Thirty seconds later, Karl regained his sight, the powder sweated and teared out of his eyes. He looked around at the crowd, urging him to leave the ring, but Karl seemed to be scanning the crowd, searching for someone. He found me on the medical stage. I stood up, and raised my right hand to him. He returned my salute, and then closed his eyes. Barely, I could see the ring lift an inch or two off the floor and move to one side, and then all at once, as the ringposts made contact with the cage it, the ring, and everything inside, blew up.

There were only two more wrestling shows at the arena before the promotion closed its doors for good. I didn't attend either show, and from what I've been told not many other people bothered to show up either. The appeal was gone. The people simply didn't care anymore. The crowd had finally seen what they'd been waiting to see for all those years.

Both Dashing Dan and the referee were fine eventually. Dan lost a significant amount of blood during the match, but he healed and continued wrestling for another ten years with a different promotion. Not that it mattered; the label "The Man Who Killed Killer Karl" stuck with him to his dying day. The referee had never been hurt at all, and he worked the next week at a different promotion's show. Neither one would say whether or not the script had been abandoned mid-match, and to this day that remains a debating point among wrestling enthusiasts everywhere.

The cause of death was officially given as a heart attack. Nobody's quite sure exactly at what point it happened in the match, but that's what the medical examiner gave. A group of technicians examined the unit used to transmit Karl's vital signs to the machines on the stage, but it was found to be in perfect working order. Assuming it always was, a dead man wrestled in very much a live manner for a little more than three minutes.

I still have my interview notes with him. The Monday after the card I put them in a lockbox and there they've sat ever since. Prime Wrestling Action wanted a detailed story covering the interview but I told them no, and haven't written for them since. When I got home after the show I looked over the notes, and remembered what had happened during the match. Nobody knew who he was; everybody knew what they wanted him to be, and he unwillingly strained to meet that image. For years, he'd been looking for a way out.

Lake Effect

Eight pairs of eyes widened at once. Two of their owners inched back from the conference room table, looking like clowns horrified by the sight of a joke gone wrong, unsure how to respond. There was shouting, pounding on the table—was that him doing that? Three of them stood up and made for the door, as the pounding became more emphatic, pound, pound, pound—

Ron Baxter jerked awake in his patio chair and looked around, trying to figure out whether or not he'd fallen asleep and how long he'd been out for if he had. As he watched a couple of boats go by on the lake, he thought about the disastrous meeting his last day at the office. The week he'd spent at this cabin had been at once relaxing and lonely. His cellphone was back in Detroit on the orders of his psychologist. The cabin had no television, radio, Internet, or even a local newspaper delivered. Ron had no car; he'd flown into Traverse City and hired a taxi to drive him the forty minutes to this cabin, just outside of Harbor Lights. With every passing day, the rest of the world seemed more vague and distant, like a place he'd been once and now struggled to remember.

A crunching sound came from around the side of the house. Someone was walking up the gravel path leading from the drive. He couldn't remember hearing a car pull up; maybe it was the car door slamming that had woken him. A moment later a woman appeared from around the side of the house. Her hair was a next of tangles, and she strained with the weight of the plastic grocery bags she had in each hand, all bulging and overflowing. She didn't appear to notice Ron sitting on the deck until she was at the foot of the stairs leading up to it. When she saw him, her expression lightened a little, and she rolled a shoulder. "Mind giving me a hand?"

Ron almost jumped out of his chair. He took one handful of bags from the woman and opened the screen door to the cabin.

"Thanks," she said, entering. "These things weigh a ton." She walked over to the kitchen area and began unpacking the bags, putting the groceries away as if she'd been here before.

Ron placed the bags he was holding on the floor beside her. "I'm sorry, but who are you?"

She stopped unpacking long enough to look at him. "Oh," she said. "Right. Margie. Margie Collins." He must have still looked confused because she continued, "Didn't Ben tell you I was coming?"

Ben was Dr. Benjamin Samuels, Ron's psychologist, the person responsible for him being here. "No."

"He didn't call or anything?"

Ron took a couple of steps backward. "No phone."

"Oh. Yeah. He never did get around to installing a phone, and there's no reception out here to speak of." She opened the freezer, frowned, and continued with her unpacking.

Ron sat down at the dining table. He wondered how well she and Ben knew each other. Clearly well enough that she could be trusted to come with food. "So Ben sent you?"

"Supposed to come here every Thursday with groceries and supplies for you for the week and check up on you, make sure you're still in one piece." She crumpled up one empty bag and put it inside another.

"And how do you know Ben exactly?"

"Lake party. A few times every season everybody who's got a place on the lake here gets together at somebody's house for a grillout. There's not too much in the way of entertainment in these parts, just the couple of bars in Harbor Lights, really. So the grillouts are, you know, the big social event. A chance to meet and greet and all that." She crumpled the last of the plastic bags and stuffed it in with the others. "Well, if you need anything, I'm just two houses down from here. The little white one with the big garden on the side." She walked to the door, opened it, and stepped outside. "Let me know if you need anything," she said, closing the door.

Ron nodded. "Okay." After she'd gone, Ron looked around the cabin, wondering why it suddenly seemed so empty and lifeless.

The cabin had a dock just large enough to tether a small boat to. Everyone up here had a boat, Ron noticed, or nearly everyone. During the day the lake was full of traffic: families taking the powerboat out for a spin, parents up front speeding along, children on inflated rings being towed along behind, bumping along in the wake; the occasional lonely rowboat, one or two people aboard holding poles and staring at the drink, willing any fish they could to come along and take a bite; rafts of kayakers, all wearing vivid neon multicolored wetsuits, staying close to the shore doing not much more than paddling and watching the scenery float by. The cottage faced east; Ron woke early a couple of times to watch the sunrise glistening off the surface of the lake, sharing the view with the fishermen, blinding them all with its power.

Ron had spent most of the week watching all of the activity. Everyone, he noticed, looked happy. The kayakers seemed fascinated both with how well everyone kept their lawn, but also with whatever wildlife showed up, rabbits, deer, the occasional otter. The fishermen, he thought, must be content in their own way, and the few times he'd seen one of them reel in a catch of any size, both the man who caught it and whatever person shared the boat with him acted like they scored the winning goal. The children being pulled along on inflated tubes were having the time of their lives, and the parents alternated between happy and concerned, happy to be out in the sun, concerned that something might happen to their child.

The day after her visit, Ron saw Margie glide by in a kayak. He wasn't sure he recognized her at first. Her hair, which had been a mess the day before, was pulled back into a neat bun, and the construction barrel orange wetsuit made a marked difference from the baggy tee-shirt and jeans she'd had on. As she passed in front of the cabin, Margie looked in his direction and waved. Ron returned it, if a bit half-heartedly. He still didn't know what to make of her. Ben asking her to stock the cabin with food was understandable; it had seemed curiously well prepared for a place that hadn't been occupied in ten months, now he thought about it, and Ron had no real means of getting more supplies. Had he been in such bad shape when he left Detroit that Ben thought he needed looking after? Ron supposed so. The meeting had gone so badly, the shouting, the crying, There must be another solution, there must be, Ben appearing as if by magic, none of the employees willing to make eye contact.

Margie picked her paddle up and moved along. Ron fell asleep again in his chair and didn't see her return. She had stopped by, though. The sun was down by the time he woke. The porch light was on, as were a few inside the cabin. Ron scratched his head as he stood, looking at the porch light. It hadn't been on when he came out, nor had any of the ones in the cabin. Inside there was a covered dish and a book on the table. Beneath the cover was a full dinner: two pieces of oven-fried chicken, an ear of corn, and some green beans. On the cover was a Post-It. "Thought you'd enjoy the book. Hope you like the dinner. Margie." Ron peeled the note off and tapped it against the table top a couple of times before sitting down to eat. Was this something else Ben had asked her to do, some other bizarre part of his therapy?

Two days later, Ron was on the patio reading the book, looking at the water in between pages and chapters, when Margie pulled up at his dock in a small boat. The book was one he hadn't read before, a murder mystery by a Detroit writer he'd read a few times, even met once or twice. He started reading it as a means of distraction, a way of keeping his mind occupied, but the further he got in to it the more he found himself caught up in the storyline, the general intrigue, the noir elements. Margie waved as she pulled in, powering down the motor, and he put the book down and went toward her. When he got near she threw one end of a rope at him. "Mind giving me a hand?" she said. "It's a lot harder to do on your own." She pointed at a metal post to his left. "Tie it around that one there."

Ron bent down and looped the rope around the hitch. To his right, he heard Margie jump out of the boat and onto the dock. She started to fasten a second rope around another hitch. "Didn't expect to see you today," he said.

"Thought I'd check in on you, see how you were getting by."

Ron finished tying a knot on the rope and stood up. Margie stood at the same time. "Why don't you come in, have a drink? I've got—well, you know what I've got," he said.

Margie smiled. Ron was almost blinded by how white her teeth were, how they almost glistened as bright as the sunlight on the water. "Thank you, that would be very nice."

As they went inside Ron said, "Thanks for dinner the other night. That really wasn't necessary. And I like the book."

"Oh, it wasn't a problem." Margie reclined into the sofa. "I just had a feeling."

He pulled two bottles of water from the refrigerator. "You just had a feeling what?"

Margie took one of the bottles from him as he sat on the opposite end of the sofa. "That you weren't much of a cook." She grinned and angled her head downward. "I stocked your fridge the day before you got here. All of the meat in the freezer was still there when I came by a few days ago."

She was quite right. Ron's expertise in the kitchen was limited to whatever could be heated in the microwave, and even then he required instruction. There'd been some pre-packaged meals. He'd been living on those. "Gotta give it to Ben. He thinks of everything."

"It was, uh—it was my idea."

Ron sipped his water to buy himself a moment to think. Margie looked genuinely embarrassed, like she'd done something she oughtn't to have, been a bit too forward. If Ben had asked her to bring him dinner there'd be no cause for embarrassment, but Ron couldn't figure out why she'd do it of her own accord. He appreciated the gesture, though. No one would have done that for him at work. No one there asked him to join them for lunch, looked in to see if he needed anything. Everyone seemed to be afraid of him, one way or another. "So what did Ben tell you about me?" he said.

Margie shook her head. "Just that someone was coming up to stay at his cabin for a while, and to make sure they had food and everything was ready for them."

"And he didn't say why?"

"Well, no, I asked if everything was alright, and he said yes, but could I do him this one favor. I figured something special was going on, and Ben did me a favor a while back." She shrugged, took a drink of water and looked out the front picture window. "Thought it'd be a bit nosy to ask why exactly. I assumed you were family of some sort, or a close friend. To tell the truth, I was really hoping it would be Ben coming. He didn't make it up here last summer either. I'd had the cottage ready to go for him for a month when he called, and I really—" Margie stopped herself and shook hear head. "It would've been nice to see Ben again. Nothing against you."

"No offense taken," he said.

The lake was empty of people. The water rippled into shore gently, inaudible. "So are you? A relative or a friend?"

Ron thought on that for a moment. He barely knew Margie, had only ever talked to her twice counting now. Telling her the truth seemed like admitting a weakness but he'd never been great at lying. "Neither, actually," he said. "I'm a patient of his."

A moment passed, then Margie's eyes widened. "Oh." She put her water down on the coffee table, her face sliding into the same embarrassed look she'd had earlier. Ron wondered how far he'd fallen in her estimation, thought telling her may have been a mistake. He could see a question, or perhaps a hundred, brewing behind her eyes, waiting to be asked. After another minute of silence that reminded him of a high school meet-the-parents date, Margie said, "I suppose you'd just like to be left alone."

"No," he said. He saw her eyes twinkle for a moment, and then not. "I haven't talked to anyone in a week. Barely left the cottage, actually. Been kinda quiet, which is nice, but after a while—" He shrugged and left the sentence hanging.

"So, what," Margie said and then stopped and started again, "I mean, how did you— I mean—" Ron could tell she was having difficulty finding the right words to ask her question without being too direct.

"I'm fine," he said. Margie looked over at him, a little relief playing across her face. "I'm just—I needed to get away for a while. Things were getting a bit too—" Stressful, he wanted to say. Demanding. Angry. Everybody coming at me from all directions, sell the company, sell the company, sell the company. "Much. At home."

"It's okay," she said. "You don't have to say anything else if you don't want to."

Ron sighed and looked down to discover that he had a death grip on his bottle of water. He put it down on the coffee table for its own safety. "It's irresistible, this place. I've sat on the porch every day, just staring out at the lake and the people passing by. It's almost like nirvana."

"So you like it here?"

Ron looked out the window at the lake, calm as anything. The sun was starting downward; the water was bright orange with the glow of it. In that moment his last meeting at the office blurred a little, the shouts becoming an indistinct grunting. "Yeah. I suppose I do."

Margie settled back into the sofa and smiled. "Been here all my life, and I can't imagine getting tired of this view."

"Is that what keeps you here?" Ron said, nodding at the view.

"Well, yeah, that. I'd find that hard to give up. And, you know—" Her voice trailed off.

Ron waited a moment. "Yes?"

Her face glossed over slightly, and almost as quickly cleared. "I just like it here."

Ron took a sip of water, certain that Margie had been about to say something else.

A few days passed before he saw Margie again. Whether that was two days or three or four Ron wasn't sure, and was even less certain he cared. The days blended together, each one as indistinct as the next, bringing with it the promise of beautiful weather, cloudless skies and barely a breeze to ruffle the trees, the nights bringing a contented near-stillness with only crickets breaking the peace, and the promise of a full night's uninterrupted sleep.

Ron was sitting on the patio, watching the world stand still, when the crunching sound came from around the side of the house again. This time he was fairly certain he hadn't fallen asleep and hadn't heard a car door slam. A moment later Margie appeared, empty handed. "Wondered if you were up for a walk," she said.

He only had to think for a moment. "Sure. Alright."

It was already dark when the taxi had dropped him off however many days earlier. Now, in full daylight, the beauty of the area could be truly appreciated. It wasn't that he hadn't noticed the trees that lined the two sides of the lawn between the cabin and the lake. He just hadn't paid them much attention. The trees along the road that all of the lake houses sat on were magnificent, full of leaf, towering above cottage and street alike. In October, he thought, the colors must be truly wondrous.

"I thought we'd just go a mile up the road and back," she said. "Is that too much for you?"

"That's fine." Really he wasn't sure. It had been a long time since he'd walked any farther than from his desk to his car, but he was feeling rested and restless.

For the first part of the walk, they discussed little issues, where they grew up, what they did, what they thought about the world at large. Margie, it transpired, had been in the same house all her life. Her parents had owned a group of hotels scattered about the tourist areas of northern Michigan. When they passed away, she inherited them and now lived entirely off the proceeds. "I've never worked a day in my life, not even in college. I don't know what that says about me." It occurred to Ron that, were he in Detroit, he might have made her an offer to buy the hotels, but at the moment it didn't seem the thing to do. She had as little clue about the outside world as he did. "I don't pay attention anymore. It's all war and paparazzi, scandal of some sort. I just can't bring myself to care." He told her as much as he could about Detroit, which she'd been to only once. Ron wasn't particularly fond of the city as a whole and never had been, but, "It's home, you know? It's where I've lived, where I've always lived. It's what I know."

By the time they turned around Ron was having difficulty keeping up with Margie, who he guessed had done this walk hundreds of times before. When they got back to Ben's cabin, Ron was hobbling slightly and feeling some small pains in his knees.

"Can you make it a bit farther?" Margie said. "I thought we might dine at my place."

That's an odd way of asking me to dinner, he thought. Margie was nice to be around, sure, pleasant in her way, amusing in her slight disheveledness, but there was no attraction on his end. Or maybe there was and he didn't recognize the emotion. The idea that he was overthinking the question struck him then. "Sure," he said.

Margie's house was as she'd described it a few days earlier: small, white, with a fair-sized garden on one side. The house looked comfortable from the outside, he thought, a bit larger than Ben's cabin and just about right for one person, possibly two. On the side that sighted the lake was a trellis arch large enough for two people to stand beneath. The remarkable thing about the garden was that it was overgrown with vines in need of trimming, and it stopped Ron in his tracks.

"You have a nice garden," he said, not looking away from the trellis.

Margie kept walking. "Yeah. Thanks." Her voice sound empty and glum. A moment later he heard a screen door swing open. "You coming?" Ron walked quickly to her front door and followed her inside. "Go ahead and have a seat," she said, gesturing to the sofa. "I'll get started."

As she worked in her kitchen, shuffling a few pans this way and that, Ron thought about what had just happened as he eased into the sofa. Had he said or done something to offend her? He didn't think so, and yet she had definitely not been happy outside at the garden. He scratched his head and looked out the picture window. The view here was about the same as at his cabin. He got lost in watching the rippling water until he felt a weight settle at the other end of the sofa.

"Dinner's in the oven," Margie said, sitting back. "I have to put some rice on in half an hour."

"Listen," he said, "I'm sorry if I said something outside to upset you."

She shook her head. "It's nothing. There's just—there's a lot of bad memories out there."

"You sure?"

Margie was silent for a moment. "I almost got married once under that trellis."

A bird chirped outside the window. A full beat passed then Ron said, "I'm sorry."

Margie shrugged. "There's a party tomorrow. Fourth of July. People have grillouts, and then there's a fireworks display. Everyone gets on their boats, goes out on the lake, watches. The party I'm going to is a nice small one, over at the Grable's place, and I was wondering—you wouldn't want to come, would you?"

Ron said nothing for a moment. On the heels of her revelation, the invitation seemed forced, out of place, a deliberate attempt to change the subject. Parties in general didn't much appeal to him, particularly where he didn't know anyone. He wondered why Margie was asking. Was she lonely and needing company? Did she think the same of him? Ron shook his head. *Maybe she just thinks you're a nice person*, he thought. *That could be it, nothing more. No agendas. Not like home.* "Sure," he said. "Sure."

Margie pulled up to his pier at six the next evening. Ron almost didn't recognize her. Her hair was pulled back in the bun again, her outfit stylish but modest and she was wearing make-up, not a large amount, but she was a woman transformed. A corner of his mind wondered if this was for his benefit or someone else's, or her own, or no one's.

"Hop on," she said, pulling up next to the dock. He stepped onto the boat and she immediately shifted into reverse. A moment later they were powering across the lake, houses flashing by on one side, the wide open expanse of water on the other. They didn't talk; Ron didn't feel like shouting over the din of the motor.

After a few minutes they pulled up behind a large house with a larger back lawn and dock than Ben's place. Two boats were already tied there. Margie pulled hers in behind one of them, and they jumped out to tether it. When they finished Ron and Margie looked at each other.

"You looked very nice," he said.

He wasn't sure but he thought Margie blushed a little. "Thank you."

A ring of laughter came from the direction of the house. "Do they know I'm coming?"

"I think they do. Our host does. Fred Grable. You'll like him. Great guy. I'm not sure what he does for a living." She'd been looking again at the moorings, but now Margie looked up at Ron. "You don't know him, do you? From down south?"

"No." He hadn't considered that possibility yet, and felt a new wave of anxiety. It was well-known within the company that he didn't have a cabin up here. The few times it had come up in conversation Ron had poo-poohed the idea. "All they do is tie a person down," he would say. "I mean, you go and buy a second place on a lake up north, then summer comes and you want to take a holiday, to Florida, say. Only you've got this cabin now, which is supposed to be for that sort of thing, and you think, 'Well, I've spent all this money on it, I may as well get some use out of it.' Before you know it, you're on 75 North headed for wherever and saying to yourself, 'Okay, Florida next year then.'"

He must have been silent for a long moment, because Margie spoke next. "Tell them you've borrowed a friend's place. It happens often enough." Ron nodded and headed toward the house, Margie right behind.

Two men were on the back patio trying to get the grill to light. Everyone else was inside, sipping cocktails and swapping stories of the winter, the goings-on of children and grandchildren. Margie made introductions as they encountered people. Everyone greeted her warmly and seemed genuinely pleased to meet Ron. They took seats in the living room and were welcomed into the conversation as easily as if they'd always been there. Ron said as little as he could about his business back home, never going into detail, using phrases and concise means of description he recited at countless charity dinners. He stole a glimpse of Margie out of the corner of his eye every couple minutes. The first few times she smiled at him, head tilted down, a slight blush on her face. He missed her leaving at one point, but a minute later she pressed a beer into his hand (his brand of choice; how did she guess?) as she resumed the seat to his right.

A moment after that a woman in a sparkling black dress built for a woman forty pounds lighter took the seat to his left. "So you're Margie's friend, then," the woman said.

Ron thought for a moment. "Friend" could mean a number of things within this context. "Yeah," he said, "guess so."

"And how long have you two been together?"

"Oh, no. It's not like that. We're just neighbors. I only met her a week ago."

"Oh," she said. Disappointment splashed on her face. "We all keep hoping for Margie. She's been alone in that house of hers for an awful long time, ever since the wedding that—"

"Helen!" Margie said from behind Ron.

"Well, I'm sorry, sweetie, but what are we supposed to think, you coming here all prettied up with a gentleman on your arm?" Helen looked Ron up and down. "And I must say, you could do worse. This one looks like he's got money."

Ron rolled his eyes. "He's at Ben Samuels's place for the summer," Margie said.

"Oh, you know Ben?" Helen shifted her attention back to Ron. "Not coming up again this year, huh? Ah, well. He must be busy. Stark raving lunatics coming to him for help at all hours. But he needs a break from that every now and then. If I've told him that once, I've told him a thousand times. And how do you know him?"

Ron started to stammer a response, but Margie overrode him. "So how are the kids, Helen?"

"Oh, great, dear, just great." Helen started talking about her children and Ron retreated to the patio. The two men had finished with the grill and gone inside, leaving him quite alone. He sat in one of he lawn chairs and pondered the trees.

A few minutes later Margie came out from the house and sat next to him. "Sorry about her," she said. "Helen can be a bit hard to take."

"It's okay," Ron said. "Just wasn't expecting it, that's all." He knew that was a lie. Margie seemed to pick up on it.

"I'm not trying anything, you know. It isn't that I'm not interested. But, well— Helen's—" She fumbled her hands.

"Closer to the truth than you'd like?"

The smile Margie gave wasn't a happy one. "I have been alone for a while. A good long while. Met a guy once at one of Fred's parties. He seemed pretty nice. We saw each other a few more times before he went south for winter, but we stayed in touch. He proposed at Christmas. I did all the planning for a July Fourth ceremony in my back yard, he fell more and more out of touch. Day of the wedding everybody turns up but the groom."

Ron looked at her and saw a tear drift down from the corner of her eye. A moment later the patio door opened, and both of them looked up to see Helen poking her head out. "Yoo-hoo, you two!" she said. "We've started serving appetizers if you wanted some."

He tried to give Margie a look that suggested they finish this conversation later, but he wasn't sure he managed it; it may have looked like a grimace. "Shall we?" he said, rising.

"Sure." Margie stood up. As they went inside, Ron saw her wipe the tear away.

They didn't stray far from each other for the rest of the night, except for a few minutes toward the end.

As the evening progressed, everyone eased into a comfortable familiarity; each person knew he or she was in the company of friends, some closer than others perhaps, but no one would be judged too harshly. Ron hadn't experienced this type of relaxation since his collegiate days, and even then recreational drugs were involved. Tonight he wasn't the principal shareholder of his own company, wasn't expected to defend his reluctance to sell the business he'd worked so hard to build. Therapy was something other people needed, people in real emotional distress. Not long after coming back inside he was drawn into a discussion about the Lions and how bad a team they would have that year. Margie entered into conversation with Helen. He caught Margie's eye once. They shared a quick smile and went back to their conversations.

Later in the evening, after the food had been eaten and a good portion of the drinks consumed, Margie excused herself. She took Ron's paper plate; she was going to the bathroom, she said, but the trash can was on the way. With Margie out of the room, somehow everything seemed a little flatter, as if some crucial element was missing. It didn't escape his attention that they were staying near each other, as if clinging to a lifeline. He couldn't tell if he was staying close to her or vice versa, but he wasn't sure it mattered. Ron let his gaze drift toward one of the windows. Night had fallen. The trees he knew were out there were barely visible. A moment later he was tapped on the shoulder from behind. Ron turned to see Helen sitting where Margie had been.

"So," she said, "about Margie."

Ron started to speak but Helen cut him off.

"Yes, I know. Nothing between you, you've both said already. But she's looking very nice tonight, isn't she? I haven't seen her all done up like that in a while. Usually she's just in tee-shirt and jeans when I see her."

He nodded his head, leaving the opportunity open for Helen to continue.

"I mean, don't get me wrong," Helen said. "She's tough. Tougher than most of the people here, I should think. But have you been up here in winter, with all the snow and the bitter cold? Can drive a person crazy after a while. Being alone only makes it worse, and she's been alone since that idiot left her at the altar fifteen years ago. Every year since then some fella from down south turns up at one of these parties, thinking, 'Oh, house party, maybe there'll be some single women there.' And they focus in on Margie."

"That really wasn't my inten—"

"Nobody wants to see her hurt again by somebody from out of town, that's all. Have you looked at her at all tonight? She's practically glowing. You must have made quite an impression."

Ron hadn't noticed. Margie seemed happy, happier than most of the people at the party, but he didn't know about glowing. On the other hand, he thought, people almost never glowed in the office, and he wasn't sure he would recognize it if he saw it.

Fred wandered back into the room then. "Fifteen minutes to fireworks, everybody. Head out and find a good spot."

People began filtering toward the back door in twos and fours, carrying their glasses of wine and beers, stopping at the kitchen island on the way out for a last snack from the cheese and vegetable tray. Ron stayed in his seat until everyone else had gone, then got up with a grunt and headed toward the back door himself. He'd gotten nearly that far when Margie's voice came from behind him. "Did I hear something about the fireworks?"

Ron nodded. "Fifteen minutes, Fred said." He looked Margie up and down as she passed him, but couldn't see any hint of glowing. "Something about finding a good spot."

"There's a good place not too far from here." Margie opened the back door, then turned and stopped. "What?"

"Oh," he said, drawing the word out for a couple of seconds. He must have been staring. "Nothing."

❖   ❖   ❖

Ron didn't like boating any more by night than he did by day. The more he thought on it, he liked it a little less. How Margie could see where she was going he wasn't sure. The moon was only a quarter full, giving off a small bit of light, but it was too dim for Ron to see any more than a handful of feet in any direction even with the boat lights on. Margie pulled the boat into a small inlet, shut the engine off, and tossed a small anchor into the drink. The nearest boat to them was easily two hundred feet away. Bits of laughter from the other boat drifted back to them but otherwise the only sound was the water lapping up against the side of the boat.

No sooner had she shut the lights off than a bang went off in the distance and an explosion of red brightened the sky. A moment later, a blue and then a green. It had been a handful of years since Ron had seen a fireworks display. He didn't see much of a point in going to one by himself, one of a very few singles in a crowd of thousands lining both sides of the Detroit River. The enchantment he felt was genuine; he had forgotten how much he enjoyed them as a child. Even the slight breeze bringing a hint of chill to the night air did nothing to lighten his spirits. Twenty minutes later, when the last of the fireworks had finally gone and the slight odor of gunpowder began to dissolve, it took him a minute to register where he was and who he was with.

"Did you enjoy them?" Margie said.

"Yes. Yes, I did. Very much. Thank you."

Margie made no move to turn the boat lights back on. "Do you mind if we stay out here for a bit? With everyone trying to get to wherever at once, this might be a safe place to be. There aren't any houses back here so no one's likely to ram us."

"Yeah, that's fine. Nowhere to be."

"Listen," she said, "about earlier—"

"You don't have to explain."

"I didn't mean to just lay all that at your feet."

"It's alright, really."

"It's just— I mean—"

"No. Really. It's fine."

Margie sniffed. Ron wondered whether or not she teared up again.

"I don't have this at home," he said.

"What? Conversation or quiet?"

"Both." Ron sighed. "I can just see it, trying to talk personal issues with one of my vice presidents. They'd wonder if I lost my mind."

Margie said nothing for a moment. "Have you? Is that why you're up here?"

"More or less. I—" Ron paused and looked at his feet, thinking of the proper phrasing, of how much he wanted to reveal, and then remembered how open Margie had been. "—snapped. Or 'lost control' as Ben would say. Or 'melted down.' Right in the middle of an executive meeting. There've been a few offers to buy the company, I've been against it, most of the rest of the board of directors are in favor of it. They—the other board members—have been hassling me to change my vote for a while now, and at the last meeting it was just one time too many. There was shouting, most of it mine, then a lot of crying, most of it mine, then people scampering for cover. My assistant had Ben to the office within the hour. That was the day before I got here."

He could feel Margie staring at him, waiting. Even the water wasn't smacking the side of the boat quite so loud, and the crickets had gone silent. After another couple of minutes, she began lifting the anchor.

Ron couldn't find the strength to even raise his head. He wondered what Margie thought of him now. That he was weak, probably, or frightening, or just angry, and which of those ideas bothered him the most? Would she stop coming to see him, become just another face on the lake? It didn't even register to him that he'd disembarked until Margie was opening a door and leading him inside, and even then it took him a few moments to notice that it wasn't his cabin, but hers.

"You're staying here tonight," she said. "You shouldn't be alone."

"Waited for two hours before I sent everyone home."

The smell of disuse that had been present when they entered the spare bedroom was barely noticeable now. He was reclined against the headboard, looking at Margie in profile sitting at the far end of the bed. The only light in the room came in through the windows, or from the kitchen.

Margie shifted a little at the edge of the bed. "He didn't call, he didn't send a telegram, nothing. And there I was, standing in the large tent behind the house, me in my wedding gown, trying to explain to the caterers that everything's off, and what am I going to do with the cake. To this day I haven't heard from him. He sold his cabin before the next summer." She wiped a strand of hair from her face. "I'm not even sure I care anymore. I suppose that makes me kind of awful. We were supposed to be married beneath that trellis in the garden. Everytime I look at it—" She left the sentence hanging.

Ron shook his head. "Would it matter after all this time? If you saw him tomorrow, say, on the street here in Harbor Lights. If he came and knocked on your door for whatever reason. Would it even matter?"

Margie sniffed. "I don't know. I suppose not. I'd just kind of like to know what happened."

"Would you have moved to Detroit?"

"Would you have sold the company?" Margie sighed, looked at the ceiling, lazily ran her hand over the comforter. "I don't know why I'm telling you this. You must think I'm a complete mess."

Ron leaned forward and placed a hand on her shoulder. "No, you're not." He looked into Margie's eyes, and he could see the future there: his summer days spent napping on the porch as the boaters drifted by on the lake, Margie among them in her kayak possibly, admiring the scenery she knew by heart; or perhaps on the porch beside him, reading a book, or inside making dinner; the nights filled with conversation on all topics, what was good about this book or that, what was going on in the world today, or perhaps just experiences, where they'd been, where they wanted to go; the winters spent in semi-isolation, snow blanketed a foot or two deep on the ground, a fire blazing in the hearth every day, Ron chopping wood for exercise, or perhaps trudging into Harbor Lights for supplies or news from the outside world; the office a distant memory.

ALBERT ♥ JULIA

Martin Mull knew it was going to rain. The trick knee he'd inherited from his father, who inherited it from his father before him, had been aching since three in the morning when a full bladder had pulled him out of a dream involving Kylie Minogue, a barge on the Seine, and fifteen cases of red wine that had been damaged by a passing buffalo herd. No one believed that the trick knee could be handed down from father to son so he said it was from an old football injury. People accepted that until someone pointed out that he hadn't played football at any point during his upbringing. The knee acted up in the twenty-four hours leading up to a big storm so he knew something was coming soon. Also he'd seen the weather report; the Hurricane Dennis coverage had been hard to miss.

"Hey! Comedian!" The bartender greeted him with the same warm call he greeted all the locals with and waved him over.

Martin took the nearest stool at the bar. The Sea Gull Bar and Grill, one of only two restaurants worthy of the name in Hatteras Village and the only one that didn't have a dress code, had been open since breakfast. Business, though, had been slow; the vacationers had started leaving the Outer Banks the night before under an evacuation order, and most of the locals were busy bracing for it. Martin had people for that. "Wish you'd stop calling me that, Phil. It's not my fault my folks named me after someone famous, or quasi-famous anyway."

"Listen," Phil said, "I got one for you."

"Okay. A good joke would be well appreciated right now."

"Nah, not a joke. A drink." The bartender reached under the counter and brought up a rocks glass filled with a dark liquid.

Martin eyed the glass suspiciously. "Is this a drink or is this five-weight motor oil?"

Phil gave him a smile. "Give it a go."

Martin picked up the glass, swirled it for a second to see if it would clear up, and when it didn't he took a gulp. A second later he spit it out again. "Ugh. What the hell?"

"It's called a Bubonic Plague. Two ounces each gin, crème de cacao, and black coffee, and a teaspoon of blackstrap molasses."

"You come up with that yourself?"

"Saw it in a detective novel new out this month. Thought I'd try it out."

"There's a reason it's called fiction, Phil." Martin took a hefty swig from a nearby glass of water that may or may not have been drunk out of by someone else first and made a face. "Ready for Dennis?"

"Ready as I'm gonna be. I'm only here until two and that's more than enough time to get home and board up my little all. And this place—" he made a regal gesture and rolled his eyes to the ceiling "—could probably survive World War III. Storm's not even due until late tonight, but you know people: give 'em half a reason to and they'll panic. You?"

Martin managed the Oceanview Motel, across the street from the bar. The three buildings had withstood a pair of hurricanes and every other storm Mother Nature had hurled at them, thanks in part to the fifteen-foot-high sandbank separating it from the beach. The hotel's name was a lie; only a few of the rooms on the second floor could actually see onto the beach and the ocean beyond, and those offered only a limited view. "The hotel's solid. All of the windows face north and the storm's coming from the south so that shouldn't be too much of an issue, and we weathered the last big storm pretty well. Just the one car got crushed by a telephone pole—nothing I could do about that. The beach took more damage than anything else. It sits at least ten feet higher than it did before Emily hit six years ago, my hand to God." The bar's phone rang then. Phil stepped away to answer it and Martin eyed the drink in front of him again before taking another sip. Upon second review it tasted kind of sweet. *That's probably the molasses*, he thought.

Phil came back a minute later. "That was your maintenance guy. Somebody's digging a hole on your beach."

The original plan was to begin excavation earlier than he did, but Albert slept past his alarm. He had spent a healthy part of the night before at the Sea Gull, drowning his sorrows with beer and trivia games along with what seemed like the rest of Hatteras Village. The bartender had taken his keys, which hardly mattered; he was staying at the Oceanview. When he finally did wake up, a little past eleven, the hangover he was blessed with was enough to make him pray for an earlier death. And he was hungry, hungrier than he had been in a very long time. What little provisions he had needed to be saved for later, during the dig. Bleary-eyed and barely upright, Albert stumbled back to the Sea Gull for breakfast. With one eye on his watch and the other on the plate glass window that opened onto a view of Route 12 and the Oceanview Motel beyond, he cut through an omelet and two mugs of coffee regular like a man eating his last meal.

"Hurricane coming, you know," his waitress said. "Well, not here exactly. Out at sea a bit. All we'll get here is the edge of it. Lot of wind, lot of rain. One thing about living on the coast, this sort of thing happens a lot. There's an evacuation order on, but all of the locals are staying." She drifted off and came back once to refill his coffee and leave the bill.

After breakfast he got his car keys from the bar and walked back across the road to the motel, stood on the small wooden platform perched at the top of the sandbank separating the motel from the ocean. Every six hours since he checked in Albert had walked out to look at the water, at the high and low tides. The high tide interested him, how far in the water came, how that might affect his digging. As if that mattered; the storm swell would bring the water in even more. Even now, when the ocean should have been in the process of ebbing, the water seemed higher than it had been since his arrival. Still, it was well clear of the bottom of the wooden stairway leading down to the beach, which was what he cared about most.

The stairway below him disappeared into the beach, handrail and all. Albert had spent part of the three days examining it and the sand in front of it. He measured the space between each step and the incline of the stairway as a whole, and pored over the mathematics: how far out from the bottom of the stairway he would have to go, how many feet down he would have to dig, how much sand would have to be moved. Some of it—a lot of it—was nothing but a guess; his memory of how tall the stairway was before it was buried was unclear.

He had come prepared. In a bag were personal essentials, all of which were now unnecessary: a hat, a pair of sunglasses, a bottle of SPF 45 sunscreen, and his car keys. In a six-pack cooler was a sandwich, a big of chips, and apple, and three bottles of water, and clamped in the same hand was a bucket and a shovel. He went down to the beach, put the bag, cooler and shovel down, and began marking off the area of excavation, drawing lines in the sand with his feet. He purposefully marked off too large an area, adding an extra two feet on either side of the stairway for elbow space as the hole deepened. As he dug he would wet the sides of the hole with ocean water to help firm them up, keep them from caving in and trapping him beneath who knew how much sand.

Albert walked to the ocean and stood knee deep in it for a few moments, bucket in hand, looking out over the breaking waves. The vast ocean, stretching out farther than he could ever hope to see, made him feel small, unimportant. This little thing he was doing today did not matter; whether or not he found what he was looking for would not change anything. It would not bring Julia back. He filled the bucket, took it back to the stair, and set it next to his things. The topmost of the buried steps was beneath three inches of sand. Digging from the center out, Albert uncovered it in ten minutes and stood on it, looking out to the ocean. Up here, on the stair, he didn't feel quite so small. A wind blew across him then, rustling the foliage growing from the dune, making him shudder, reminding him of their last night together.

The morning after, Julia woke before Albert. It took her a few moments to remember where she was. She hadn't paid a whole lot of attention to the room décor the night before; they hadn't even turned on the lights. Beside her, Albert snored quietly, his hair tousled. The alarm clock on the bedside table said it was just after seven. *Dammit*, she thought. *If I get home fast enough I can get in before Mom notices I've been out all night.* She decided to walk home; it was half a mile away, and Albert looked so peaceful where he was. She dressed and left the room as quietly as she could. Albert would understand. Besides, her parents barely tolerated her dating him. Him bringing her home at this hour of the morning would only leading to a fight.

She was maybe halfway home, walking along the right-side shoulder of Route 12, when a car came up from behind her, the driver fumbling in his passenger seat for another cassette and steering with his knees, drifting slowly onto the same shoulder Julia was walking on. By the time the driver looked up and noticed her it was far too late to do anything else.

Martin watched the man dig for a moment, surveyed the damage, and spoke. "Excuse me, sir?"

Two steps had been cleared. The third, Albert thought, would be exposed before much longer. He had, to this point, worked largely undisturbed. People cresting the dune from the hotel side noticed Albert working below and walked down the stroller path on the other side of the handrail instead.

"Yes?" Albert kept digging.

"What—what are you doing?"

"Digging."

"Digging." Martin descended to the stair three above where Albert had begun unearthing. He tried to fathom what was going on before him, why anybody would be digging up a stairway on a beach, but nothing occurred to him. "For what?"

"Something."

"Something." Martin tapped his foot a couple of times and rubbed his hands together. He felt warm, but that might have been the after effects of the Bubonic Plague. "Sir?"

Albert drove his shovel handle up into the sand, standing it on end, and leaned himself against the handle. "You the Manager of the Oceanview?"

"Yes, I am. Martin Mull at your service."

Albert squinted. "Like the comic?"

"Yes."

"My apologies. I'm Albert Hicks. I believe I contacted you a week ago about wanting to borrow a portion of your beach for a day. Checked in a couple of days ago."

Martin smiled and the two shook hands. "Ah, yes. Mr. Hicks. Room 201. I figured you'd just be building an extra large sandcastle or something, but then one of my maintenance people said there was somebody out here digging a hole at the foot of the stairs, so I thought I'd come and have a look."

"I should have let you know I was starting today, where I was going to dig." Albert turned his attention back to the sand beneath him and started to dig again.

"You know there's a hurricane coming? You should have done this yesterday or the day before, evacuated with the rest of the tourists."

Albert kept digging.

Martin waited another two shovelsful of sand before speaking again. "So what are you building? A sandcastle?"

"Not exactly."

Three a.m. Giggling, they pushed open the door to Room 201. Julia twirled herself into Albert's arms and kissed him as the door swung shut behind them. The smell of the smoke from the bonfire dissipated from them as if it had never existed along with the rest of the world. Within seconds they were horizontal, side by side on the queen size bed, and after a pause and a meaning-filled look they kissed again.

They had neither one of them seen a member of the opposite sex nude, other than a game of I'll-show-you-mine-if-you-show-me-yours when they were seven and neither one counted that. Both wanted their first lovemaking experience to be with the other, but when it came right down to it they felt more awkward than anything else, starting with the first kiss. They'd kissed before and often, but it hadn't been expected to lead to anything. This time it was foreplay, and both entered into the first one feeling as scared as someone going on stage for the first time. That they saw themselves as best friends ahead of being lovers only complicated things.

"You taste like strawberries," Albert said.

"Lip gloss," Julia said, and kissed him again.

His problem was nerves; his shaking hands running up her sides and under her shirt made both of them giggle. Her problem was modesty; finding herself down to her underwear in front of a man for the first time, she wanted a blanket. Albert felt the need to compensate somehow, like he too should be in his underpants.

He started unbuttoning his shirt when Julia put her hand on his. "I'm scared too," she said. She undid the remainder of the buttons and ran her hands down his chest as Albert tossed the shirt aside. "Do you mean it?" she said.

He blinked. "Mean what?"

"What you wrote out there. Albert loves Julia."

"Yes, I do. Very much."

She pulled him down to her and kissed him again. After a few moments, she took his hands and gently guided them to her breasts. Then, the next awkward moment: Albert attempting to undo the clasps on Julia's bra, cursing after the third unsuccessful attempt.

A laugh later, she helped him.

Martin looked over his shoulder at the building nearest him. Room 201 was on the second floor, closest to the beach. "Huh."

Albert was sitting next to him, eating one of the sandwiches he'd packed and looking out at the water again. It had receded some but not much, and the sky to the south started at cerulean and ended at royal blue.

"Did you request that room?"

Albert nodded and kept eating.

"We wonder, sometimes, what goes on in the rooms. It's part and parcel of working in the hotel industry. And we know, or we suspect we know. First time anybody's confirmed it."

On either side of the pit, three local families that had heard about somebody digging up the Oceanview's beach and come to see it happening, and stayed to offer not only moral support but physical as well, helping to get the dug sand out of the way and bringing buckets of water to help firm up the wall were themselves taking a break too, the children using the dug-up sand to make castles, the parents reading magazines and ignoring the oncoming storm.

"So where did you go? Afterwards, I mean. The next morning," Martin said.

"Shipped out as planned. I had orders to report to Fort Sill the next evening. Got dressed, drove up to Norfolk in a rented car, flew out."

Martin looked at the pit. "I remember hearing about a girl getting hit by a car not too far from here a long time ago. Can't remember her name."

"Julia McManus."

"That's right. Julia Mc—" Martin's eyes widened, and he turned his head slightly toward Albert. "That was your Julia, wasn't it? She was walking home from here."

The nod Albert gave was crisper and shorter than the last one.

"You didn't know, did you?"

"They told me three weeks later. Sergeant pulled me into a room and told me, said they'd only found out themselves right before they told me. I'd been writing, getting no response. My Dad split when I was a kid and Mom was so tanked most of the time she barely knew what planet she was on, so the only way I was gonna hear anything was from her folks and they didn't like me either."

Martin shot him a look.

"They had money. I didn't. My Sergeant knew about Julia, knew I hadn't heard anything. He got a hold of the local paper from here, saw the obit, made a phone call to confirm. I flipped. Trashed his office. They pulled my visits home and shipped me overseas the day after basic ended. Eight years in Korea watching a border nobody's fighting over anymore."

Martin nodded. He tried to understand how anybody could be so cruel as to keep the news of Julia's death from the most important person in her life apart from her family.

Albert took the last bite of his sandwich and a sip of water from a bottle. One of the children nearby giggled, the sound swallowed whole by the worsening tide. "I miss my friend," he said at last. "That's what she was, before the girlfriend thing. My best friend. And they kept her death from me, kept me from coming home and saying goodbye, sent me over to that God-forsaken place. Not nobody deserves that."

"But doing this," Martin said. "This pit. I don't understand. What are you doing this for? What are you trying to find?"

Albert stood and picked up the shovel again. "Three words on a stair."

Two thirty a.m. The bonfire on the Oceanview beach was dying. The crowd, which had started at a dozen local teens four hours earlier, had thinned to a half dozen, Albert and Julia and two other couples. The smuggled-in booze was gone and the other two girls were starting to drift off, so they and their boyfriends said goodnight and left Albert and Julia alone on the beach.

"Lovely night," Julia said. "You can actually see the stars out."

"Yeah." Albert had been drinking soda for most of the night. Even so, he was trying not to drift off himself. He wanted to enjoy every minute with her that he could before leaving in the morning for Fort Sill. The rental car he was driving to the airport was already in the parking lot of the Oceanview. "Listen," he said.

Julia looked at him. In the moonlight her eyes glistened.

"I got something for you. Well, not got so much as did."

She smiled. "Really?"

He stood and offered her a hand. "Come on." They walked over to the stairway leading up over the dune and back to the beach. Albert shone a flashlight at the bottom step. "I did this earlier this afternoon."

Julia bent over and looked. Into the front of the step the words "Albert ♥ Julia" had been carved. "A random act of violence? You? The day before you join the Army?" She kissed him on the cheek. "I was thinking."

Albert raised his eyebrows.

"We've known each other since we were kids, and we've been together forever. And I know we agreed to wait until we got married to do anything—well, I agreed and you went along with it—but I don't want to wait anymore."

He cocked his head slightly.

Julia held up a room key. The number on the plastic marker was just visible in the fading firelight: 201. "And we should go there. Right now."

Albert was too dumbstruck to do anything but follow.

"Who is this girl he's talking about anyway? A girlfriend? Is her body down there?"

The crowd around the pit had widened to a dozen families. The newest arrivals were filled in by the ones who had been there for awhile, and everybody was pitching in where they could. Martin was sitting on the first step that had been cleared, engaging Albert from time to time in conversation. He wasn't sure why Albert trusted him more than anyone else there—when someone other than Martin asked a question it went unanswered—but he felt honored and obliged to listen.

Albert was starting to lose faith. The eighth step down in the sand did not have the inscription. Neither did the ninth. But he'd been uncovering the handrail along with the stairs, and so long as that kept extending downward into the sand Albert held out hope. He drove his shovel into the sand once more and heard the familiar thunk of metal on wood. Hurriedly, he brushed away the sand from the top and front edge of the stair as he had with all the others.

"Found it."

Albert had no sooner wiped away the sand from the inscription than the skies opened up. Rain started pouring down harder than it had all day, and he became aware that the skies were the wrong shade of navy blue.

"Hold tight, Albert. We're gonna get you your stair," Martin called above the sound of the surf and the rain. He walked down into the pit with the handsaw he'd borrowed from the maintenance man an hour earlier. Albert stepped up from the bottom for the first time in hours as Martin cut away at the planking. Fifteen minutes later, it was done. He held up the stair, looked at the inscription, and handed it to Albert. The group of people around the pit cheered as they packed their things. A minute later everyone had run for cover but the two of them.

"Thank you," Albert said. He hadn't noticed the rain, had no idea how thoroughly soaked he was.

Martin put a hand above his eyes for protection. "Come in, Albert. Come in from the rain. You're done here."

They looked down at the place the stair had been. A clap of thunder echoed through the air. "No, I—I think I'll remain here a while."

Martin nodded, offered a handshake, and started up the stairway out of the pit.

"Wait," Albert said. He came up the stairs, fumbling to get his wallet out of his pocket. He opened it, pulled out a picture, and gave it to Martin, who squinted to see it in what light there was left.

"Is this her?" Martin said, trying to protect the picture from the rain. "She's beautiful."

"Tell her parents I'm sorry. If they come." He walked back down the stairs, down to the bottom of the pit, and sat down, holding his stair close.

Martin looked down at him for a moment, then turned and ran back toward the hotel.

The hotel didn't escape as unscathed as Martin had hoped. The loud crash he heard just after midnight was part of the balcony in front of three second story rooms tearing away, completely stranding one room with no way to reach the ground. No one was in there. It was Room 201, the room he'd given to Albert, the one Albert requested to have, the one where—

Martin climbed the dune to the beach. Albert's pit had partially collapsed in on itself, and what hadn't was filled with water. The beach was covered in flotsam dumped there by the storm, driftwood mostly along with some larger rocks. There was no sign of Albert. Martin scanned the beach as far as he could in both directions. Turning back to the hotel side he saw that the Sea Gull across the road was open. The clean-up effort wouldn't notice the fifteen-minute delay.

Unsurprisingly, the restaurant was empty. A couple of servers were wrapping cutlery at a table and Phil was sorting glasses at the bar. Martin took the nearest stool. "Didn't expect you to be open today."

Phil shrugged. "Damp, but mostly undamaged. We got a generator working out the back to at least give us a little power, try and salvage some of what we got in the fridge before it goes bad. And Route 12 is completely out. If a few locals come in, maybe take their minds off of being completely cut off from the mainland, that isn't a bad thing."

Martin gave a small nod and looked at the row of bottles on the counter behind the bar. "Bubonic Plague, if you would."

"You finally trying to be funny?"

"No. That's what I want."

The bartender raised his eyebrows and then started putting the drink together. "So what was the story with the guy on your beach yesterday? Boy proves his love for girl by digging up a stairway?"

"Something like that."

Phil gave a small chuckle. "Can't say that's a new one." He added the teaspoon of molasses to the drink and slid the glass in front of Martin. "How does this one end?"

Martin picked up the glass, held it at eye level, and waited for the answer to go away.

AFTER THE WAR ENDED

After the war ended—after the contents of the house were loaded into a moving truck and directed to a place three states away—the first thing Bill did was take off his coat, lie on the living room floor, and soak in the quiet. He watched it go to make sure, stood at the curb and witnessed the truck pull out of the gated community, turn left onto the main road, and disappear. When it didn't come back within five minutes he knew it was gone, and proceeded with the undressing and the soaking. He let the quiet consume him. The last time it had been so still was in the days before Jamie and Bill moved in. Even Jamie had been quieter in those days. Not completely quiet, but certainly when she spoke you had to be in the same room with her to hear what she was saying. Now merely being within a city block was enough. The only peace and quiet connected with Jamie Randolph was when she slept, when she had just a hint of a snore, and the house was as peaceful, if not as empty, as it was now. That was where it had gone wrong, he thought. That was where the marriage fell apart. Too much noise. Not enough quiet. The furnace came on, responding to the outside temperature, adding another unwanted layer onto the quiet. Bill got up, shut it off, and lied back down on the carpet.

Jamie would never have approved. A man should look proper at all times, she said. A man should look respectable, and that begins with the current attire, head to toe: well-groomed hair; complementing shirt, tie, and slacks; matching shoes and socks. The clothes make the man, influence who he is, how he behaves, how he carries himself. A well-dressed man is respected by his peers and admired from the moment someone meets him. She'd been spewing out little bits of garbage like that for years. That she'd been saying it at volume ten only made the present silence sweeter. Bill, for the life of him, couldn't figure out how wearing a jacket and tie would make him a more efficient worker, for example, or feel any better or different about himself.

He lied there for ten minutes, then an hour, and by dusk he was contemplating the mostly virgin walls, kept white at Jamie's insistence. She didn't want anything as trivial as wall color distracting from her selected furnishings, and she refused to install a piece in a client's home that didn't look good in her own. The living room became a rotating display of various sofas, chairs, and assorted sundries. If a particular fabric didn't work on a particular sofa, that was Bill's fault, wasn't it? He had designed both the fabric and the frame for Thompson Furniture, hadn't he? Never mind that the sofa simply didn't look good in a room painted white. Or that it had been provided by the company below cost. Or that when she insisted on returning it—which she did more often than not—Bill lost a little bit of face in the company, with everyone from the factory workers who wasted their time on a returned sofa up to his boss, the owner of the company.

There was no furniture in the living room anymore, and the white walls brought out the true personality of the room: this was a quiet space, and it lulled Bill Randolph to sleep.

Sitting on Bill Randolph was the thing to do. If a person entered a home and saw a Bill Randolph in the living room, ready and waiting to conform to the contours of his or her backside, one could be assured that the home was among the finest in the community. Mothers would redecorate entire rooms in Bill Randolph for their single daughters—everything from the wallpaper and paint trim to the sofa to the glass vase with molded plastic water and fake flowers on the end table—hoping that said daughter would bring home a boyfriend, who would see the Bill Randolph and think, "This is an amazingly together woman. I have to get to know her better." A home without Bill Randolph among the upper classes was a home steadfastly avoided. People had ways of finding out. Mailmen talked. E-mails were exchanged. Without any Bill Randolph, one might as well belong to the bourgeoisie.

John Thompson, owner of Thompson Home Furnishings, Inc., wanted nothing more than to own the largest furniture manufacturer in the country. When he interviewed Bill fifteen years previously, it was obvious from the sketches and drawings provided that he had talent. Almost immediately, John started having visions of grandeur. Since inheriting the company from his father, it had done little but lose money, slowly at first but more steadily as time went on. What the company needed was an icon, a brand name that consumers could latch on to and canonize if necessary, and right here in front of him was someone who could help it happen. So what if Bill Randolph wasn't an established name?

John signed Bill to a contract, set him up in an office, and gave him the nearest thing to carte blanche in the company: come and go as he pleased, work at home if he felt like it, but the quality designs had to keep coming. Within two years the company started making a profit on the Bill Randolph line of upholstery. Over time, the line expanded to include fabrics, paint, wallpaper, decorative accessories, general home goods (bath towels, placemats, and flatware, amongst other things), and, in stores that very day, his and hers perfumes.

All that was missing was a cooking show on the Food Network and perhaps a hip-hop record, something upbeat and drenched in synthesizers, something that the daughters of his target audience could get into.

What John found puzzling—John and the rest of the Board of Directors—was Bill's absence from the launch party for the perfumes the night before. Humility and shyness were two of his known traits—Bill typically worked with his office door closed and rarely ventured out into the offices or the factory—but not turning up for a product launch was unlike him. He couldn't possibly have forgotten the date. It was a tradition; every product in the Bill Randolph line had debuted on that date. At that moment, six business days after the contents of the Randolph house pulled away in the back of a moving truck, John Thompson, owner of Thompson Home Furnishings, Inc., was on his way to the office of William Randolph—"Bill" to his friends—to get an explanation for his absence the night previous.

Even if there was one to be gotten Bill wasn't there to give it. Judging from the amount of interoffice mail stacked in his in-box, he hadn't been there in several days, John guessed. Had Bill taken that vacation John had been pressuring him to take for who-knew-how-many years? But surely he would have said something to that effect. Perhaps not, John thought, but surely it wouldn't have scheduled over the debut of the new scents. Had he called in sick? John would have asked Bill's supervisor, but that was himself, and he'd just came back from a month-long trip to China, trying to get the billion-and-some people there interested in the joys of Bill Randolph, and perhaps line up some cheap labor.

Maybe something was wrong at home, or within his family. That he could understand. Maybe whatever it was was so urgent that Bill had to leave right away, and hadn't had the time to tell anyone where he was off to. John gave Bill another day to check in or make an appearance, and then he would get hold of Bill's wife.

Bill was drifting off for his hourly nap, this time in the third upstairs bedroom, the one that overlooked the driveway at the side of the house, when the doorbell rang. Each room had its own sound. The design of the room, the textures of the floor, walls, and ceiling, whether or not the main and closet doors were open, all of this contributed to the overall personality of the room as expressed by its ambient sounds. Jamie hadn't noticed that, but then she wouldn't have. Jamie was too busy making her own noise to pay attention to what was already there. Empty of furniture and empty of Jamie, though, the natural personality of each room blossomed into maturity, giving the new and exciting personae.

Bill opened the windows, and let in the outside world, enhancing the texture of the sound, two calms coming together to create one as perfect as a heartbeat. He slept on the floors of the various rooms of the house, taking his pillow and blanket to a new location each night like a nomad, dozing off to the unique sound each room had to offer.

But now he heard the doorbell.

It was fascinating lying there on the floor of that bedroom with the window propped open, listening to the sound of the asphalt below. It had been lain a decade earlier; he could still remember the two days it took to put all the asphalt down, how the smell of fresh tar invaded everything in the house from the bedclothes to his underclothes for weeks afterwards. Now the sound of it, still settling in the early evening sun, drifted up and in to this bedroom that saw little use when it was full of furnishings, where Bill was preparing to ignore the doorbell until it rang again. "Oh, good Lord," he said, pulling himself up from the floor and starting toward the front door.

The man on the other side of the door shivered into his three-piece suit. It had been a mild winter, if not a bit chilly, and people that left their homes without their coats on wished they had remembered to take it. The man kept his hands in his pockets, jingling his pocket change like he was waiting for the right bus to turn up. The first two things that came to Bill's mind were "encyclopedia salesman" and "religious zealot," but then this man had always given off that impression. "Bill," John said, trying to sound cheerful and failing. "You're home. Good."

Bill pondered what effect leaving the front door open all the time would have on the sound of the living room. He watched as John jingled his pocket change again, realizing there wasn't going to be a handshake offered.

"We were concerned about you," John went on. "You haven't been into the office for a few days, and you missed the launch party for the perfumes two nights ago. I thought I might check in on you, make sure everything's— okay—"

Bill forced a smile that felt like it belonged on a circus clown. Some time later, he supposed the smile had made him look like a maniac, and that it may not have been the thing to do.

John was peeking over Bill's shoulder, into the empty living room. Bill brought the door closed enough that the opening wasn't quite wide enough for his face. He hated nosy people. Them and gossips. People who have so little going on in their own lives that they feel the need to ask you and yours about every little detail, every little thing going on in your life. He thought Jamie might have been one of those people had she not found interior decorating. She was one of those people, come to that. She only started designing a room after long talks with the client about his or her life. There would be nights she would come home from an appointment and go on and on and on about every little detail of a family he would never meet. "I'm fine," Bill said.

"Good," John said, "good. I'm glad to hear it." He took a few steps back and started down the steps off the front porch. "Well, I— thought I'd let you know we— miss you at work. And if you could— let me know what's going on and when you're coming in again—"

"I'm fine," Bill said, and closed the door. He reopened it as soon as John had driven away. This room sounded better that way, and then he wondered: what does the third upstairs bedroom sound like at dusk?

"He's mental," John said at dinner. "That or he's hiding something."

John loosened his necktie, the stuffed bell peppers were so hot. Ellen, still basking in her promotion to Chief of Thoracic Surgery at County Hospital outside of town, was so backed up with administrivia and learning her new job and working seven-day weeks she barely knew coming from going, and was engrossed in paperwork at the other end of the table. In only three weeks on the job, the black rings under her eyes had become permanent features of the landscape. Her hair, once full of bounce and life, now needed twice the amount of hairspray to keep its form. So tired and engorged by her job, the heat of the dinner was completely lost on her.

"I'm sorry, what?" she said, closing one over-stuffed manila folder and opening another.

"Bill. Bill Randolph." John's voice was sullen, dropping half an octave in an attempt to hide his anger. He was used to people paying attention to him, including his wife. Especially his wife.

"Oh? What about him?"

John rubbed the bridge of his nose. "He was all funny today when I went to his house looking for him. He hasn't been in to work for days, but all he said was, 'I'm fine.' He didn't come outside. He closed the door so far I couldn't see his whole face, but dear— I think the house is empty."

Ellen didn't respond, eating the rest of her dinner like a vacuum cleaner pulling up so much dust. John wondered if anything he'd even said had registered. He was surprised he'd been able to get her attention at all, a small victory in comparison to most of the dinner discussions since the promotion. Those victories were getting fewer and farther between, inversely proportionate to the thoughts that this marriage of career-minded people had gone as far as it was going to go. He filed the thought away to discuss with his therapist in their next session.

"I think you should go over there," he said.

"Where?"

"The Randolphs. I think you should go over there and talk to him, find out what's going on."

Ellen looked up at him over the top of her reading glasses. "It wouldn't do any good. You know him better than I do."

"It'd do more good than if I went."

She blinked at him.

"The man's worked for me for fifteen years, been the only designer our company's ever had, and we've never talked outside of work. He's an island unto himself. Sometimes he'll strike up a conversation with my secretary, but most of the time he stays locked up in his office. He's never talked to me about anything personal, and, you know, maybe you'll have better luck at it than I will. I just can't shake the feeling that something's horribly wrong there, and somebody needs to talk to him and find out what it is."

Ellen sighed.

"I'm asking you to do this one thing for me, Ellen. Please. Just go and talk to him."

"All right," she said. "All right all right all right." She drew in a deep breath and let it out. "Just let me relax, will you? For just one minute. Can you do that? Let me finish my supper and I'll go. All right?"

This woman reminded him of Jamie a little. Very little. But enough. This woman was singleminded like Jamie. She wasn't loud, or particularly overbearing. That was the difference between them. But both women were determined. When Jamie started on a project she kept working on it until it was just so, complete, finished, perfect as only Jamie Randolph could make something. Bill could see a lot of that in this woman as well. She had come in and introduced herself—Ellen Thompson, John's wife, they'd met at one of the company Christmas parties, remember?—and started right in on the questions: why were all the windows and doors open, was Jamie all right, why was the heat shut off, when would Jamie be coming back, what had happened to all the furniture. She had taken her time getting to that question, but Bill had been watching her shift her weight from one leg to the other from the moment she walked in the door, so he suspected her leg cramps had something to do with her desire for a chair. Her knee-length skirt, her pantyhose, and her modesty kept her from kneeling or sitting on the floor. Or maybe it was her professionalism. He wasn't sure he cared. She hadn't taken off her coat either, after Bill made no move to close the windows and doors.

"I can't pretend to know what you're going through, whatever it is—"

Her voice reminded him of Jamie, soft, melodic, confident beneath. That was the old Jamie, the one he'd fallen in love with in college. They were both design students then, an isolated pair in a school full of business and pre-med students. They had every class together out of necessity, and their study dates became just dates after a couple of months. He'd courted her for two years before proposing. It was only after the wedding that she became so demanding and undesirable. And loud. What did this woman know of that?

"—What is important, though, is that we keep living, keep being who we are, make our own lives go forward—"

Forward. That was a funny one. Forward to him in college had been a wife, kids, a modest house, and a career in design. There weren't any kids, and the house wasn't really all that modest—none of them in the gated community were anything short of "spacious"—but otherwise things had mostly gone Bill's way. Forward to Jamie was supposed to have been the same thing, except that her career as an interior designer had spluttered at the best of times. Every now and then a client would be completely satisfied with the selections Jamie had made for them, but more and more frequently it hadn't gone nearly so well. She started complaining more often right around then, started wondering why people couldn't see her genius, started getting angrier at Bill and his rapidly expanding lines of homewares, started talking louder. Forward to Bill now was peace and quiet.

"—and some day you may learn to love again—"

Bill only knew Ellen Thompson by reputation. He'd seen her name in the paper a few weeks back in connection with County Hospital—she was running some part of it now or some such—but not otherwise. There may have been a meeting or two at the product launches, but certainly not at the holiday parties. He didn't go to those. All that ever happened was a bunch of drinking and loud music, and since he enjoyed neither one there wasn't a reason to go. And now here she was, lecturing him about getting on with his life, prattling on about emotional recovery like she had a clue. She couldn't. To her, all of these feelings, this recovery she kept on about, wasn't anything more than conjecture. John was still married to her. John hadn't left her a goodbye note without so much as an apology.

Bill saw the first few tentative snowflakes fall from the sky. That had to be a wonderful sound: snowfall. He walked over to where the front door stood open. "Get out."

"—it's all for the beg your pardon?"

Bill jerked his head in the direction of the front lawn. "She's gone. Glad she's gone. Better that way. Get out."

Ellen blinked a couple of times then took her purse from the kitchen counter. "But Bill, there's nothing here. No furniture, no heat, no nothing. Just bare walls and carpeting, Bill." She'd been walking towards him across the living room floor. "You can't really want that."

For the first time since she turned up, she stopped talking long enough for Bill to hear the house. That was what had been missing from the scene. "Hadn't noticed."

❖   ❖   ❖

"He. Kicked. Me. Out."

There were more words than that. John could hear them all perfectly well, but those were the four most often repeated. Those were the four that every other thing she said was supposed to support. Her rant more than tripled the duration of the original five-minute encounter, examining it from every angle that seemed to favor her. Bill Randolph, she said, had been short with her, obtrusive, abrasive, ill-tempered, terse. He was obstinate, obdurate, adamant. He hadn't listened, hadn't cared, hadn't heard a word she said, and, as she'd been saying from the moment she opened the door from the garage, he had, without warning and/or probable cause, told her, in no uncertain terms, to get out.

She finished, her face the red of a bullseye, and stomped toward the bedroom. Through the front window, he could see the snow falling faster, the first signs of accumulation showing on the lawn. The roads through the gated community would start to ice over presently, if they hadn't already. John contemplated going to Bill and asking for an explanation, but it would have to wait until morning.

By dawn eight inches of snow had fallen, topped by a half-inch layer of ice. The city and everything in it would be staying home. The plow company hired out by the Community Planning Board might and might not get the snow cleared from the roads before noon. Through the front window, John could see that the crews had made a valiant attempt at keeping up, but the bigger of the two deluges, the one that came an hour before dawn, with all the freezing rain and ice, had proven too much for them. John and Ellen were snowed in.

He found Ellen in the kitchen, sitting at the counter, splitting her attention between half of a grapefruit and the morning newscasts. "You see the snow?" she said. "Weatherman says it's supposed to get worse. Another four inches today, more ice on top of that. Windchill's supposed to hit ten below."

Instantly, his thoughts went to Bill. Bill had had all of his windows open when John was over there, and yes they were still open when Ellen left, she'd said. He walked into the front hall, pulled his coat and boots from the closet, and walked out the front door. He doubted Ellen even noticed.

It took him fifteen minutes to make the normally five minute walk to the Randolph house. As John had guessed, the windows were all open as wide as they could get, and the front door was propped open by a two-foot deep snowdrift. The entire of the front lawn was pristine, the ice covering the snow, creating a slick, glistening surface. Where exactly the front walk was under it all was a mystery.

"Bill?"

Each step across the front lawn was an exercise in how high John could lift his knees. He didn't walk up the front steps so much as he climbed up the drift. Once he got inside the front entry he kicked as much snow out of the way as he could and closed the door. Some of the snow was still inside, but he doubted Bill would mind.

"Bill? You there?"

John started with the ground floor: living room, dining room, kitchen, half-bath, two offices, den, garage. Empty. No Bill, no furniture. A door that probably led to the basement, a stairway up to the second floor, a doorwall with snow drifted halfway up the closed half, a screen door that looked like a sieve with snow piled through it, and no footprints anywhere near it. John went up.

Bill was beneath his simple blue bedsheet in the smallest of the upstairs bedrooms, curled up fetal against the wall opposite the open window, teeth chattering, skin blue, wide awake. "John," he said. "I—"

"It's okay, Bill. We'll get you warmed up in no time." John was already taking off his coat.

"I heard it, John."

John stopped where he was, arm nearly out of one sleeve, and made eye contact.

"I heard the snow falling. I heard it."

William Randolph—"Bill" to his friends—was admitted to County Hospital an hour later. After the 9-1-1 call went through, a plow party was organized, and within minutes a path had been cleared from the front of the gated community to the Randolph house, giving the ambulance a way to get through. John watched from the hallway as the EMTs cocooned Bill in flannel blankets, and then piled the bundle of Bill onto a stretcher, into the ambulance, and away. John watched it go to make sure, stood at the curb in the same spot Bill had watched the moving truck go, and when the ambulance turned left onto the main road and disappeared John started the long walk home. He would get Ellen to pull some strings, have Bill put under psychiatric observation, preferably hers.

John worked well into the evening the next day. There was some minor damage control to be done, members of the press asking for clarification on the Bill Randolph situation, what was he in the hospital for, was there a situation at all, did he have a statement and such. John hung up the phone on the last one well after dark. By the end he was performing by rote, the answers coming before the questions were finished.

He pulled up in front of the Randolph house on his way home. It was dark except for a light from an upstairs room. Must have left a light on, he thought. He shut the engine off and walked toward the house. He would turn the light off. That's all. Make sure the house hadn't been tampered with. Then go home. Right? Right. Everything would be just fine, and John could go home and sleep. Nothing to worry about. Nothing to see here.

He stopped at the front door and looked back toward his car. He just stood there, listening for any activity from within, signs of life that shouldn't be present. There was a light breeze that night blowing through the trees, making the small sound like air coming through a hole in a bicycle tire. Somewhere, maybe half a mile away, he could hear a salt truck rumbling down the main road. The sound of it vibrated through the trees and reached him there on the front porch. He cleared a spot in the snow, sat down on the front steps, leaned his head against the wall, and listened. Through the siding he could hear the inner rumblings of Bill's house, all speaking in one voice as hollow and rumbling as an earthmover. And when morning came, and someone jostled him awake, and a woman's voice said his name, "John? John? What are you doing here?" it didn't matter to him who the voice belonged to. All he knew was that it was too loud.

RESERVATIONS

A car passed outside, Dopplered itself toward and then away from the house. Children played an indeterminate game in the faraway.

He looked at her again, rocked back on his heels, then forward. Back, then forward. She sat on the couch, hands joined in her lap, undressed.

"No—" he said.

The last of the day filtered through the blinds. Particles of dust wafted through the yellow-orange light, on their way to nowhere.

She did not make eye contact. To do so would have been a mistake. Best to keep her head down, her hands clasped, her clothes off. That might distract him.

"—seriously—" he said.

In between the words the quiet stretched. The children giggled, the traffic buzzed, but all were vague and distant, afterthoughts.

He sought for clues in what she was and wasn't saying and wearing and could find none. She perched on the border between ennui and apathy. Whatever her response, she would be nothing more nor less than a passenger.

"—where do you want to go for dinner?" he said.

Her hands gripped and ungripped each other. Her shoulders tensed and relaxed. Her eyes rolled clockwise as she let out a breath and prepared to give her answer.

What she wasn't sure of, what she was never sure of, was whether or not it was the correct one.

"I—" she said.

"—don't know."

Then silence.

Meeting Monica Seles

Todd was hitting the ball well. He'd done well in a couple of key tournaments, was starting to get a national reputation, and had just picked up an agent. "You realize you're a bit old to be doing this?" I asked him across the net. "Most tennis players are considering what flavor their retirement will be when they reach 27, and you're just now going pro?"

"Age is a state of mind, Terry. Now serve the damn ball." Todd in a nutshell. His focus, application, and dedication were remarkable, commendable, and something of a pain to his closest friends. His favorite sport, all through his early childhood, had been baseball. He had several years of little league under his belt, and then he saw some coverage of Wimbledon on TV one afternoon, showing Monica Seles getting a three-set win in the first round. "I'm going to be a star tennis player," he announced at dinner that night.

"Wonderful, dear," Mom told him, and passed the mashed potatoes anyway.

And he meant it. The next day he biked down to the Tennis and Racquetball Club a couple of miles from here and asked how much lessons cost. That was his first setback: $40 an hour. He was 16 years old, had no job, and didn't have enough money to be able to float that kind of outlay every week. That should have been that, except no one anticipated how much ass-kissing Todd managed to find the time to do, certainly not our parents, who I think paid for the lessons if only to shut him up.

I served the ball, kind of. It floated over the net in slow-motion and landed out of bounds. Todd shook his head and came forward a bit for the next serve. I served again, and he smashed it straight at me so fast I barely had time to jump out of the way. I watched as it bounced into the court-surrounding fence. "Nice," I said, walking over to the other side of the court.

"Can't you serve any better than that?"

"No. I'm not the aspiring tennis player here, remember? Love-fifteen," and was about to serve the ball when Todd's cell phone went off. He ran over to answer it, while I walked around the other fenced-in courts collecting all the balls he'd blown by me.

By the time I got back, Todd gave me the news. "I'm going to Indian Wells."

"Indian Wells?"

"California. The Newsweek Champions Cup. One of the Tennis Masters Series. They play a tournament there every year, and my agent was able to get me into the qualifying rounds."

"Congratulations." I drank from my water bottle and thought, Indian Wells, qualifying. Whatever.

"Monica will be there, too."

"Oh."

The rest of us didn't find out until a couple years later exactly why he took up tennis to begin with, and even then it was by accident. "You've gotten pretty good at this," I told him at his Pizza Hut dinner, celebrating Jackson High's winning of the High School State Tennis Championships. "Here, the rest of us thought you would be the starting third baseman for the Tigers, but no, you're gonna be a tennis star."

"Damn straight," he replied, and would've actually gotten to the beer had Dad not smacked his hand an inch away from the pitcher. He excused himself and he went off to the bathroom. Five minutes later he hadn't come back, so I went after him. I walked into the men's room and saw him standing at the urinal with his wallet propped open on the pipe fixture above it. He was staring intently at the picture, and muttering in a low voice. The picture was of Monica. Not really wanting to interrupt a private moment, I turned around and went back to the table.

"Why would Monica be at Indian Wells?" I asked him. "Isn't she slightly of the wrong gender to be playing in a Tennis Masters Series event?"

"They have both a men's and a women's tournament there."

"Ah, right. Should've guessed."

"Hopefully, she'll do well. She only got as far as the quarters this week in Scottsdale, so maybe this will push her to do better." His voice took on a reverent tone when he spoke of Monica's accomplishments, as if each one was a moment in history to be savored by one and all.

Todd had wanted to meet Monica for years, certainly since he started taking tennis lessons, but all of his best-laid plans for getting anywhere near her had come up short. Even the odd autograph signing session hadn't panned out for him. "I assume you have a plan," I said.

"Not yet, but something will come to me."

This would be the first time Monica and Todd would be in the same facility at the same time as players. Once, as a Christmas gift, our parents had gotten him plane tickets and three session passes to the 1991 Australian Open, which Monica won, but due to a variety of scheduling conflicts, weather, and what the passes were actually good for, he didn't actually get to see her play. He did, however, get a Monica poster, which became the first of several.

He got a call back from the agent after he showered, and though my brother and I are close, I prefer it when he dresses before making travel statements for me like, "You're coming to California."

"Beg pardon?" and averted my eyes.

"She made plane reservations and all the whatnot for two people, and I need a hitting partner anyway, so I told them you'd come. Besides, we've been booked to stay in the same hotel Monica's staying at."

It was the hitting partner bit that seemed bogus to me. He hadn't asked me to do that since his "controversial" loss at an important tournament eight years ago. He had scouted, he said, his next round opponent who supposedly hit "a masterful drop shot to win an obscenely high percentage of his points." For three hours, Todd had me hit nothing but variations of drop shots at him and, duly prepared, he went out and lost. The opponent hit nothing but lob winners over Todd, who spent every point charging in waiting for a damn drop shot. This was, of course, my fault, but on the upside he bought a can of tennis balls that had all been signed by Monica from a sports memorabilia merchant, so the week was not a complete scratch.

I briefly mentioned the incident, but he casually brushed it off. "I was young."

"You were 19."

"I was upset."

"Yes, well... don't take it out on me this time, okay?"

"Fair enough."

Todd slept through most of the flight. What usually did it for him was reading Monica's autobiography. I don't know how many times he's read it, but he's got six copies now, counting the one he just bought on an Internet auction site, which was an autographed edition. He's already looked into renting a safe-deposit box.

My parents said very little when he quit baseball for tennis, and even less when his desire for all things Monica spilled over into his everyday life. They didn't say anything when I started taking writing classes either, although they were hoping at least one of their sons would be a doctor or a lawyer. They told us, after the fact, that they thought it best that we made our own ways in the world, and though they may not have agreed with what we wanted to do with our lives – Todd in particular; being a sports star was not their idea of a career – they stayed out of our way and supported us where they could.

Having said that, they still never saw Todd play a match, nor read any of my books.

❖   ❖   ❖

"The rule is what?" I asked.

"Very simple, Terry. The promoters put us up in this hotel free of charge for either two nights, or until I'm out of the tournament, whichever comes last. And two nights is plenty of time, because Monica's already here."

"Really?"

He pointed skyward. "Two floors up. She's scheduled practice time for right after my match starts, and she's scheduled fourth on the main court, so she should be lounging about when I finish my match."

"Which is when?"

"Tomorrow morning, 10 am sharp," which meant a wake-up call at an ungodly hour, probably 6:30 or something, on top of a nice case of jet lag. Thrilling. And this crazy bastard brother of mine would want to wake, shower, go right on over to the complex, grab a practice court, and have me hit balls at him up until time.

Todd's a morning person. He'd play at dawn if he could talk the tournament organizers into it. He was scheduled to play at 10 am at a tournament a few years back, it started raining at 9:30 and didn't stop until 3, and in the meantime Todd got himself so worked up over not playing that when he finally did, he couldn't.

Fortunately, the forecast was good.

6:30 comes early, though, especially when it's only 5:15. "Wha—?" I grunted as Todd nudged me awake.

"Get up," he said. "I can't sleep."

"That's funny. I can," and I rolled back over.

Todd kept talking. "What if I meet her?"

"So what if you do?"

"I mean, what am I supposed to say to her?"

"'Pardon me. Sorry I got in your way.'"

"We have so much in common, I almost feel a kinship with her."

I turned back over to face him. "You're not Slavic, and you've never been on the cover of a magazine. Other than playing tennis, what on earth could you possibly have in common with Monica Seles?"

"April 30th."

On April 30, 1993, right around the time Monica was getting stabbed in Hamburg, Todd was waking up on the morning of his 20th birthday. When the news broke here in America, the family was getting ready to go out and give him a birthday lunch at Ponderosa. I saw it on ESPN right before we left, but didn't tell Todd until we got back. It would have spoiled the occasion.

On April 30, 1994, he left the house before daybreak, and nobody saw or heard from him until the following morning, when he pretended that nothing had happened, that everything was, in fact, beautiful. After that we just celebrated his birthday a day early, which he didn't seem to mind too much.

"Okay, so the stars were in alignment for a day. What else?"

Todd fumbled for a second. "Never mind. Go back to sleep."

I rolled back over, and thought of something else to say. "Perfect. I'm losing sleep over a girl you've never met."

Todd woke me back up in an hour, and we went ahead to the complex. We were assigned a court, and started hitting balls at each other. After forty-five minutes, he wanted a break. "Sorry about waking you up last night."

I was willing to let it go before, but since he brought it up, "I understand desire, okay? Lust, obsession, whatever... I think we all feel that for something on one level or another."

"Is that what you think of me? That I'm obsessed with her?"

I knew I shouldn't have used that particular word. "If you are, then you need to put it aside until lunchtime. You have a match to get ready for."

"You didn't answer the question."

"Todd, I don't know what to call your feelings for Monica. I really don't. Neither do Mom and Dad. We've all tried to be supportive, and let you indulge yourself to extremes, but all we get back is Monica."

"Monica Seles is a strong and courageous woman." His face was getting red.

"Right, and you've been worshipping the ground she walks on since 1989. You know things about her that even relatively well-educated sportscasters don't know, and probably a few things she doesn't. What else are we supposed to think?"

"Blow it out your ass."

"Happily, but let me say this first. Whatever it is you feel, fine. We love you, we care about you, and we don't want you making a fool out of yourself." Todd grabbed his racquet bag and stormed off of the court, headed for the men's locker room. I followed in hot pursuit. "Just what is your problem, anyway? You wanted to know what we thought. Now you know."

"Get the hell away from me," and Todd started trying to outwalk me.

I let him go, calling after him, "Fair enough. I'll be in the stands."

Todd's match started bright and punctual at 10:05. His opponent was Russian with a name with a million consonants in it, so I didn't bother trying to learn it. Todd got off to a pretty good start. He was using his lucky racquet, a store-bought men's Yonex that Monica had autographed for someone some-where sometime and Todd had picked up in another Internet auction, and that was doing wonders for him psychologically, up until the string broke. He was up big in the first set, smashed one down the sideline, and PING! I heard it up in the 12th row, but then I was one of maybe 20 people watching the match, so it's not as if there was a crowd to drown it out. Todd looked down at the racquet and frowned. As he went back to his changeover chair, a ballboy came up to take the racquet off to the stringer's tent. Todd looked at the boy for a moment, then told him something in a low voice and pointed up at me. The ballboy nodded, then ran up into the stands and gave the racquet to me. "Your brother says to make yourself useful and run this off to get restrung. You know where it is?"

Strings break. That's part of the game. A while back a couple of guys fig-ured they'd capitalize on that and set up shop at all the tournaments. They charged a hundred per racquet and made a killing. Usually I did his restringing, but with professionals in the building, "Yeah, I know where it is," and took the racquet there.

The two fellas at the stringer's looked surprised to see somebody who wasn't a ballboy or a player. "Who're you?" one asked.

"Terry Murphy. Just dropping off a racquet for Todd Murphy."

"Who?"

"Potential qualifier. He likes a good tight tension."

"Two hours," the fella said and took the racquet.

I turned to leave and nearly collided with a woman coming in. I had opened the door to go, wasn't paying attention and BAM! there she was. "Oh, pardon me," I said stepping aside to let her through.

"Thank you," she said, coming in. I closed the door behind me and was half-way back to the stands before it even occurred to me that it was Monica Seles.

They'd only managed to get four games in since I'd left, and Todd had man-aged to lose them all. They played another point, and I figured out that his collapse was directly tied to his not using the lucky Monica Seles-autographed racquet. Clearly aggravated, he lost the next two games and the first set.

His breakdown became complete in short order. On the first point of the first game of the second set, the Russian hit a well-placed drop shot. Todd made a headlong dive for it, overshot badly, and did a header into one of the poles holding the net up. The sickening metallic thud echoed though the stands as I stood up. Todd twitched for an instant, then lay still. After a couple seconds, when it became obvious he wasn't getting up, I started running down the stairs to the court, only to be stopped by a security guard. "That's my brother!" I screamed, holding up my pass, and he let me through.

Two trainers and the net umpire had already huddled around him, as the Russian looked concerned — but not too concerned — from the far baseline. I ran up and knelt beside Todd. He was unconscious for what seemed like forever. A moment later, the head referee and two paramedics brought a gurney up, and they carted him off. The knot on his forehead had already started to grow.

There's not really much to tell after that. He regained consciousness in the ambulance, and although he knew his name, he didn't know what city he was in or what day it was. He thought he was still at home three days earlier. That got him kept overnight for observation, and he wasn't released for another day after that, after which we promptly taxied to the airport and flew home. He was defaulted and lost the match, of course, but he managed to make the evening news.

I probably did the nicest thing I'll ever do when I lied to Todd on the way home. I told him before he'd gone on court for his match, he ran into Monica in a hallway. "You met her, you know. Monica."

"I did?"

"Yup. You met her at the stringer's before your match started."

"How'd I do? What'd I say?"

"Well enough. You said sorry for running into you, you said you were a big fan, she thanked you and went about her business."

"Cool," and he went back to sleep with a smile. He doesn't know that she won her match that day but eventually lost to Martina Hingis in the quarterfinals, although I'm sure he'll find that out someday. He also doesn't know his chance meeting with Monica at the stringer's was actually mine, and I don't intend to tell him.

TORNADO IN A BOX

We created a tornado in a box. A real one, high winds, lightning and thunder, all of it. To make it look more realistic, we put in a miniature plastic cow and a small replica of Dorothy Gale's house that would fly around and around the funnel. We could almost hear the mooing and the crunch of the witch when the house landed on her. Almost.

We wanted to sell Tornado in a Box. First there was the research: would anyone want to own one? They could put it on a mantle, say, or a bookshelf, the box, and start it up at parties or perhaps on romantic evenings if they were with those sorts of people, although that wouldn't be our preference. What we envisioned were children using it, learning from it, sticking their sisters's Barbies in it along with the cow and the Gale house. So we tested it first on children. They loved it. They learned from it. They watched the cow and the house go around and around, and when we offered them a choice of extra stuff to put in they went for the Barbies. Even the girls. Then we tested it on the adults. They thought it was interesting but they didn't go for it. Nobody wanted it for their mantle or bookshelf; apparently we didn't test those sorts of people. All they wanted to know was how much it would cost, would it be within everybody's gift budgets.

We needed to manufacture Tornado in a Box. The parts themselves weren't that big a deal. We wanted everything to be made in America because one thing the adults did say was that that would look better on the box, the outer box, the box we sold the Tornado in a Box in. We didn't have to search too far for the box components or any of the things that made up the tornado, but we ended up having to send off to Malaysia for the cows and the Gale houses. We didn't want to do any false advertising, so we started an Internet meme that the United States was about to annex Malaysia. It caught on. People took it seriously. The White House issued denial after denial. We didn't feel bad about the advertising anymore.

We needed somewhere to manufacture Tornado in a Box. The first three we made in our garage, even the miniatures which were perfect if we do say so ourselves. But our garage would not be big enough to keep up with demand. We needed cheap land, and abandoned warehouse maybe. We searched far and wide. We found space in this little town called Liberty that was an on-again-off-again tourist destination. They were happy to have us. Good for commerce, they said. Clears up that little problem of the closed-up semi-truck repair garage on the edge of town. All farming and no manufacturing made for a hard sell for people to move there. We said we would help with that.

We had to set up the assembly plant for Tornado in a Box. The materials came in, the boxes for the Boxes were printed, "Made in the USA" in a prominent place. We hired a dozen workers and taught them: put this, this, and this in the Box, put the Box in the box, close the box. Done. There were no problems with the training. We were happy about that. Also, twelve new jobs in Liberty, so they were happy about that. People were talking too: what was going on in that closed-up semi-truck repair garage on the edge of town? Chatter at the Starbucks was high. Nobody knew who we were when we went in for our latté, which made us happy.

We had to distribute Tornado in a Box. We made arrangements to have it sold in all the big box stores. We shipped dozens, hundreds to each big box store. We had been manufacturing for months by then. The Tornados were restless. We had set a price for it that we were fairly certain people would pay. The retailers were excited. Tornado in a Box would be the next big thing, they said.

We had to advertise Tornado in a Box. We built a website. We made print ads featuring adorable rented children marveling over the lightning and the flying cow in the Box. We made commercials with people who chased tornados for a living. One of them looked into the camera and said, This is the easiest tornado I've ever chased and the funnest. We test-marketed all of it. People liked it. People loved it. People wanted to put one on their mantles and bookcases.

We sold Tornado in a Box. We sold a lot of them. A lot. We had hoped to move maybe two or three units per store per week. We had not anticipated most of the stores selling out on the first day. This was a problem; we had no back stock to speak of. We expanded our converted semi-truck repair garage. We hired and trained more workers. More jobs for Liberty. They were happy about that. "Manufactured in Liberty" was put on the boxes. They were happy about that too. The back orders were filled, and sold, and filled again. We were rich. We gave back to the community. We gave everyone in town a complimentary Tornado in a Box. Liberty renamed the center of town Tornado in a Box Square. There was a celebration. People came. Bands played. Children got sick on elephant ears. Everyone was happy.

We did not anticipate the problems with Tornado in a Box. We were surprised when we got the first phone call, from somebody in Liberty no less: their Tornado had escaped from the Box. That wasn't an issue, we said, the Tornado should fizzle out after a while outside of the Box. No, they said, it had been free for three hours and showed no signs of slowing. We went right over and sure enough there was the Tornado smack in the center of the living room, a tissue and a live mouse in close orbit. We didn't quite know what to say. The Tornado came in our direction but we stepped out of the way. It went by us and out the front door we'd left open by accident. We offered a replacement Tornado in a Box to the customer. They declined. On the bright side, their mouse issue was solved.

We had hoped that was a singular occurrence for Tornado in a Box. It wasn't. Three more in Liberty broke out by the end of the day. The next day another half dozen escaped. The mayor called us. We assured him the Tornados would dissipate on their own. He accepted that. We kept filling orders. The next day the phones rang more. All local, all escapees. Why wasn't this happening in Milwaukee, we said, why wasn't this happening in Tucson? We were worried. Another two days and the mayor called again. Please come down to Tornado in a Box Square, he said.

We had not expected the sheer violence of Tornado in a Box. We went to the Square, to the steps of the county building, and saw a dozen of the escaped Tornados on the front lawn, twisting away, sucking up little bits of dirt and grass. There were news cameras. The mayor's spokesperson made a statement. No one interviewed us. No one knew who we were. We were happy about that. But the tornados were not going away. Two of them collided with each other. They combined. They made a bigger Tornado.

We lived in fear of Tornado in a Box. We made phone calls: stop manufacturing them, let the back orders go unfilled. More escaped. More joined together. The phone calls came every minute. A Pekingese was in the grasp of a waist-high one out by Old Man Johnson's farm. A parking meter was spinning around another one that had taken up residence just outside of the Starbucks that nobody wanted to go into for fear of possibly being sucked up by the Tornado. There was small destruction of public property but nobody was hurt and no buildings were damaged. Still, people were upset. This was not what we wanted from Tornado in a Box, they said. Lawsuits were filed. We weren't quite anonymous anymore. A few days later they had combined into one great big one, big and powerful as a real one. It sucked up some things around the courthouse, around Tornado in a Box Square, then it made its way to the edge of town and destroyed the converted and expanded semi-truck repair garage where we made Tornado in a Box. One second standing, the next rubble. And it left town. Dropped all the local things it had picked up and left town. It's out there somewhere.

We are bankrupt because of Tornado in a Box. We settled the lawsuits with all of our money. We replaced what we could, carpets, fish tanks, SUVs. The town changed the name for the center of town back to Liberty Square. The mayor asked us to leave. We left. When we got to Cincinnati, we went into a big box store. They had a Tornado in a Box. We checked; no one had reported any problems with them. We bought it. It's the one on the mantle. It's all we have left.

ANOTHER SUNRISE

The panga stopped fifteen feet short of the beach. The drive killed the motor and turned to Eric. "*¿Es este un buen lugar?*"

Eric nodded. He knew the driver would have taken him across to another beach if he'd asked but the five hundred yards in distance wouldn't have mattered any. He swung his legs over the side of the panga and jumped down into the foot-deep water. The water felt nice around his toes. The driver grunted as he lifted one of Eric's two wet bags and handed it down to him. "*Espero que hayas empacado lo suficiente,*" the driver said.

Eric slung it over one shoulder with a little difficulty and pulled the second one over after it. The sudden added weight nearly put him on his knees. He reached up to shake the driver's hand. "*¿Tres días?*" The driver nodded. Eric went around the front of the panga and gave it a push backward. The panga's small outboard motor came to life, and the driver turned it around and headed back for the yacht that had dropped them both off. Eric watched it go for a moment before turning back to the beach.

Eric looked up and down the beach for a moment. He'd hoped to be greeted by a colony of sunning sea lions but there were none to be found. Perhaps they were on another beach or— He looked at his watch: 3.15. They were out feeding and playing. Later, toward dusk, they would come back in and lay out for the evening and sleep. *This would be a good place for some sunset pictures*, he thought. *Facing west, the sea lions in silhouette... perfect.* He walked to the back of the beach and dropped the wet bags at a place where there would be just enough space to pitch the tent between two clumps of scrub. He turned back in time to see the yacht start moving. In two minutes it was gone around the edge of the island. There was nothing but ocean now in front of him clear to Indonesia. The surf crashed in and out, in and out.

Eric yawned. He'd spent the last two days flying, Detroit to Miami to Guayaquil to Baltra Island, three thousand miles in a straight line, and though he'd already been in the islands a full day jet lag was starting to assert itself. He pulled the tent from one of the wet bags and twenty minutes later was asleep inside it.

He was woken by a bark. It didn't register at first what he'd heard. His dream had provided an interesting framework: He'd been sitting at his mother's bedside in the hospital, watching her life drift away like so many unfinished sentences, and the heart monitor which had been beeping away like it usually did barked like a sea lion instead. It was on the second one that Eric woke up. He looked around his tent in confusion. *No, no sea lions in here.* A quick glance at his watch showed he had been asleep for an hour. There was plenty of sunlight left, and pictures to be taken.

It was as he was unzipping the tent to go outside that he heard the bark again, several in a row, searching, insistent, plaintive. He slid out and looked around for the source. In the time he was asleep, the beach had filled itself with sea lions. They lay on the sand, enjoying the late afternoon sun in clumps of threes and fours and fives. He watched one for a moment as it rolled from one side to the other, its now-exposed flank half-covered in caked-on sand. The business voice in his head reminded him that this was what he was here for, this wildlife in front of him acting naturally as anything, but the barking noise coming from nearby silenced it.

A moment later he spotted the source: a sea lion pup crawling in his general direction along the beach. Every six or seven feet it would stop and look around for a moment before continuing, barking all the while. *It's looking for its mother*, he thought. *It's gotten separated.* Eric knew enough to know this wasn't a good thing. Alone, with no mother to feed and protect it, a sea pup didn't have a very good chance of survival. As he watched, the sea pup went over to one group of four adults and tried nestling up to one. The barking stopped for a moment, then the adult shifted and growled and the pup scampered away, rejected.

It made its way past Eric, not even noticing him, and tried again to cuddle up to two other groups of adults, rebuffed both times. It was as it was coming back toward him that Eric noticed what was really wrong with it: a large gash was open just above its right rear flank, and while it wasn't bleeding, the wound was deep enough that the pup couldn't use either of its back flippers. That was what had seemed wrong; it had essentially been dragging itself along. And that was probably why the other adults were rejecting it: not only was it not their child, but it was injured to boot.

Eric sighed and watched as it made its way back up the beach, eventually disappearing behind some scrub and moving out of earshot a moment later. There was nothing he could do for the pup. It was illegal to touch the wildlife within the park, or to alter the natural course of events in any way. *But even if I was able*, he thought, *what could I really do*? He wasn't a vet or even remotely qualified to try and heal the pup, and he was quite frankly afraid of the consequences if he tried. This opportunity he'd been granted was a rare privilege.

Screwing it up in the slightest was not an option. He took a moment to look over the sleeping sea lions to find a few that looked particularly photogenic, and raised his camera.

The elevator doors opened onto a waiting area. *Convenient*, Eric thought. *Don't have to go searching around for your loved ones.* His brother Todd was in a chair next to some windows looking out onto an overcast sky. As Eric walked over Todd stood up, and they shared a brief embrace before taking opposing chairs. "Sorry I couldn't get here sooner. Flight was delayed. How is she?"

Todd shook his head. "She was awake last time I was in there. Grandma and Grandpa are in there now."

Eric looked out at the sky, hoping that the clouds would provide some sort of comfort. "Spoken to the doctor?"

"He came out a minute after Grandma and Grandpa went in." He took a moment, cleared his throat, hung his head. "Tonight, sometime, he thinks. Middle of the night at the latest."

"How did we go from six months to a year two days ago, to six weeks last night, to— to—?" Eric shook his head and flung his arms outward and let them fall on the armrests.

"Mom— wasn't being entirely truthful with us. The six month diagnosis was three months ago."

Eric's sigh was nearly tangible.

"Well, you know Mom. Deflects all the time. Doesn't want anyone to worry about her."

"Yeah, but still—"

Todd shrugged. "Nobody knew. You, me, Grandma, Grandpa. Nobody."

"How'd they react when they found out?"

"About as well as you'd expect." Someone spoke over the intercom for a moment, looking for a doctor. "When are you leaving again?"

"Week from tomorrow, probably. I can push it back a week if I have to, take care of whatever has to happen here." Eric paused for a moment. "That seems callous of me."

"No. Or at least I don't think so. Maybe getting back to work might be for the best."

"I can delay it, you know, if you need any help arranging things."

"Doesn't look like I will. Mom left a fairly comprehensive list in a file on her computer, places where arrangements have already been made, people who need to be called. She's been planning this for a while, apparently." Todd took in and let out a deep breath. "You should go. Really. Mom would want you too."

Eric nodded. When he'd gotten the contract to do the Galápagos National Park calendar, the first person he'd called was his mother. Her words of praise still echoed in his head when he thought about it. They were deafening now. Images of the family visit to the Galápagos filled his dreams for nights on end. He'd been looking for a reason to go back for a long while and here was one that had the bonus of being on someone else's dime.

Todd looked at his watch. "Damn, I've gotta go. There's some things at the restaurant that need dealing with. I shouldn't be but an hour. Call me if anything happens."

Eric looked up at his brother and said okay, and a minute later he had the waiting area to himself.

Somewhere, behind one of these walls, my mother is dying, he thought. He looked at each of the three walls in turn as if expecting to be able to discern where exactly she was by some divine inspiration. After a moment of this, he went back to looking at the grey clouds outside and thinking about his forthcoming trip to the Galapagos. It still felt kind of odd and somehow heartless to be dashing off almost as soon as the funeral was over. And yes, maybe getting right back to work was for the best. Maybe. But then he'd never lost a parent before. His father didn't count; he'd gotten in the car one morning when Eric was two and Todd was five and not been heard of since, and how could he mourn a man he didn't remember?

A few minutes later his grandparents came through a door and greeted him. "Todd left a while ago," Eric said while getting what passed for a bearhug from his grandmother. "Something he had to take care of at the restaurant. He'll be back after a bit, he said."

"Your mother was asking after you," his grandfather said. There was no judgment in his voice. "She's the second door on the right. We haven't eaten, so—"

"Go on. I'd like some time alone with her."

His grandmother nodded and sobbed, and his grandfather led her off toward the elevators. Eric went through the door they'd just come through and went to the room they'd indicated. His mother was lying in the only bed in the room, her eyes closed. A nurse was standing next to the bed, fiddling with some tubes. "Family?"

"Son," Eric said. "Younger son."

The nurse nodded. "She drifted off a few minutes ago. She's been in and out all afternoon. I'll be back in a while to check on her again."

With the nurse gone the room was quiet. The monitor above her bed showed that her heart was still beating, but slowly. Her bed sheets shifted slightly at each inhale and exhale. Without those two things it would be difficult to tell from a distance if she was still alive. An oxygen tube was attached to her nose and another one—for water? feeding?—was in her mouth.

He took the seat next to the bed and looked at her. She had on a scarf to hide her scalp. Her hair was long since gone, the first casualty of multiple rounds of radiation and chemotherapy. This was not the woman he remembered. That one was stronger, resilient, upright. That one would tell you what she thought, not to hurt but merely to state her opinion. Looking at his mother in this condition was hard, almost insulting.

A few minutes after he sat down, it occurred to Eric that maybe he should do something. Hold her hand, perhaps? That's what other people seemed to do in this situation: sit at the bedside, hold hands, and look concerned. Well, he was concerned, so all that seemed perfectly manageable. Eric reached out and put his hand on top of his mother's. A few seconds later her eyes opened. He smiled but it felt weak and insincere, and it didn't reach his eyes. He wanted to say something but all of the words he could think of seemed inadequate.

"Eric," she said, her words slightly garbled by the tube in her throat.

"Hi, Mom."

There was a long pause as she inhaled and exhaled a couple of times. "I'm going to die. How do you feel about that?"

He blinked a couple of times, and the tears started down his cheeks. "Not good, Mom."

The amazing thing about being on the equator was that the sun rose and set at the same time every day. Eric knew the sun would go down at six, leaving him in darkness until six the next morning. But there were hardly ever clouds in the sky over the islands, rain virtually unknown. Even the oldest people in the islands, as the Park Director had told him in Puerto Ayora his one night there before coming to Fernandina, could not remember the last thunderstorm, could remember volcanic eruptions much easier. The result was clear nighttime skies and, on nights like this one with a full moon, near perfect illumination. Out here on the island, the lack of light pollution made it that much easier.

Eric had set up a small gas stove a few feet in front of his tent. He'd had a negative experience a few years earlier doing a safari shoot where the guide's idea of a "filling, tasty" meal were some MRE's left over from the Reagan administration and ever since then, on nights when he knew in advance that room service was not an option, Eric made sure to have a heat source, something to boil water in, and attempts at reasonably good meals. Tonight's dinner was a rice and bean concoction he'd been experimenting with. It was filling and tasty, if not completely satisfying. Tonight, for no particular reason, what he really wanted was baked macaroni and cheese.

In the hour and a half of daylight that he had left after his nap he snapped off something like three hundred shots. He spent about half the time with the sea lions, all of whom seemed thoroughly disinterested in the guy with the camera. After that he followed the shore south for a few hundred yards and found a colony of marine iguanas sunning themselves on an outcropping of hardened lava. He was looking forward to reviewing the shots later that night on his laptop; he was fairly certain there was one of an iguana spitting salt water from its nose, and that would look good for a main picture for a month. Eric didn't see the injured sea lion pup during that time but it wasn't far from his thoughts. A couple of times he lowered the camera from his face and looked around, expecting to see the pup appear from behind a bush. Or maybe not; the iguana colony was a solid two hundred fifty yards away from his tent, and the pup wouldn't drag himself that far.

Eric finished his meal and walked over to the surf to rinse out the small pot he'd cooked it in, winding his way between sleeping sea lions. As he was walking back, a glint under a piece of scrub twenty feet from his tent caught his eye. *A trick of the light*, he thought. *Something somebody dropped found its way under the brush*. It was as he unzipped the flap to his tent that he heard the bark, softer than earlier but every bit as insistent. He turned and looked at the bush again. There was nothing for a few seconds, so he finished unzipping the tent. Again the bark came. Eric took out his flashlight and aimed it at the bush. The source of the glint became clear: it was the injured sea lion pup from earlier, the light bouncing from its eyes. The two stared at each other for a long moment before the pup crawled out from under the brush and into the campsite. It stopped a couple of feet from the stove, barked again, and rested.

Eric tilted his head sideways, pursed his lips, and turned the flashlight off. In the clear moonlight he didn't need it to see the pup anymore. "Well, hello there," he said to the pup. He knew the pup couldn't respond, and he felt a tad foolish talking to an animal, but he thought he saw the pup look in his direction so he kept on. "Never did find your mother, I take it. Well, no, obviously you didn't. Otherwise you'd be with her."

Eric sat on the ground, directly opposite the pup, and frowned.

"So what got you? What—what happened to your hindquarters there? Did you scratch it on something? There's coral in these waters and that stuff's pretty sharp. I knew a fella once cut himself pretty bad on some coral while he was out scuba diving. Or did one of your siblings do that to you, roughhousing? Maybe one of them pushed you into the coral? Or is that from your mother, trying to calm you down?"

The pup looked at him, turned its head to the side, then put its head back down on the sand.

"It was a shark, wasn't it?" The area around the Galapagos was home to the white-tipped shark. Six feet long from tip to tip, snorkelers looked on them with awe and comfort, knowing they could tell people they'd swum with sharks when in reality the sharks weren't any longer than the average man and wouldn't have been able to do much damage to a human. A small sea lion pup, though, would probably resemble lunch. "You swam too close to it, didn't you?"

The pup looked at him again, head slightly raised, and then it didn't.

"And somehow you've been separated from your family. Only makes it worse." Eric sniffed then opened a thermos and poured himself some coffee. "Or did they abandon you? Did they think you were done for, or tainted, or—?" He swirled the coffee around in the plastic lid that doubled as a cup. "Doesn't really matter, does it?"

The bark from the pup was not strong. It was more of a plea than anything else.

"You're going to die. You know that, don't you?"

The surf crashed in and out, in and out.

Eric took another sip of coffee. "Yeah, I expect you do." He swirled what was left around the bottom of the cup. "You're welcome to hang around if you want." He snorted. "Like that'd be up to me anyway. Can't stop you from staying or going. Can't even touch you. But I know if I was you I wouldn't want to be alone. No, sir, I wouldn't." He spread his arms expansively. "*Mi camping está su camping*. That's what I'm saying."

The pup looked nonplussed.

"And maybe," Eric said, "your mother will turn up. I'll stay up with you, too, if that's what you'd like. Would you like that?"

The pup lifted its head for a moment, looked at him, and put it back down.

"Of course I will." He drank the last of his coffee and stared out at the water. "As long as you need me."

Eric wasn't dreaming of anything when the hand on his shoulder woke him up. It took him a second to recognize his surroundings but he was used to that. Years of traveling for his photography had taken him pretty far afield, to some places that seemed like living daydreams and to others that formed the basis of every nightmare. It wasn't until he looked to his left and saw his mother in the hospital bed that he remembered where he was and why.

"Sir?"

He turned to look at the person speaking. An older woman in pink floral scrubs was looking at him through bifocals.

"Visiting hours are over. You'll have to go."

"I'm her son."

The nurse nodded and removed her hand. "I believe it. You've got her nose and chin."

Eric rubbed his eyes. "What time is it?"

"Twelve thirty. Give or take a minute."

He was a little surprised he wasn't wide awake. Two days earlier he'd been in Moscow, snapping off photos for a new fashion line, when the phone call came to tell him just how bad off his mother was. He hopped the first place he could and flew back to Detroit, forty-eight hundred miles in a straight line, but his body should have still been on Moscow time.

"I can get you a blanket and pillow," the nurse said. "I know the chairs here aren't all that comfortable."

"I'd appreciate that. Thank you."

Eric turned back toward his mother as the nurse left the room. The monitor over her bed showed a constant but slow heartbeat and blood pressure on the low end of things, but to look at her it was hard to tell she was still alive. Her breathing was shallow and it seemed an hour between breaths. She was asleep or unconscious, Eric couldn't tell which. He wondered, idly, what she was thinking or dreaming about just then, if anything, and if she'd be able to tell him what that was when she woke up again. If she does at all, he thought.

He felt another hand on his shoulder. This time it belonged to Todd. "Sorry I took so long," Todd said. "Problem with that place is that they can't seem to make any decisions for themselves, so when I turn up I get asked every damn thing they've been wondering for however long. I like being needed, but there's a limit to that."

Eric nodded. "It's alright. You haven't missed anything."

Todd took the seat at the foot of the hospital bed and looked at the monitor. "No change, I take it."

"No." Eric relaxed back into his chair. "The nurses keep asking me whether or not I'm family."

"Well, you haven't been around but today. I've been in and out of here for the last few days visiting, so most of them have seen me by now. You, not so much." Neither one said anything for a moment, while the monitor chirped softly in the background. "How long since the doctor was in?"

Eric looked at his watch. "A couple hours. Prognosis didn't change any."

"I don't like this."

"I don't like it much either, not being able to do much of anything but sit and wait and watch. And I hate it that there's nothing I could do anyway."

Todd looked at his mother, and then at the monitor again, and said nothing.

"She told me she was dying." Eric clasped his hands in his lap and looked down at them. "Asked how I felt about that. I told her not good. I think she wanted to say something else but she wasn't hardly awake, so."

Neither brother said anything, each one avoiding the other's gaze.

"She bought me my first camera. Believed in me when everybody else in the family thought I was nuts to try and make it as a photographer."

"I know." Todd sighed and looked at his brother. "I know."

"I could make a list a mile long of all the things I want to tell her before she goes, of all the things I should have said. I would rather the last thing she heard me say is that I love her and I wish she wouldn't go."

"Same here."

"And it just burns me that I can't. That I'm on this incredible hot streak with my work and it doesn't mean a damn thing. I'd trade it all in. I'd let it all burn if it would buy me another sunrise with her so I could say it, say everything I want to, listen to her talk to me again." He took a deep breath. "I want to punch something."

"It won't help."

Eric looked at the monitor, and then at his mother. "She's not going to wake up, is she?"

A long pause, then, "No."

At about ten Eric pulled out his laptop from the second wet bag, uploaded the pictures from his camera, and started going through them, deleting the blurry ones and starting to correct some of the better ones. He marked the few he thought would be ideal for the calendar: a nice shot of three sea lions grouped together on the beach, sand caked to the back of the one nearest the camera; a group of flightless cormorants that just happened to line themselves up in such a way as to resemble a group of bowling pins; a Galapagos penguin that he hadn't expected to see on this island; and the shot he really wanted of a marine iguana spitting salt out of its nostrils directly into the camera as part of a defense mechanism. The exercise felt empty, though. He tried not to look at the pup if he didn't have to. Every few minutes he did glance over to see if there were signs of life. The pup for its part shifted positions a few times during the night but otherwise slept.

After a few hours he closed the laptop and stared at the pup. "Still with me?"

The pup did nothing, but he saw it inhale and exhale.

"Good." He put the laptop on the blanket next to him. "Sort of a déjà vu element to this, you know? My mother was in the hospital last week. Cancer. Started as breast cancer, spread to her shoulder, her back, her brain. Of course we didn't know the middle bits, that it had spread. Didn't find that out until the day she went into the hospital. Nothing anybody could have done for her by then. Nothing I could have done for her anyway, except pray and wish her well. Doesn't seem quite enough, you know?

"So I sat there at her bedside last week, watching her. All night. I might have slept an hour or so, I don't know. Anyway, I was sitting there, hoping she'd wake up again, hoping I could get in one last conversation with her, tell her all the things I never got a chance to say."

The pup may have shifted a little. In the half-shadow it was sitting in Eric couldn't tell.

"What are you thinking? What—what would you have told your mother right now if she were here? Okay, yeah, a few barks, but what would that mean?"

He looked up at the stars. Even the dimmest ones were visible in the clear night sky with no light pollution to mask them.

"She didn't make it either. To dawn. Missed by about half an hour. Had an eastern facing window, blinds open, ready to greet the new day. She would have liked that. Would have liked to have seen the sun again."

Eric found Orion in the sky, the three stars in a line that make up his belt, the one part of the constellation he could identify.

"Where are you tonight, Mom? Where are you when I need you?"

The pup shifted a little but stayed silent.

"Listen," he said, looking back at the pup, "I'm sure she'll come. She'll find you. She misses you too." He didn't have any real conviction in his words, but in the pup's place he would have wanted to hear them. "Give her time. When the sun comes up she'll start looking again, and she'll find you."

The surf crashed in and out, in and out.

"You'll have plenty of days together. I can feel it." But he could feel himself drifting off to sleep even as he said it, and a few minutes later both of them were gone completely.

❖   ❖   ❖

"I feel so bad for Eric."

The sun had been up for half an hour. Phone calls to all the relatives had been made. Several of them were in the waiting room, some flitting from group to group as if at a cocktail party. One of them—Eric knew precisely which—said that sentence which drifted across the air to where he and Todd sat on a sofa, ignored by everyone, and then followed it up: "He lost the only real parent he's ever known."

Eric sighed. "I'm grieving," he said at the voice. "I'm not fucking deaf."

"Relax," Todd said. "Let it go. It isn't— important just now. They've lost someone too. They've lost a sister, an aunt,—" He looked across to where their grandparents sat, their grandmother stone faced and done crying, their grandfather weeping the first tears either one of them had ever seen on him. "—a daughter."

"Yeah, but look at the rest of them. They're not even sad." Someone chuckled in one corner of the room but it stopped almost as soon as it started. "Do they even understand what's happened?"

Todd shrugged. A low murmur filled the area as conversations carried on, all of them steadfastly avoiding the brothers. "We all grieve differently. It's both universal and unique unto the individual."

Eric looked down at the carpet, a beige sisal worn nearly bare by countless people in the same position he and everyone else found themselves in now. Todd said something then but Eric wasn't paying attention. It took a jab in the ribs to bring him out of his idle staring. "What?"

"I said we should eat something soon," Todd said. "It's been a long night."

"Yeah."

"Supposed to be a gorgeous day. First day of spring and all."

Eric looked at the window. Someone had drawn a translucent visor but sunlight still filled the waiting area. "Why do I find no solace in that?" The two of them sat there, Eric looking out the window, Todd examining the drop ceiling, for another minute before Eric spoke again. "So what's the next step?"

"Funeral home's been on standby for a few days now, and she bought the spot where her urn's going to go months ago."

Eric nodded.

"We'll do the proper placement of the urn after you get back from the Galápagos. There's an engraving she wanted to go on the side of the box that hasn't been taken care of yet." Todd ran a hand through his hair. "I'm assuming you're still going."

"It's either that or hang around here being miserable. And like you said, Mom would want me to go."

Another two relations got off the elevator and were greeted by some other relations. Three minutes later the newest arrivals had made no effort to speak to the brothers.

Eric stood up. "I can't take this anymore. I'm going for coffee."

Todd rose. "Think I'll join you."

They went to the elevator, thirty-five feet in a straight line, unstopped by anyone, and pressed the down button. "Think we'll be missed?" Todd said as they stepped on and hit the button for two floors down.

As the doors slid shut, Eric shook his head.

Eric woke up with a jerk and started spitting sand out. It wasn't the first time he'd fallen asleep on a beach, or even outside of a tent he'd erected, but the waking up was seldom pleasant. Things had a way of getting into his mouth and nose, and more than once the inability to breathe because of that was what woke him. As he cleaned the sand from his eyes, he thought about the dream he'd just had, reliving the long night from the week before. It had haunted his waking moments ever since. That it had crossed over into his sleeping hours disturbed him.

The funeral happened two days before he got on the plane for Ecuador, four from this morning. It had been stately and dignified, mostly, until the floor was given over to the grievers to offer their remembrances of his mother. What was offered wasn't so much reminiscences but stories that related to the deceased tangentially at best by people that didn't look sad at all. The lone exception was Todd, who spoke for ten minutes about growing up with her guidance and support. Eric declined the opportunity to speak, and skipped the after-party entirely.

The pup was still where it had been when he fell asleep. That was a bad sign and he knew it. He checked his watch: 7.30. The sun had been up for an hour and a half, another bad sign. He looked over toward the main beach: empty. All of the sea lions were in the water, feeding, playing, learning.

Eric crawled across to where the pup lay. It was still breathing, but barely. "You made it," he said. "You saw the sun come up."

The pup blinked up at him and then closed its eyes.

Eric stood and walked out to the beach. There were no sea lions at all, none. Not even the young had stayed behind. He watched for a minute, hoping to see one emerge from the surf, but none did. He turned and went back to the campsite. The pup had gone. Tracks from where it had been overnight led back to the bush he'd found it under the evening before. Eric peeked beneath the brush and saw the pup, its eyes closed, its body still.

He sat down in the sand, facing the bush, and felt a tear come to his eye. "You didn't deserve this," he said. "You didn't deserve to die alone. Someone should be here to mourn you."

The surf crashed in and out, in and out.

"I will."

SEA OF TRANQUILITY

We weren't sleeping much, either one of us. We went through the ritual, Pat and I. I brushed and flossed and got into bed and read while Pat took her contacts out and applied a pore-cleanser to her face. She joined me in bed, switched off the lights and we discussed the events of the day before heading to our own sides of the mattress, dreaming about sleeping. Pat would lie on one side, adjust her pillow every few minutes, then turn over on her other side and repeat. I just stared at the ceiling, counting the ripples in the texture until the relief came. I beat her to sleep most nights, she tells me.

I woke up at two o'clock one morning, can't remember why, and she was gone. She'd been gone a few times before. I found her in the kitchen usually, sitting over a freshly brewed mug that was guaranteed to keep her awake the rest of the night. If I found her late enough, toward four or so, she was making breakfast for herself, scrambled eggs, bacon, toast. That morning, the morning I woke up at two, she wasn't there. In the kitchen. She wasn't in the living room laughing at an infomercial. She wasn't in the bathroom sobbing on her knees in front of the toilet. She wasn't in the house.

I found her in Hempstead Park, two blocks away from our house, where she and Jack would go every few nights to get away from the glow of the village and stare up at the stars. They would pack a few snacks and spread out a blanket as Pat taught him about the stars, about the constellations and the mythology that explains them. It was quiet time together for mother and son, it got them out of the house, whatever—they were enjoying themselves, and it helped Pat feel closer to Jack. They took me along because I was the only one strong enough to lug the telescope to and from the park. Pat is five-foot-nothing; the silly thing's bigger than she is. I don't know what Jack's excuse was other than he was carrying the picnic basket and the blanket. They would've used it at home except our neighbors on both sides have outdoor lights.

The last time they'd had me do this for them, the celestial object of their affection was the moon. Pat aimed and focused the telescope and stepped back to make room for Jack. "There," she said. "Have a look. Beautiful, isn't it?"

"Wow," he said, muffled a bit by the telescope. "What's that big empty spot there in the center?"

Pat looked in the telescope. "That is the Sea of Tranquility," she said and launched into an Apollo 11 history recitation straight out of her planetarium presentations.

The park seemed the obvious place for her to go. She'd been doing a lot of that in the days prior, day and night, eyes to the sky as if she were waiting for some sort of astronomical signal. I found her fetal on the metal merry-go-round, green and red silk pajamas intact, asleep. One of us had to be, I guess, or deserved to be, so I carried her home and let her do the rest of it in her own bed.

She made her way into the kitchen at eight the next morning. I thought I'd do something nice for her and make breakfast: eggs, bacon, and my attempt at pancakes. She stood there in the doorframe, with a look like she thought she'd crashlanded on Mars or somewhere. "Have a seat," I told her. "The eggs are almost ready."

Pat scratched her hip and turned to go. "I have to get ready for work."

"Sit down. You're not going. I called in for you, told them you weren't ready yet, you'd be in tomorrow or the next day." I would rather it was closer to a week given the night before, but I couldn't tell her that. She hadn't been in for eight days. Another one or two wouldn't hurt.

"Tom, you had no right," she said, but there was nothing behind it.

"Pat, you look like hell. Now sit down and have some breakfast."

She sat at the kitchen table and I placed a mug of fresh coffee in front of her. The rings beneath her eyes were red and black enough that no amount of make-up could hide her lack of sleep. In between scrambling the eggs and flipping the pancakes, I caught glimpses of her adding cream and sugar to her coffee like she was underwater. Her stirring took so long that I had her breakfast plated by the time she finished.

I put the meal in front of her and watched her ponder it for a solid fifteen seconds before she said, "Thank you," and that in a quiet tone. She'd used up all her energy walking to the kitchen.

"Go back to bed, Pat," I said.

"Can't. Wasn't asleep anyway."

"Go back to bed."

She went. I ate the breakfast.

Pat listens to Pat. That's how it is, really. It might seem from the outside that she listens to me, but we established without saying so very early on in our relationship that what I would say to her was more suggestion than instruction. I'm not complaining. Half the time she did the right thing by ignoring me. Jack knew that too. Jack knew that Mommy did whatever she wanted no matter what Daddy had to say about it. When he worked that out at age eight, it became fascinating watching him play one of us against the other. He would ask me for something, hockey lessons or some new toy or some such, and I'd say no.

A couple of days later, I'd be rearranging my schedule all the same so I could pick him up from practice, or trying not to trip over the newest thing in the living room that makes more noise than anything should. All thanks to Mommy.

What – what do I do?

I could have made it through work that day. I wouldn't have been worth a damn, a two-hundred-forty pound lump for one and all to avoid, but I would have been there. That would have been a welcome change, being there as opposed to where I had been for a week. Work as opposed to home. All the past eight days had done was reinforce how bored I was within my own four walls. Nice place to visit, but living there was terrible. I had visions of Pat waking up and disappearing while I was gone. Lord knows where she'd turn up if that happened, wearing her pajamas or something else that screamed, "I'm not well, do as you will to me." That I'd found her in the park, that her energy had gotten her as far as the merry-go-round and no farther, had been an educated guess, but still just a guess. Where would she be next time? The playground at school? The field where Jack played his little league games? I couldn't do it. I couldn't leave her alone.

I spent the days rediscovering soap operas, their twists, their turns, their incredulity. Spouses cheated on one another, parenting children with the baby-sitter who turned out to be a long lost cousin. After three days of that I redis-covered the off button and turned to our bookshelves and read, one eye on the text, the other on the hallway leading back to our bedroom. Pat then had to go past me to get anywhere else in the house or outside. She kept mostly romance novels on the shelves, little things only slightly larger than my hand, with as much thought put into them as the soap operas. I stomached four in a two-day period and gave up. The alternatives were in the horror genre, vampires and spooks, things from the early days of King and Rice. Somehow my stomach and heart couldn't fathom pulling one off the shelf, let alone attempting to read one. It would be the romances or nothing.

I think, most of the time, Pat just lay in bed, tossing and turning and praying for sleep. Or something better.

A fella down the hall from me at work lost one of his kids the year before last. Leukemia. Very sad thing. He didn't have the luxury of going from upbeat to suicidal in a fleeting moment, poor guy. He had to have it drag on for I don't know how many years. You could see it in him, the eyes getting more and more sunken over time, the wrinkles on the forehead deepening, the graying of the temples, the growing reluctance to talk about his only son. I'd ask him every now and then how his boy was doing, if the leukemia was in remission or any other good news. When I started working there his answers were, "He's good," or, "He's fine. Doing well." Over the next couple of years the answers came a little more slowly, seemed a little more forced. I could see him tense up when I asked about it. His eyes would widen a bit, like somebody'd just nudged him with a pitchfork, and he'd sit for a long moment before shrugging first and saying, "All right." It was never more than that toward the end. "All right."

He was gone from work for two weeks and some when his son passed away. When he came back, he looked like hell, as if he hadn't slept in a year and he was down to three brain cells that weren't on speaking terms anymore. He was, you know, just there, less worthwhile than parsley on a cheeseburger platter, not worth a damn to the company, but he wanted to get out of his own house. I know how he felt.

I'd fallen asleep in the easy chair pondering the news events of the day and dammit if she didn't sneak out on me. Not in the bedroom, not in the bath, not in the kitchen. The only upside was that I'd finally gotten a little nap, for all the good it'd done.

She was in one of the swings in the play area at the park, a few dozen feet away from the merry-go-round I'd found her on before. The other three swings were occupied by children busy trying to psych each other out with how high they could go before jumping off. That there was this woman in the fourth swing just sitting there, staring at the gravel, was of no consequence. So long as she didn't get in the way or remind them how what they were doing was dangerous, they didn't care.

At least she'd gotten dressed first.

I walked up and stood in front of her swing. "Pat?" I said, hands in my pockets. She didn't acknowledge me. "You okay, honey?"

The children next to us kept playing, swinging and shouting about how one of them was going to break his neck jumping from as high as he was. But he didn't listen. By then he'd gotten a lot of momentum going, and when the swing peaked at six feet in the air, he jumped, arcing in a feet-first dive, and landed safely. Pat watched all this from the comfort of her own swing and let a tear form in one eye.

I held out a hand to help her out of the swing. She took it, stood up, wiped away the tear. "Did he know any of these?"

She knew he didn't. Jack's friends were in and out of our place constantly, invited or self-invited to countless dinners, sleepovers, baseball games in the backyard. They called us Mr. and Mrs. Hertzman when they called us anything. They knew enough to chew with their mouths closed, keep their elbows off the table, admit when they broke a neighbor's window, deny it when they broke ours. They had been absent since the funeral. "No, honey," I said. "Too young. Jack's friends were older." Pat nodded, and I led her home.

Actually, that's not entirely true, that bit about the friends being absent. Two days after the funeral Jack's girlfriend Tina turned up to claim some things of hers. "He borrowed, like, a couple of CDs last month. I just—you know, thought I could get them," she said after I let her in the house.

"Sure," I said. "They're probably in his room. Help yourself."

Tina was a sweet girl. He'd brought her home maybe the year before, did the whole meet-the-parents-dinner thing wherein she didn't say a word and made eye contact with me and Pat twice each. Jack tried like never before to initiate conversation, get Tina to talk about what she was into, and I swear the transformation Jack underwent that night—from self-involved teenager to out-going conversationalist—was a stunning and, as we discovered the next night, singular experience when he talked about Jack and nothing but. I'm fairly certain that Tina found her way back to Jack's room at least once, and Lord knows what they did in there. She seemed to know the way; Tina went ahead down the hall to Jack's room as I sat back down on the couch and resumed reading a fifth-rate romance called The Pleasures of His Flesh.

Maybe a minute later she came back to the living room. "Mr. Hertzman?" she said behind me.

I didn't look up. "Yeah?"

"I was wondering, could you, maybe, you know, go in and get them for me?"

I marked my place in the book, walked down the hall, and got as far as putting my hand on the doorknob. We didn't have any plans for Jack's room—still don't. We hadn't touched it, hadn't opened the door. There was too much of him in there. I had my hand on the doorknob and I couldn't turn it. Dust was probably already gathering inside on everything, from the clothes in his hamper to the cable TV on top of his dresser, from the bookshelf to the desk. In months it would become an allergist's wasteland, a dust bunny paradise in an otherwise spotless home. Jack would never have suffered it, nor would he have suffered our entering his room without him. There was everything of him in there, and out here, right next to me with this look on her face like a rabbit who's being teased with a carrot it's not even sure it wants, was his girlfriend. She just wanted her CD's, and she wanted to violate—wanted me to violate the sanctity of Jack's room. An image flashed in my mind of what must have happened a minute before; she'd stood where I was, hand at the ready, primed to turn the knob, and frozen like a Medusa victim.

"Can we do this some other time?" I asked, hand still on the doorknob.

She took a minute. "Yeah, sure, no problem," she said and left. I pried myself away and went back to my book.

I tried again with the cooking to lure Pat out of the bedroom. Half an hour later the steaks were sizzling over the coals. Pat trudged herself into the kitchen as I came back inside with dinner. She sat down at the table which I'd set while the food was cooking and waited blankly as I put the plate of beef in front of her, and I wondered for a few moments if it had registered that I'd made her favorite. She got around to saying, "Thank you," and ate like she'd been fasting for a week, which wasn't too far from the truth.

We went through the same motions after the steak was eaten. I brushed my teeth, climbed into bed, and stared at the ceiling. Pat applied the whatever to her face, took her contacts out, came to bed and tossed and turned. We pretended as if each other were asleep, preferring to be alone in our miseries.

At two thirty Pat got out of bed, put her robe on, and walked out of the bedroom. I stood up and followed. She walked through the house to the kitchen and out the back door, fluffy house robe, green and red silk pajamas and all.

I got dressed and caught up to her where I expected to: on the merry-go-round in the park. She was staring at the moon again, clutching the metal pole attached to the platform, the one children held on to and screamed for their lives in joy as the merry-go-round spun and spun.

"Pat, you can't keep coming back here," I said.

She looked down at the dirt track around the merry-go-round, her expression saying, "I can and I will."

"You need to come home, Pat. You need to sleep."

Pat looked up at the moon. "Where do you think he is by now?"

I looked up at the sky, to the full moon that shone in the bright darkness like a beacon guiding someone home. The moon Jack died under was half full, a sign of a life not yet complete or completed. "Right now, he's standing on the Sea of Tranquility, gazing at us through the highest power telescope heavenly money can buy. He's looking at us, moving constellations on the face of the Earth, and he's smiling because one day his mother will stand beside him, and see what he's seeing, and be in just as much awe as he is. More importantly, though, they will be happy just to be together again."

Pat stood up and buried her face in my chest. "I miss my son, Tom."

"I know, honey. I know."

That was how I walked her home, leaning against me, both of us crying, and when we got there we slept for hours and hours. We went back to our jobs the next day, received what consolation our co-workers could give us, and by degrees came back around to the business of living. When we open the door to Jack's room—a couple of months from now, I think—it will probably be me who goes in. There's a large phosphorescent poster of the moon on the wall directly opposite the door, and seeing that would be a bit much for Pat.

Some nights I look at the sky, at the moon, and I see my son, his face, his smile. And years from now, when I remember how to forget—

THE AUTHOR

Peter Barlow grew up in suburban Dayton, studied at Miami University for a while, relocated to Michigan, finished college remotely at Vermont College and Fairleigh Dickinson University, and now leads a quiet life with his family in suburban Detroit. This is his first collection.

www.ingramcontent.com/pod-product-compliance
Lightning Source LLC
Chambersburg PA
CBHW080730020726
47503CB00010B/2864